The Call

P.D. Viner did some theatre, film and created the award-winning range of SmartPass guides for Shakespeare and the classics. Then he decided to kill people, and has never been happier. Check out his best-selling *Sad Man* and Dani Lancing crime series. He will kill again soon.

Also by P.D. Viner

The Call
The Choice

The
CALL

P.D. VINER

hera

First published in the United Kingdom in 2022 by

Hera Books
Unit 9 (Canelo), 5th Floor
Cargo Works, 1-2 Hatfields
London, SE1 9PG
United Kingdom

Print ISBN 978 1 80032 849 5
Ebook ISBN 978 1 912973 83 5

Look for more great books at www.herabooks.com

Printed and bound in Great Britain by Clays Ltd, Elcograf S.p.A.

Chapter One

Mia

I can't breathe.

Calm down, Mia, hold it together.

It's almost midnight. Time is running out. I wish I didn't have to call – Christ, I wish I didn't – but I can't do this alone. I need Ben. I need my husband. I reach out to the phone again, though now my hand is shaking too much to pick it up.

Breathe, Mia.

Oh god, please don't let this be the end, I'll do anything to make this right... anything... please.

Breathe.

I have to calm down, I need the world to stop spinning. My lungs are on fire. I'm holding my breath, like a petulant child, because I want to freeze time and keep the new day from starting. I want to push it back, just a few hours, to before all this happened. That isn't much to ask, is it? A second chance?

Oh god, Ben, I'm so sorry to pull you into this mess, but I need you. You're my lifeline, my phone-a-friend, and I know you'll come, like a true hero – like Sir Galahad, or Romeo or John Wick. You'll come because you love

I

me. I know you do, because you've told me so a trillion times.

'*I love you and I will always come when you need me, even if I have to cross an ocean or break into hell itself, I will come. It will always be the two of us against the world.*'

He said that before he put the ring on my finger, in front of all of our friends and everyone that loved us. That was twenty years ago. Christ, where did the time go?

Our wedding day was beautiful. We were married by a lake, in an ancient stone circle. Ben made the confetti himself, from old law books he'd bought and shredded. He gave every guest a little bottle of bubble liquid and when the celebrant said '*You may now kiss the bride,*' a hundred thousand bubbles floated into the air. It was magical. I wore a dress that floated like tissue paper, and Ben was in a suit the colour of oil on water. Our friends sang us songs and we'd rented doves, and someone brought a peacock, and afterwards there were fireworks and a ceilidh and… oh my god. I haven't thought about that day in such a long time. Haven't recalled how truly wonderful it was. I'd forgotten how much we loved each other.

We wrote our own vows – of course Ben's were off-the-scale romantic and I knew that I'd never be able to match him; that I could never show how I felt, or express it like he could, like a poet. I knew that I would always lose to him at the game of love. So what I said, in front of everyone, was:

'*You want me, you got me.*'

People laughed, '*Just sooooo Mia,*' they said, but it was honest and true. I was his, and I couldn't imagine that changing. Not then.

Ben's vows were next, and of course they were epic and eternal and beautiful and haunting… there wasn't a dry eye in the house. Not even mine. Bloody romantic idiot.

But tonight – well, I've broken it, haven't I? Trampled our marriage into the dust and… *oh god*. What have I done to him and what have I done to *us*? When he knows the truth, about what I did, who I am… Will he still love me?

It's all such a fucking mess. Sometimes life gives you lemons, but you can't make lemonade because there's no sweetness left in the whole wide world, only sourness and bitterness and hate. Only the stench of blood and death and… *I can't breathe. I can't…*

I would do anything to put this right. Anything. What are the stages of grief? Shock, denial, anger, bargaining… I'm absolutely at bargaining. This can't be it – I will not let this be the end of me, the end of *us*. Please. Just give me one last chance.

I grab the phone, as the final sands of the day drain away. Midnight is striking. I have to get hold of him. I need him.

Wake up, Ben.

'*Ben!*' I scream.

Chapter Two

Midnight

Ben

'Wha—'

I'm suddenly awake. For a second I'm lost, but then I realise I'm at home, in bed, though I feel groggy and a little weird. I think I just had a nightmare, but I don't remember what happened in it except... *Mia*... Mia shouted my name, and that's what woke me.

I try and sit up and, *oh Christ*, I'm almost sick from the room spinning. It's like being on a boat in a storm. My stomach's pitching, and my head's cracking open; I need some ibuprofen, and about three pints of sweet fizzy Berocca. And I really need to brush my teeth, as my mouth tastes like something died in it. I breathe deep, and let the rollercoaster finish its loop-the-loop and calm down. When I'm okay again, I reach out into the gloom, grab my glasses and search for my phone. It should be next to the bed but I can't find it.

'Mia?' I whisper into the dark, but there's no reply. 'Mia?' I call louder, but there's still nothing. She isn't here. I sit up carefully, and realise that I'm lying on top of the bed, not under the covers. I'm in my underwear, which is a stupidly snug Siouxsie and the Banshees T-shirt (as I still haven't lost my lockdown tummy), and I'm wearing underpants that are fifty shades of grey, and not in a sexy way. I don't understand what's going on. Where's Mia? What happened last night?

By the dim glow of the digital clock I can see it's 12.03. Why am I in bed so early; did I get really smashed tonight? I try and drag my memory out from whatever rock it's hiding under, but there's nothing there. I don't know why. I stretch my arm out again, feeling for my phone. Maybe it fell and— *what's that?* In the gloom, I can just about make out a cut on my hand, a jagged scratch crusted with dried blood. Underneath, there's a wash of black, like smeared ink. It doesn't hurt, but it looks like it would have hurt like hell when I did it. I have no memory of it happening. No memory of anything at all.

And then I hear something, a burble from another room in the house, maybe downstairs, but I think it's Mia talking. She'll know why I'm in bed this early and why I can't remember what happened tonight. She's not a doctor, or a mind reader, it's just that in our marriage she's the practical one – I mean, we both wear the trousers, but hers fit properly.

'Mia,' I call, as I roll off the bed and steady myself, letting the dizziness settle down. I can't hear what she's saying, but I know it's her. She must be on the phone, and at this time of night it can only be Sandi – an old friend whose life's a total car crash. I'll go and find Mia; if she can't talk, then I'll just kiss the top of her head, and then get some drugs to stop my brain exploding. Sounds like a cunning plan.

I walk out onto the landing. There's no sound. I can't hear Mia anymore. The house is cold – like, really freezing. Mia's always chilly and I'm always hot, so turning

5

the heating on is a constant tug of war between us. Normally she wins, so I don't know why it's off, or why it's so bloody dark. I can't see a thing, but that doesn't matter; I know the house like the back of my hand. On the wall to my left are our wedding photos, in old antique silver frames that we found in a little junk shop in Exeter. Next to them is a doll in a glass case. On our wedding night we stayed in a bed and breakfast and the owner's daughter made these woollen dolls, so we bought one and framed it. Then there are two paintings of Mia's parents, and then an old photograph of my grandmother as a beautiful fresh-faced twenty-year-old on a fruit-picking holiday in Sussex. Below that there's an old table with a lamp on it that my great grandfather made, and to the ri—

'*Jesus*,' I trip on something, right at the top of the stairs and fall forward. My arms cartwheel as I topple headfirst into the blackness. I shoot my hand out, grabbing at the bannister, and swing into the wall. *Ouch*.

I'll have a nasty bruise there later, but it's better than breaking my neck. My heart's racing. I don't know what I fell over, but whatever it was, it shouldn't have been there. I don't know how or why, but something's changed. The feel of the house is different, like I don't belong here, as if it isn't my house anymore.

Downstairs, I call: 'Mia!' But my voice just rattles around in the empty hallway. What's going on, did I sleep for a year? Have I missed another virus, the Triffids taking over, a zombie attack? What the hell has happened?

'Mia,' I yell. 'Mia, where are you? I know you're here, I just heard you.' But there's no reply, nothing. I flick on the light in the hallway – I should have done that upstairs – and everything looks normal.

'Mia?' I call again, but there's still nothing, so I push open the living room door. I expect to find her on the phone, frantically waving me away because there's some new crisis with Sandi, but the room's empty. *Where is she?* I turn to explore the rest of the house, though stop as something catches my eye. There's a tiny green light, flashing in the corner of the room. I have no idea what it is; I've never seen it before. I go over and bend down to look.

'Huh.' It's the answering machine. I'd totally forgotten we had one. Only scammers and chuggers call on landlines these days, I don't even remember what our home number is, but the light's flashing; there's a message. I push the play button.

'You have nine new messages. First message recorded today at twenty-three, twenty-two hours,' a cold, mechanical voice tells me. *Nine?* The first one plays.

'Ben... Oh Ben, where are you? I need you. I need help, oh god, I need help. Pick up the phone... pick up the—' Beep.

'Message two.'

'I am in so much trouble, Ben wake up... Please wake up... WAKE UP!' Beep.

'Message three.'

'Ben... Ben, answer the phone. I'm sorry to call. I don't want to drag you into this but I need you. I need you.' Beep.

Mia's voice chills me. Normally she's so calm and collected, but now she sounds desperate, full of panic. It's not like her. And why did she call the landline and not my mobile? I don't—

'Message four.'

'Ben? Ben? BEN?' Beep.

'Message five.'

'It was an accident but… *Christ*… Ben, there's so much blood…' She begins to cry.

I feel nausea bubble up in my throat, and I run, only just making it to the kitchen sink before I'm sick. Behind me, I can still hear her voice – the panic rising – and I realise it was her message that woke me. She called out for me, and somehow her voice worked its way into my dream. Somewhere she's alone, scared – and she needs me.

I cup my hand under the cold tap and splash water across my face. From behind I can still hear her, and as the last message plays she sobs:

'Ben… I need you. Help me. PLEASE HELP ME!'

And like the most annoying earworm, the line repeats and repeats through my head, spreading into the fault line of my headache, and blowing it open with dynamite.

Ben… I need you. Help me. PLEASE HELP ME!

I have to find my damn phone. I look in all the places I'd normally leave it – my bag, my coat, the kitchen counter – nothing. *Damn*. Let me think…

'What was I wearing last night?' I ask out loud, even though there's no one here to tell me. *Think, bloody think.* I try to fire up my memory, but there's just a yesterday-shaped hole in my head.

'This is crazy!' I yell at no one, as I search through my wardrobe, looking in every trouser pocket, every jacket and coat, even the ones I know I haven't worn in years, but it isn't here.

'Bloody—' I grab the door to slam it closed, but at the last moment I catch a glimpse of something. I kneel and squint into the depths of the wardrobe.

'*What?*' It's my best suit – the Paul Smith – and it's been rolled into a ball and stuffed right at the back. I lean inside, stretching as far as I can, like reaching into some second-rate Narnia, and pull it out. It looks like shit. Why didn't I hang it up? It cost a fortune; I only wear it for my most important meetings. Why the hell is it all balled up in the back of the wardrobe like this? I'm so angry with myself.

I unfold the jacket. I'm gentle with it, like it's a baby or a bomb. As I try to ease the wrinkles out with my hands, I feel weight behind the lapel. I slide my fingers into the top pocket and pull out my phone. For the briefest moment I wonder why it's there, but then that's blown away by anger, as I realise it's almost out of charge; there's merely the tiniest sliver of red, winking at me from the top right corner. *Idiot!* I want to hit myself, what the hell is wrong with me? We bought the green cable and put it in the hall for this exact situation. Mia even wrote that dumb sign: *for the sole use of Ben the forgetful*. It's there so I can't ever complain that there isn't a cable when I need one, so why didn't I use it? I must have walked right past it. Why am I such an idiot?

There's barely a flicker of life, maybe one per cent of battery, if I'm lucky. I hold my breath and go to my contacts. I open my favourites, there's only one number, and I call my wife.

Zjeeep – Zjeeep – Zjeeep. Zjeeep – Zjeeep – Zjeeep.

From somewhere in the house, I hear a phone ring.

'What?'

I walk back downstairs, following the sound, like a rat searching out the Pied Piper. It feels like it should be April the first, and Mia's gonna jump out and scream 'Fooled you!' but it's only February the tenth. And this isn't funny.

As I move, I can hear the phone get louder; I'm getting warmer.

In the hall there's a cupboard for winter coats, scarves, gloves and wellington boots. The ringing's coming from inside.

Zjeeep – Zjeeep – Zjeeep.

But, as I put my hand on the door handle, it stops – fades to nothing.

Zjeeeeeeeeeeeeeeeeeeeeepppppppppppppp..........

I look down at my phone, as the last breath of life flutters out of it, and the house is quiet again.

I pull open the little cupboard door. Inside there's a nasty smell of must and damp. I can't help but imagine the spiders and woodlice that call it home. The thought makes my skin crawl; I hate insects. I screw up all my courage and reach inside, snaking my fingers through the umbrellas, wellies and tattered old waterproof jackets and... *there*. I can feel the handle of something under a pile of coats. I pull at it, dragging it out into the light. I see what it is and... *What the hell is going on?* It's her handbag, the new one she bought in the new year sales. It was expensive, some designer label she likes, but it's definitely hers. I could identify it in a police line-up any day. Christ, that's morbid. *Don't think like that.*

I open the bag and tip it upside down, shaking the contents out onto the carpet. There's her phone, purse, keys, make-up... everything. Her whole life is here; but she never goes out without her phone. She's always checking emails, posting tweets, doing quizzes, counting steps, liking things, sharing stuff; she's glued to her phone. Even when she goes running it's strapped on her arm; I don't understand why she'd leave it tonight – and why it was hidden?

I open the purse. All her bank cards are inside, her driving licence, loyalty cards, stamps... Something is terribly wrong. Mia is like the ultimate Girl Guide, always prepared, always has her stuff with her; she doesn't go anywhere without it. So what's different tonight?

I slide my fingers into the little pockets and pouches in her purse, and I can feel that there's something there, folded in the compartment, hidden behind her credit and debit cards. I pull out two hundred pounds. My stomach swirls, and a feeling of dread slides through me.

I check again, but it's clear that everything that should be in her purse is here. Nothing's missing – except maybe one thing. There was a photo that used to sit in the little plastic window at the front, but now it's gone. It's possible that she took it out some time ago, maybe she didn't want to see it every day, but I doubt it, because it was a photo of—

Ring ring...

I'm lost for a moment. I look at the phone in the bag, expecting to see the screen lit up, but it isn't ringing, and I can't work out what's going on.

Ring ring...

'It's the landline, you idiot!' I finally scream at myself, as I scramble up and run to the living room. Damn, I'm slow tonight.

Beep. The machine picks up.

'This is the home of—'

'Hello, I'm here, don't hang up...' I snatch the receiver from its cradle and yell: 'Mia, Mia?'

'Ben?' Her voice is tiny, thin, barely there.

'Mia.'

'You're there – I'm so glad – I thought you wouldn't wake up. I thought I was alone.'

'No, I'm here, I heard you call me.'

'Thank you,' she says softly.

'Mia, what happened?'

'Ben, he… he's dead.'

I open my mouth, but nothing comes out, like my brain is glitching. *Dead*. Someone's dead. I know I should have a response to that but it's like my head is just full of white noise.

'Mia, I don't underst—'

'If I could just go back, I would. It was one second, Ben, just one second and it was done. How can everything change in one second?'

'I don't…' I dry up. 'Mia…' I say as gently as I can, '…tell me what happened?'

There's a pause, and then a deep breath, and she says: 'He's dead; it was so quick., I couldn't… I couldn't stop it.'

'Don't blame yourself, awful things happen, it's just life. Have you called the police?'

There's a pause, and I wonder if she heard my question, but then in the smallest of voices, she replies, 'No.'

'That's okay, I'll call them, where are you; are you the only one there?'

She doesn't say anything so I try again.

'Mia, are you the only witness, is there someone else with you? Was it a hit and run?'

'Ben, you can't call the police.'

'Has someone already called them?'

'No… that wasn't what I meant. Ben you can't call the police. We don't need to involve anyone else. I just need you.'

'I…' The white noise gets louder. 'I don't understand.'

'Just you and me Ben, the two of us against the world, remember?'

'Of course I remember, but—'

'Ben, I'm sorry to do this, I wouldn't if there was any other way, but there isn't. So I have to ask you to help me, and you must promise not to call anyone,' she insists.

'But what's going on? I don't know wha—'

'Swear to me, Ben.'

'Mia, that's—'

'Just the two of us against the world.'

I pause. I remember saying those words like it was yesterday, and not thousands of yesterdays ago. 'Where are you, Mia?'

'I'll tell you, but you have to come alone, you swear?'

'But I don't—'

'You have to swear, Ben? Cross your heart?'

'Okay... of course I swear.'

'And you do trust me, don't you?'

'Yes.'

'And you love me?'

'Jesus Christ, Mia, you know I do. Please tell me what happened.'

'Okay...' She breathes deeply. 'It was an accident, Ben, it was an awful tragic accident. That's what's important. I didn't mean it.'

'Mean what?'

'To kill him.'

'Kill?' The word shocks me, she'd said *dead* before, but *kill* is different. It's not finding a body or seeing a guy collapse in the street; it isn't passive, or distant. *Kill* is close and violent and trouble – *kill* will worm its way into your soul. 'Who... who did you kill?' I ask.

'It doesn't matter, not the details,' she says. 'But you have to know that it was my fault. It was an accident, but it was my fault.'

'Did you hit someone?'

'Kind of.'

'Have you been drinking?'

She pauses. 'Yes.'

'Christ.' My brain is spinning – what to do, how to make this okay, how to be safe? 'We can get a lawyer, if it was an accident then the police will see that, the forensics will show what happened; tragic accidents happen all the time, it's okay, Mia.'

'No, it isn't,' she snaps, sounding brittle and on edge. 'Ben, I know how the law works, so no police, I just need you to come and help me.'

'I… I said I would, didn't I? It's… it's just…' I flounder a little and my head won't stop pounding. 'I just want to know why… I mean, did you hit someone with the car?' In my mind's eye I see a stretch of road with black skid marks – brakes applied too heavy and too late – a body in the road. I see Mia in our car; there's a dent in the wing, and a crack that spreads through the windscreen, like a family tree expanding out to the very tip of the glass.

'Car?' she says, like it's a word from some foreign language she's never heard before. 'Hit someone with the car… no.'

'Then what happened?'

'You'll see when you get here, just come. I need you.'

She needs me. 'I'm coming, don't worry, It's you and me against the world.'

She breathes a deep sigh of relief. 'Thank you.' Her voice is lighter for a second, and then I hear it shift as she draws up her strength. 'I need you to bring me some things.'

'Like… like what?'

'Things I'll need, that we'll need… to make this right.'

I have the sensation of falling. 'What am I bringing you?'

Very calmly, articulating each word, she says: 'Kitchen spray, bleach, rags, towels – a lot of towels – and we'll need bin bags, black ones and the garden waste ones that are stronger, and tape – strong tape – lots of it.'

'Mia…' I start but the rest of the question just dies on my tongue. I want to ask *why, why do you need these things?* But I'm afraid of the answer. There's only one reason I can think of, and it makes my stomach churn.

'And bring some of the old lockdown masks and marigold gloves. And I need a change of clothes, dark and baggy, with a hood – I need a hood.'

'Mia… this is a joke, right?' But she doesn't laugh. 'You're scaring me.'

'You said you'd help.' There's an edge to her voice, a mix of anger and frustration. She doesn't want a debate, she wants loyalty, and I've always sworn I would be there for her. I can't let her down, even though I think we should call the police. So I tell her: 'I'll help, it's just that I don't understand what's happened. You said there's a dead man, but it wasn't a car accident?'

'No, I didn't bring the car. It's still outside the house.'

'So wha—'

'I pushed him, and he fell and hit his head.'

'Pushed?' I ask, suddenly feeling disconnected, like my reality has shifted and I don't know what she's saying? 'You pushed him?'

'It was an accident – that's it.'

There's a sharpness in her tone that tells me not to ask any more – and to be honest, I don't want to ask more. I'm frightened by what she might say next.

'I didn't do anything wrong Ben.' She snarls at me, a mix of anger and desperation. 'It wasn't my fault, but… but there's blood, there's a lot of blood, so I really need you to bring towels.'

'Towels?'

'Yes, for the blood. Ben, you need to concentrate. Maybe you should get a pen and paper, to write down what you need to bring. I can go through the list again slowly.'

'I just…' Cold creeps through me. She's moving too fast, pushing me into a corner without telling me what's happened. I have to know more about what we're dealing with. 'Who's dead?' I ask.

'I don't know his name, Ben, it doesn't matter.'

'But Mia—'

'He was hurting me, okay?' She flares in anger and then that dies away and she sounds scared. 'He hurt me, Ben.'

'Hurt you? But Mia—'

'Ben, he hurt me. I pushed him away and… and now I need your help, without you bombarding me with questions. You get that don't you?'

'Of course, I do, but—'

'Please, just come, bring what I asked for… and…' She pauses and I hold my breath, as I sense that something even worse is coming. 'There are two more things I need.' She drops her voice. 'A hammer and a carving knife… the sharpest one we've got.' She says it low and clear, no fear, she might just as well have said: *pick us up some toilet paper and milk on your way home*, but she didn't… she asked for *a hammer and a carving knife*. I can't breathe.

'Where—' I start, but the phone goes dead.

I find an old Adidas holdall, a kit bag from when I used to play squash – though that was at least ten years and twenty pounds ago – and I start to stuff it with all the things she asked for. I'm trying to stop thinking about what it all means, because that's a rabbit hole to fall down. I've binged enough serial killer box sets to know that she must be planning to clean up a crime scene. She's going to wipe away all the evidence she was there; bleach away all fingerprints and her DNA. What else could she be doing? It's unreal; the thought of it makes my stomach squirm. It's like I'm in some knock-off Tarantino movie. Either Mia's gone mad, or this is some crazy twenty-years-married test, to see how much I love her – how far I'll go for her. *Jesus Christ.* Is she crazy – or even worse – is she sane?

The last thing to go in the holdall is her change of clothes: a pair of leggings, a shirt, a black hoodie, and running shoes. And me? I change into a navy hoodie and black jeans. Then I go and find my old pair of prescription sunglasses and put them on. I look stupid, like I'm in the throes of a mid-life crisis and should have a teenage girlfriend and a sports car. I put my normal glasses back on, and then just sit and try to stop thinking about the bag with the bleach and the knife and the hammer. *Christ.*

Five minutes later the phone rings. I snatch it up before the first ring's finished. 'I'm here.'

'Do you remember that time in Exeter, in that cottage?' Her voice is breathy, a little husky.

'Yes, but I don't—'

'I can't get it out of my head… I don't know why.' She sounds a little spacey, dislocated, like after you come round from an anaesthetic.

'There was that rabbit,' I say.

'Yes, yes, of course there was, I'd forgotten.'

I remember that trip to Exeter like it was yesterday, even though it was more than twenty years ago. 'You hit it, with the car; its legs were broken.'

'It was in such pain.'

'We ended it.'

'Yes.'

There's silence.

'I couldn't do it,' she remembers. 'Back then, I froze.'

'I did it for you.'

'You put it out of its misery.'

'Yes… it was a kindness.'

'There aren't enough kindnesses in the world,' she says, and I feel very heavy all of a sudden.

That weekend in Exeter had been a turning point in our fledgling relationship. She'd been driving, and hit a rabbit. Like in the cliché it hadn't moved, just sat transfixed by the headlights. It was Mia's fault, so clearly her fault, but I said nothing, I didn't point the finger. I just helped when it was most needed; I ended the poor creature's life.

Before that, I don't think we would've lasted as a couple. She thought I was a bit of a wimp − kind of a pushover − fun, but probably not long-term partner material. But when push came to shove, I killed for her − like a knight of old fulfilling a quest to earn his fair lady. But that was more than twenty years ago, and a badly injured rabbit is not a human being that's been pushed and hit its head and…

'Ben, what are you thinking?'

I don't answer, but instead ask, 'Where are you, Mia?'

'I'm in Earl's Court.'

I'm so surprised that I'm mute for a few seconds. 'What are you doing there?'

'I…' she makes a strangled sound. 'Ben, don't ask, just come.'

'Where exactly are you?'

'I'm at seventy-four Hastings Road.'

'Are you at somebody's house?'

'I… Just get here, Ben.'

There's nothing for a moment, then I say: 'Okay.'

'Thank you.' She sounds tired, like she could curl up and hibernate.

'I'll find directions—'

'Don't look the address up on your phone, or the computer, or anything,' she insists. 'Don't look at any maps online. There mustn't be a record of this, nothing to link either of us to this address. Do you get that, Ben? Nothing.'

'So how do I find you?'

'The old-fashioned way,' she half-laughs. 'There's an *A to Z* on the bookshelf in my office. It's old, like from before smartphones, but nothing around here has changed that much in years; even an old street finder should get you here.'

'Okay.'

'Ben, please understand how important this is – you can't leave a trail. Everything depends on that.'

'This is crazy, Mia, you know that, don't you?'

'I'm sorry, Ben, but if you love me, please do as I ask.'

'Mia…' I start, but what is there to say? 'I'll be there in twenty—'

'Don't drive.'

'What?'

'Get a cab from a rank, walk into Wimbledon. You mustn't order one, and don't pay by card or on an app, just use cash.'

'I don't have any cash.'

'In… in my purse, there's some cash. It's in my bag and that's…' There's what seems like a guilty pause. '…in the cupboard under the stairs.' I hear the annoyance in her voice; she hadn't wanted me to find the bag, to see that she'd left the house with nothing, but she must think she has no alternative now. 'Take the money, leave the purse. Don't bring anything with you – not even your wallet. No ID. Nothing that can identify us. Don't wear any jewellery, nothing.'

'Mia, this is insane.'

'No it's not, this is the only sane thing to do. If we want our lives back, if we want everything to be normal again, then this is the only way. I've thought everything through, Ben. This is the solution.'

'But I don't even know what's happen—'

'Can't you just trust me?' her voice is both brittle and poisonous in the same second. 'I'm sorry – god, Ben, I'm so sorry, I'm falling apart here. Please just come. Walk to the rank in Wimbledon, get the cab to take you to Ellis Road. It's just a couple of minutes from there to where I am, and it's mostly residential streets that are pretty dark and empty.'

'Why can't I come straight to you?'

'There are CCTV cameras everywhere, Ben. You can't just come here directly. Get out at Ellis Road, and look down as you walk, cover your head; you don't want to be seen. You're a ghost… bring nothing that could identify you and don't talk to anyone or make eye contact. No one should remember you.'

'Mia—'

'Ben, our lives depend on this. You can't have anything on you that can be traced back to us. At the end of tonight, if anyone asks—'

'You mean if the police ask?'

'If anyone asks, we're going to say we were home all evening.'

'But—'

'All evening.' She cuts me dead. 'Ben, if we mess this up… we'll lose everything.'

Chapter Three

Ben

I walk. The air is cold, though at least it's not raining. I try to keep from thinking about what's happening – about the dead man and the hammer and knife in my bag – so I start naming all the superheroes that have ever been in the Avengers. Then I try and name all the X-Men and then it's the less well-known teams like the Defenders and the Inhumans and the Champions and… *there's a dead man and my wife and a hammer and a kn—* No, think about something else, anything else…

–

I'm out of breath by the time I reach Wimbledon, which really shows how out of shape I am. Of course I keep promising myself I'll exercise – you know, a proper regime at the gym and jogging and all that – but the reality is that I get a deadline from work and I reach for the Hobnobs. I have zero willpower, and I'm over forty, so it's all downhill from here.

There's a pub near the station that stays open late, so there's bound to be some cabs parked outside, waiting for drunk students to stagger out. I head over there to grab one.

'Ellis Road, Earl's Court,' I tell the driver as I slide into the backseat, and he enters the address into the satnav and pulls away from the curb. I put the Adidas bag on my lap and hold it tight, like a sleeping baby. There are no words from the driver, as we tear up the hill towards the common. It's a pity, as it would take my mind off what's in the bag and what Mia plans to do with a hammer and a carving—

Superman, Batman, Wonder Woman, Aquaman, Flash, Green Lantern and... bleach, black plastic bags— *Oh Christ*, I can't stop the thoughts coursing through my head, I really wish I hadn't watched all those seasons of *Dexter*... I mean, she has to be planning to cut the body up and— 'No!'

'What?' The driver turns and looks at me with big eyes. 'No? What, you want me to drive another way?'

'No, no, sorry... I didn't mean to... nothing, just... nothing.'

He shakes his head and turns back to the road; he thinks I'm crazy. He's probably right. I didn't mean to say anything out loud, but this is insane. We're not violent people: we've got a direct debit for Amnesty and Greenpeace; we volunteer on litter picks; every Saturday we go to a farmers' market and then do the *Guardian* crossword in a café. Okay, so when we were younger, maybe it was a little different – on our second date we were chained to railings outside the foreign office – but that's what students do. Back then we thought we were going to change the world; we were young and in love. Oh my god, I remember that every time she yelled '*No blood for oil!*' or '*Stop the war!*' I'd get an erection. She was so hot, and I was on fire for her. Jesus, it was all so much easier back then. Nothing got in the way of our ideals. I was going to change Bush and Blair's minds with satirical cartoons, and she was going to use the law to fight for civil rights, become an advocate for the oppressed. What naïve kids we were. And where have we ended up twenty years later? I draw bloody car adverts, and she's a corporate lawyer – we're both sell-outs. But are we the kind of people who take a hammer and carving knife and… I mean, are we? Really, is that what we've become? Is this the point where we crawl into the gutter? *Jesus Christ* – and what would *he* think? What would Gandhi do?

But I know – right – the Mahatma wouldn't cut up a dead body and try to dispose of it, because that must be what's going on here. It's the only explanation, what else could she possibly want a hammer and knife for? What else could this be? I should call the police, before it's too late, before it all gets out of hand… I should… I should… but I promised Mia I wouldn't. I promised her. *Us two against the world*.

I watch the streets skitter by, as the cab races up the hill, and hits the outskirts of the common. We're surrounded by trees; the headlights make them look like skeletons, waving swords and spears; an army of darkness. If someone were to step out of the woods now, the car would plough into them and kill them. It would be an accident, awful and tragic, but an accident all the same. I'd call 999 and ask for the police and ambulance. They'd come and immediately take charge; it would be out of my hands. The police might even say *thank you*, and *what a good citizen you are*; and I could be proud I'd done my civic duty. The ambulance would remove the body, and the police would clean up the mess. It wouldn't be up to me to scrape the dead body off the road and into a bin bag – that isn't how the system works. I'm a law-abiding citizen. I recycle. I'm not a criminal, but I will be if I follow Mia. I think she's crossed the line, and she'll pull me with her if I don't…

Oh Christ. My stomach clenches and I quickly wind the window down.

'It's a hundred quid if you're sick in my cab,' the driver barks.

—

It takes a little over twenty minutes to reach Earl's Court as there's no traffic at this time of night. I pay the driver, giving him a small tip, so I don't stand out in his memory. As the taxi draws away, I pull the hood up over my head and shrink down a little, trying to blend into the shadows. I will be no one. I imagine myself homeless and unloved, like the guys I see around Waterloo station, in their cardboard boxes and stained old sleeping bags. Even when they beg, their eyes are cast down, so I do the same. Invisible. In the shadows. Head bowed all the way.

I pass little shops that are mostly closed, but there are a few convenience stores still open, for those with the late-night munchies, or active nicotine addictions, or those who just need a drink to get through the night. On a corner, there's a small twenty-four-hour store with a big bucket of roses outside. The sign above says it's almost Valentine's Day; actually it says 7, 6, 5 — 4 days, like a countdown to love. I'd forgotten romance was in the air. For Valentine's we always go to the same restaurant. It's kind of our thing; a little Italian place owned by a lovely old couple who've been married for fifty years. I always order the melanzane parmigiana; it's like a gourmet good luck charm, except for last year when we both drank too much and argued. The meal ended with Mia throwing a drink in my face and storming out. I've done nothing about booking it this year. It's probably too late now.

I pick one of the roses out of the bucket and smell it. There's no scent of anything, except maybe a chemical tang from the water. The thorns have been stripped away; the stem's denuded of everything except the blood-red petals. Maybe I should buy a bunch... but that's a dumb idea, isn't it? *Hi Mia, here are some flowers, and the hammer and carving knife you wanted.* Do you take flowers to a dismemberment? *Argh*, my stomach pitches; that was the first time I've allowed myself to think that word. I must not forget that a man has died tonight.

I drop the rose back into the bucket and move on, my head bowed again, my feet shuffling; I'm back to homeless zombie. I turn the corner into Hastings Road, and start to count off the buildings until... number seventy-four. '*Oh.*'

That isn't what I expected number seventy-four Hastings Road to be, but I was fooling myself, because I know Earl's Court; I've been here many times and know it's been dodgy for decades. It's full of bedsits and hostels, it's where the immigrants live, the people that work in Chelsea and Kensington but can't afford to live there. It's also where the men who work in the centre of town come for sex by the hour, with prostitutes of any colour, creed, sexuality or proclivity. And even though I knew all that, I still hoped number seventy-four would be a regular house. I mean, number seventy-four sounds like a normal home, right?

And deep down, I'd pictured the man who was dead – and in my head he'd been old and ill; slumped in a chair with a half-smile on his face, like he'd been released from terrible pain. And next to him, Mia as some kind of Florence Nightingale, or a walking Dignitas clinic – an angel of death with a heart of gold. I'd hoped that this unknown man's death was clean and neat, like a pet hamster dying of old age. But, of course, it isn't and it won't be. I know that now, as I look across the street at seventy-four Hastings Road, and see that it's a hotel. My hand starts to shake.

Mia

The water's so hot that it's boiled me like a lobster. I've scrubbed and scrubbed at my belly and thighs, but I can still feel him on me. In some places I'm raw, bleeding, but I still don't feel clean. I might never feel clean again. I've been standing in the shower for so long, watching the water swirl around my feet, but at last I've stopped crying. No more tears; not for me and certainly not for him.

I don't know myself tonight. I don't know why I did what I did. Why the hell did I take such a risk? I've known my whole adult life to be careful of men. Since puberty there's always been a part of my brain on the lookout to make sure I'm not putting myself in danger – we all do it: all women know that a situation can escalate quickly, and even men you think you know can change without warning. Why did I take the risk and come here? I ask myself that question, over and over – but I'm scared of the answer. That's why I stand in the boiling water and let it scald the pain away. I stand here for so long… Until I finally turn the tap off and stand, shivering, as the steam snakes away through the small white tiled room, and the air turns cold.

'Come on Mia, move!' I hiss at myself, knowing I have to get going, but I'm so sluggish. *Just another minute…* like staying in bed after the alarm has gone off. *Just another hour…* but this is not as simple as staying in a warm bed. Next door is the man I killed, and if I'm going to make it through tonight I need to cut out the part of me that feels, that pities, that shows remorse; and in particular, the part that wants to roll over and play dead. Tonight I have to fight like never before. I can fall apart later; maybe tomorrow I can allow myself the luxury of empathy and sympathy. Over time, maybe, I can even make some sort of amends – work every other weekend in a soup kitchen, or give thirty per cent of my wages to charity – but that's for later. Right now I have to harden my heart, and wade through the blood. I can do it. I will do it. There won't be two victims in this hotel room tonight.

I grab a towel from the small shelf to the side of the showerhead. It's thin and harsh, like the kind of towel I'll get in prison if I mess this up. I wrap it tight around me, and then I have to walk back into the bedroom and…

Oh fuck.

The floor is a lake of blood. He floats on it, like an island in a scarlet sea. Even dead he still looks gorgeous, though the cheeky smile has gone, and the twinkle in his eye and—

Oh god. Tears pour down my face – so much for being empty.

'It's okay, you're okay,' I tell myself as the waterfall washes me away.

I sit on the bed and lay the thin towel in my lap to catch my tears. I don't know if they hold DNA, but they must do. There's probably an episode of *CSI* where they caught someone because they wept on the body. So I catch them just in case, because that's what television has taught me: that I can't be too careful. When I leave this room there must be no trace that I was ever here. No cell of skin, not a single hair, no surface touched by my hand. I can't even trust gloves; I know they can't always hide your identity. I have to consider everything – every bloody thing – because even the smallest, briefest, touch of my body in this room can leave enough of a trace of my DNA to burn my life down.

See, Dad, television is educational – it's taught me all the traps, and all the problems of covering up a killing. I hope it's also shown me how to save myself from spending the rest of my life locked up, because I will not give this bastard that power over me, not after what he did.

I look over at the ugly digital clock by the bed. It's 12.45. Ben will be here soon. Ben... I'm so sorry that I'm dragging him into this shitstorm, but I know he'll come, because he's loyal and kind and decent; but that's also why this will hurt him so deeply. I'm asking him to show his love for me by doing something vile – and after tonight he will hate me and I don't blame him. I've trapped him. It was mean of me to use his wedding vows like that, when he wrote them with so much love, because I'm pretty sure neither of us mentioned anything about helping the other cover up a killing. I don't think that comes under *in sickness or in health and forsaking all others*... and the *forsaking all others* part – well, that just opens a whole new can of worms, doesn't it?

Fuck. The tears start again. What was it my mum used to say? '*Tears are good, they drown the devil.*' Well, I don't know about that. Life is so complicated these days, there's both devil and angel in everything now.

–

I stop crying at last. I fold the towel and put it on the floor. I stand up; my legs are a little like jelly. I see myself, naked, in the mirror on the wardrobe. I look thin. My mum would have said I was stringy, like a bean. It's the running; I think I might be addicted to it now. I can see my ribs for the first time since I was a teen, but I'm not weak because of it. I'm in control of my body, and I've made myself strong and fast. Tonight I had to fight, tooth and claw, savage and bestial and I won. And that's how I know I can do this. I can survive tonight. I will walk away from this. I nod at the warrior in the glass across from me. *Only one victim here.*

Even though it makes me feel dirty, I have to put the dress back on, the one I wore tonight. Before this evening, I have always loved this African-print dress. I call it my parrot dress, because it's wild and colourful; it hugs me tight, like a second skin, making me look naked – more than naked, perhaps – and every time I've ever worn it, I've seen the men eyeing me, salivating, calculating if they should make a move; like lions attacking a gazelle. And the truth is that I liked that. I did. I liked the effect I had on them. When I put it on, just a few hours ago, it made me feel great, sexy and powerful, but now, I want to burn it. I hate the feel of it, moulding itself to my body; I don't want to feel anything hugging me tight. I want to wear a sack, something that hides me. I don't want to be a woman, not now, maybe not for a long time. That's what he's done to me, what this night has done to me. What I am fighting against.

The room smells. I know that. I still smell, no matter how hard I've scrubbed, there's still the iron and rust of blood in the air; there's still the cloying sweetness of sex, and the bitter sweaty fear that lies underneath it all. There is still the stench of him.

I wish I had a cigarette. I gave them up fifteen years ago, I had to, and I haven't gone back to them. But now I could chain-smoke an entire pack of filterless, high-tar cancer sticks; even the ones with the pictures of tumour-encrusted lungs on the pack. I would smoke all twenty of them down to the butt. I'd let each one burn my fingers and light a new one off the dying embers of the last. *Oh god, oh god, oh god…* how do I stop my brain whirring?

I spy with my little eye, something beginning with… B…

It's blood, of course it's blood; that's all I can see, even when I close my eyes. I have to go downstairs – get away from the blood – and watch out for Ben. He'll be here any minute. Poor bastard.

I walk slow and sure, like I'm heading to the gallows. I walk down the flights of stairs to reception and then as quickly as I can, I pad silently over and peer through the glass of the old revolving door at the street outside.

I'm shocked by how normal everything is in the outside world. I see a hen party walking past. The bride is completely smashed. She can't walk straight; her brides-maids have to hold her up. Her T-shirt says *kiss me quick, fuck me slow*. It makes me feel queasy, frightened for her; she's so drunk that she couldn't defend herself if a man took her T-shirt as an invitation – as a challenge.

'She asked for it.' That would be his defence at trial, if it even got that far, because so few do. So few women have the tenacity to fight against such a screwed-up system and get their time in a courtroom. And what about me? What would I say in my own defence? What will I tell my husband, when he arrives and asks what I'm doing in this cheap, shitty hotel? How will I explain what I've done tonight? And the dead, naked, man on the floor upstairs, how do I explain that?

Then I see Ben, on the opposite side of the street. He's here, and it's time for a reckoning.

Ben

The Lampton Hotel. It looks like it's been converted from a Regency town house. It has a striped black and white awning that dips over onto the street, and chequerboard tiled steps that lead up to a slim entranceway, with a beautiful old revolving door that looks like it should lead into Harrods or Fortnum & Mason. But the illusion of opulence is shattered by the sign that sits in the window to the left of the door. In a stuttering, garish neon it reads '*Vacancies*', and below it is a piece of card, and on that, in thick Sharpie, is written: '*Any length of stay available*'. It may have once been a *nice* hotel, but now if you scratch the surface, you'll find there's a dirtiness and seediness. It's obvious that nowadays the hotel exists on bookings by the hour. A meeting place for quickies, affairs and assignations. A house built on lies and spunk.

So, I have to ask myself, why is my wife here? Though of course there's one obvious answer: she's having an affair and it's ended tragically. Maybe he had a heart attack, maybe she screwed him to death. Just thinking that makes me feel unclean but – *damn* – why am I here? How the hell can she drag me over here like this? I don't want to see her dead lover. I don't want to know about her affair. *Jesus Christ*. With my head pounding and my eyes stinging, I step onto—

'Watch where you're going, you stupid bastard,' a cabbie yells as he swerves to avoid hitting me, his tyres screeching like a banshee.

'I'm sorry,' I call to the driver, but he's already gone, probably still swearing at my stupidity. My heart is like a pinball machine in my chest.

'Sorry,' I say, but I don't know who I'm talking to anymore. Sorry... sorry... sorry, all I ever say is sorry. I'm always so bloody sorry; it's exhausting to be sorry all the time.

Finally, when my heart's stopped ricocheting off my ribs, I cross the road and step onto the pavement, looking up the stairs at the revolving door. I could turn around, except I know I can't, and I won't. Instead I step into the—

'*Jesus.*' The door shudders and jams, as someone stamps a foot into the mechanism, trapping me in the centre, like a rat in a trap. I look through the glass and see—

'Mia?'

She looks at me, her face dark and intense. Her hair's damp, pulled back tight at the scalp. Her lips are thin and harsh, no colour in them at all, and her jaw is set and stern. But then her lips crack into a sad smile. She looks glad to see me. I think.

She slowly raises her finger to her lips as if to say *quiet, now.* I nod and she moves back, so I can step inside the hotel. Automatically I reach to hug her and—

'No,' she pushes at me, panic in her eyes. I step back; she looks afraid of me. *Of me.*

'Mia, I'm sorry...' I raise my hands, palms up, like I surrender.

'Ben I didn't, I just...' She's shaking. She looks like she's barely holding it together. She whispers to me, 'This isn't the place to talk. Follow me, look straight ahead, don't look around, don't look back.' She leads the way. I follow. What else can I do?

The hotel reception is small and uncared for, I can see that the marble floor was once magnificent, but now it's chipped and pitted from years of cases and bags being dropped on it. There's a large window that looks out onto the street, with a pair of red velvet curtains that, once upon a time, might have been expensive and lush, but now are blotchy from years of sunlight. In front of the window is a sofa that's faded in places and it looks like threadbare sections have been filled in with ink.

Mia walks quickly to the stairs, by the side of reception. She aims for them like a missile, but I can't just go straight ahead, I'm like Lot's wife – I can't follow the instructions. I have to look back. My eyes slip to the left, to the faded wood of the reception desk, with a stain that stretches across the front and looks like blood. Behind it there's a tall man, hunched over. His uniform hangs on him, at least two sizes too big, a name badge reads: *Ali*. He looks like he's in his late twenties or early thirties, but from his posture he could be an old man. I see all this in a fraction of a second. Mia must sense I'm not following, and she hisses.

'Ben!'

The man looks up. Ali's eyes meet mine and I'm actually shocked for a second, as they are so full of pain, he looks like the weight of the world lies on his shoulders.

'Excuse me—' He starts to ask me something, but Mia grabs my arm and hauls me off to the stairs.

The light in the stairwell flickers and casts a green light over everything, like in some crappy zombie movie. I follow behind her, and for the first time look at what she's wearing. I don't recognise the dress. It's really bright and fancy, not the normal thing she'd wear to work. Her outfits are usually more sombre. This is vibrant and colourful and… sexy. It's definitely sexy, hugging her tight as she moves. I'm sure I've never seen it before. And I remember my Paul Smith suit, all balled up in the bottom of my wardrobe. Was there some event tonight? Were we both dressed up for something? I try to remember, but last night is still a giant hole in my head.

Mia stops at the third-floor landing and holds the door open. I walk out and… *yuk*, the carpet's sticky, and the walls look like they needed a fresh coat of paint ten years ago. Mia stops in front of room 303 and turns. I can see the cogs whirring in her head. She's thinking about whether she should send me away, whether once I get inside I might panic and make this worse. She's also thinking about the man on reception – will he follow us up? I can see the thoughts crashing round in her head, as she weighs up all the possibilities. I reach out slowly to take her hand. I don't want to spook her like I did downstairs, but then I see that there's a stamp on the back of it, a black square, just where the wash of black ink was on my hand – where my hand was cut.

'Mia, how—'

But that thought is swept out of my head by the shock of seeing, poking out from the sleeve of her dress, dark bruises like blossom on her skin.

'Jesus. The bruises, Mia?'

She pulls her sleeves down further, looking a little ashamed that I've seen the angry blue flowers on her arms.

'Ben, thanks so much for bringing this.' She points to the Adidas bag in my hand. 'But you can go now, just leave the bag,' she tells me solemnly.

'I can't, you know that,' I tell her.

'It's okay I...' A look of pain shoots across her face. 'You don't need to come inside the room. I can do it myself, now I have what I need.'

I could turn around and go, maybe five or ten minutes ago I would have just handed over the bag... but not after seeing the bruises on her arms, and the shattering tiredness in her eyes. I think that, if there's any chance that we can keep our lives and marriage intact, then it's time for me to fight alongside her. I have to make a stand.

'Ben, what are you doing?' she asks me, as I suddenly sit on the floor and take off my right shoe.

'Ben, this isn't the time for playing silly buggers.'

I drop the shoe and then pull off my right sock and shake it out into my hand.

'What are you—?'

A ring drops into my palm. It's white gold and has a pattern of tiny leaves on it. Perhaps they were a little finer twenty years ago, it has worn slightly, but you can still see them clearly. It's one of a pair. A matching pair.

'Please don't do this,' she says.

'Where's the cage?' I ask as I hold the ring up.

'This isn't a game, Ben.'

'Where's the—'

'Fuck you,' she says with real anger.

'— cage?' My voice is level; I don't ask with any malice or anger, I just ask. Her jaw tightens – she hates me for a second – and I can see that she just wants me to go. Tough luck.

'Do you have it?' I ask.

She answers by holding up her hands, and wiggling her fingers in a lacklustre display of jazz hands. She isn't wearing a watch, or a bracelet – in fact, no jewellery at all. She's not wearing the ring.

'Where is it?'

'I don't—'

'Where?'

She grinds her jaw so tight I think it might snap. 'You are such a… it's at home.'

'When did you take it off?'

'It doesn't matter.'

'It does,' I tell her, and it really does, to me. I want to know when she took her wedding ring off. 'So when?'

She doesn't say anything. I put my ring back on the second finger of my left hand. She told me to come without any jewellery, and I got that. I knew why – anything we wear can be used to identify us, so we shouldn't wear anything we aren't happy to get rid of, throw down a drain if we have to. But I couldn't leave my ring at home, I have worn it every day for twenty years. Even when I broke my hand, I wore it round my neck. So I have to ask: 'Where is it, Mia?'

She looks at my naked foot. I think she wishes a hole would open in the ground and swallow me up. 'It's in my bedside table,' she admits finally.

I look away from her, trying to keep my disappointment hidden. What I had wanted to hear, was that it was in a secret pocket, or in the lining of her bra, somewhere near, so she could put it back on after she was finished with him. But it isn't. She left it at home. She took it off to pretend she was single, so she could pick someone up… so she could…

'The cage,' I say in a small, timid voice.

'It's a stupid game,' she explodes.

'You taught it to me.'

She looks daggers back at me, like I'm immature or something, and maybe I am. But this is the bird and the cage, and it was the first game we ever played.

–

We met at university. It was the start of my second year, and I'd moved out of the dorms, into a shared house in town. It was fancy, like proper fancy, and we had a moving-in party. At about midnight, there was an argument over who had brought a bottle of champagne. It was me. My mum had given me six bottles; she'd said that was the way to win friends and influence people. I'd hidden a bottle at the back of the fridge, but this really obnoxious girl found it, and started to open it. She told this vacuous-looking handsome guy that *she* had brought it to the party. She was taking the credit for my attempt to be sophisticated, and this guy was lapping it up. She was going to get the champagne sex that was rightly mine.

'It's my bottle, let go,' I yelled at her, but she called me a 'fucking dick' and wouldn't let go. So we pulled back and forth and... the bottle exploded. The cork shot out, and it was like fizzy wine fireworks night. It shot everywhere – we both got soaked. I was angry, but the obnoxious girl just laughed and laughed. I hated her. It was Mia.

I had to take her to my room and lend her a towel and some clothes. She went through my wardrobe, and found this tuxedo, which I'd bought in a charity shop, but hadn't had the confidence to wear. She put it on, with a pair of my boxers, and she looked amazing. Ever since that night, androgynous-looking women in men's suits have been my major turn-on. I have wanked over Julie Andrews in a tux in *Victor/Victoria* so many times it is not funny.

Wearing my tuxedo, Mia left to re-join the party (FYI: I never got the tux back), but about half an hour later she came and found me. In her hand she had both the cork and the metal top from the bottle of champagne. She called them the bird (the cork) and the cage.

'These two things go together, they're no good alone,' she said. 'So, this is yours...' and she gave me the bird-cork, and she pocketed the little wire cage. 'If I see you and I produce the cage, then you'd better be able to show me the cork right that second. If you can't, then you owe me a bottle. And we'll make it *good* champagne. Okay?' and she smiled at me, like a shark smiles at sardines. 'And it works the other way around too, so you might want to come and find me some time, and test whether I have the cage.' She grinned, and of course I nodded like an idiot, feeling incredibly turned on by this girl in my clothes, and excited by any suggestion I might get to see her again. So the game was set in motion. Then she disappeared. Of course, by the next morning, it was all just a hazy half-memory, and I knew I wouldn't have the courage to go and find her. So, I forgot about Mia and fell back into university life.

But a few weeks later, at about ten p.m. on some random Thursday, she turned up at my house and presented me with the cage.

'Where is the little baby bird?' she asked and, of course, I had no idea where it had gone. 'I win,' she crowed, and sent me down to the off licence for a bottle of champagne, a tube of Rolos (she ate the whole packet, even the last one) and a packet of Rizlas. When I got back, she was in my bed. She'd gone through my record collection and made two piles; one that I could keep, and one that had to go to the charity shop the next day. The charity pile was about ninety per cent of my records.

'But you can't hate ELO,' I said.

'Are you fucking kidding me?' she said, as she expertly rolled a joint on the sleeve of *Blue* by Joni Mitchell (it had been my mum's and I was allowed to keep that one).

'Are you going to pick Jeff Lynne over this?' She pulled the duvet back, to show me she was wearing my boxer shorts – and only my boxer shorts. I kept my mouth shut and got into bed. The next day, half of my books, most of my records, and all my DVDs went to Oxfam. I had never been happier.

But now I hold up my wedding ring – the bird – and ask her to show me the cage – her ring. It's a test. Marriage is always a test.

Mia

Of course he has it. Even though I said no jewellery, he had to bring it in his sock. It's fucking romantic abuse, that's what it is; he's setting me up to fail, like so many other times. He can always out-love me; always shows me more affection than I show him. He buys better presents, knows when we first did this, or went there or experienced that. He always remembers games we played, films we saw, or music we danced to. He remembers every fucking anniversary like a romantic idiot savant. Fuck him and his bloody thoughtfulness.

'I don't have my wedding ring,' I tell him with as little emotion as I can. 'It's at home and I will tell you all about why it's there, but that has to be later.'

'I need to know what's happened tonight. You need to tell me now.'

'No I don't – fucking hell Ben – we don't have time for naval gazing. We have to act now. So what's going to happen, is that I'm going inside this room now. You can come too or you can leave. If you leave, then please be as quiet as a mouse, and don't talk to reception or call the police. But if you stay...'

I can't finish the sentence – what do I say? *If you stay you will find out what a bitch I am. You will hate me and discover how full of rage I am, how bitter and twisted I've become, and what a stupid risk I took tonight. If you enter this room I will hurt you, and I will break our marriage.*

I look down at him, still sitting cross-legged with one shoe off, like a toddler at a birthday party, who's only now realising there's no cake and is trying to keep from having a tantrum. His face is fatter than when we first met; it's soft. He used to have an edge; there was a sting in him. He was funny and could be really caustic – together we could be so mean – but always, *always* so fucking funny. And that was why I fell for him; he could take it, he could take me, and all the shit I threw at him. He took it all and kept smiling, laughing and joking – kept coming back for more. I didn't think he was the man for me, not at the start, but he wore me down. He did it by making me laugh, and he was so funny because he understood that both of us were damaged. We'd both weathered our parents' stormy break-ups and knew that tug of war with the kids as the prize. We saw the pain in each other, and tried to heal it. That was what made him such a scabrous cartoonist; at least until living the high life wore away at the rough edges. We enjoyed each other so much... but when did he last make me laugh? And when did I last make him laugh, or even smile?

I kneel down next to him. 'Don't come inside,' I tell him, and then I kiss his cheek. I'm scared to be alone but I'm even more scared for him to see past the door. 'Go home and wait for me.' I mean for it to sound enticing, but it sounds more like a threat.

'I'm staying.' He ties his lace and gets up. 'I made promises,' he says, still trying to show that he loves me more than I love him. Let's fucking hope that's true.

'Then, you have to promise not to panic when you get inside,' I tell him.

'I can't—'

'Promise not to scream, at least,' I say, level and flat, and he responds with a pout, like he always does when he thinks I've slighted him.

'I don't scream,' he says.

I roll my eyes because I remember the Vampire ride at Chessington, and how he screamed like a little girl, and that awful family from Middlesbrough laughed at him. I should remind him of that, but this isn't about winning points; I just need him to *not* freak out when we go in.

'Trust me?' I say.

He frowns, and across his face, like on a cinema screen, I see the flicker of tens of thousands of micro decisions to trust me over the years – trust me on this movie, this restaurant, this new peanut butter – a million give and takes, the compromises of twenty years of marriage, and they all come down to this.

'I trust you,' he says.

You shouldn't, I think, but I say nothing. Instead, I hold the keycard against the lock. It flashes green for a second, and I push the door open, holding it for him.

'Remember that I loved you,' I tell him, and hold my hand out to take his. Together we enter the room.

Chapter Four

Ben

Oh my god, the blood.

It lies glossy and thick, like honey that's spilled and spread – a sticky ocean, which covers most of the floor. It's seeped out of his head, and forms a corona around his skull, which then widens out like a comic-strip speech bubble that says: *Good grief!* I'm immediately ashamed by that thought – I wish I could un-think it – because it's so frivolous and callous. A man is dead.

'Are you okay?' Mia asks, as I reach out to hold her arm so I don't fall. I nod, my vision blurs a little and I feel the shakes run through me.

'I… I… thought that when you said a man was dead,' I stammer. 'I… I imagined an older guy.'

'No, he's not old,' she says.

'No, he's young,' I say. 'And he died from violence.' I don't look at her, but I feel her body tense. 'And he's naked,' I finish, without even knowing if I mean it as a statement or an accusation. I don't know what to do; this is something that will change the course of our lives, maybe it already has. It could be that our future will be forever determined by this moment – everything will be classified

43

as either *before the body* or *after the body*. I have no idea what happens after tonight ends.

I drop the Adidas bag, making sure it isn't close to the edge of the blood, and bend down. The dead man looks like he's in his early to mid-twenties, fit and muscular, not like a body builder, but you can see that he works out and takes care of himself… took care of himself. His chest is shaved; his legs and groin are smooth too. On his chest there's a tattoo of a red heart, with three names written inside: *Claire, Lilly and Harry.*

'Who are they?' I ask, pointing to the heart.

'I don't…' Her anger suddenly flares. 'Don't get all Jiminy Fucking Cricket on me, Ben. I don't need a walking conscience, I need someone to help clear up this room so we can get out of this mess.'

'And I will but—'

'No buts and no questions, just help me!'

I see panic in her face, all mixed with guilt and anger and even a dash of shame. I get that she's scared but I hate that she explodes like this. Like she's the alpha dog and thinks I should just do what she wants. But this isn't just some minor disagreement, like deciding where we go on our holiday, or what shelves we get in the living room; this is a dead man and Mia doesn't get to decide what I can and can't know about him and what happened. I have to be able to ask questions and the big one is, *why is there a young naked man in a hotel room with her?* Especially when he's so fucking good-looking. His jawline is strong, and he has wavy brown hair and his eyes are hazel… were hazel. I wish they were closed. It's horrible to see them blank and staring; if it wasn't for the emptiness in them he could be asleep. Empty eyes, and the lake of blood that's poured out of his head.

'Oh shit.' I start to retch.

'If you're gonna be sick, vomit in the bin, there's a liner inside.' Mia grabs the little wastepaper bin and hands it to me. I don't want to be sick in front of her.

'I'm okay,' I tell her. 'It's just that I haven't seen blood, not like this.' Not so much of it on the outside of a person. And I hadn't realised that it could be so sticky, or that it would smell so strongly – sweet, like rotting fruit, but earthy and metallic too. It's heady and quite overpowering. I breathe through my mouth and feel the nausea pass. I put the bin down.

'How old was he?'

'Oh come on, Ben, it doesn't matter how old he was because, unless you've acquired the powers of time travel in the last few hours, it's done and he's dead and there's no changing it.'

'I get that, I just hadn't, I just…' My words fade into nothing. Both of us are raw and afraid of what all this means. Suddenly I feel incredibly tired, like I'm a clock-work toy that's winding down after a lot of frantic running around. I look at his heart tattoo again. It stands out so bright against his bloodless skin. 'Claire, Lilly and Harry – they're probably his family.'

'Maybe. I don't know,' she says without looking at the body.

'Well, they're obviously people he loves. I mean, maybe they're brothers and sisters, but they're probably his wife and kids. They don't even know that he's dead.'

'And?'

'And… I don't know. I just… what are we doing with him?'

Her jaw tightens and she stands a little taller. There's a flash of the lawyer now, as she outlines her plan. 'We are going to wrap him up in plastic, clean the room until there isn't a speck of our DNA in here, and then we go home.'

'But, when they find the body—'

'They'll have no clue who did it, but it'll look like professionals, maybe a contract killing,' she says.

'So his kids might think he was mixed up with something really criminal?' I ask, horrified at the thought.

'Perhaps.' Her voice is brittle. She knows that what she's suggested is wrong.

'I don't like it.'

'No of course you don't. What would you rather they think?'

'I don't… I mean, I guess… they should know the truth.'

'The truth?' she says, almost like it's funny. Then I see her eyes darken like a storm's coming. 'Should his kids know that he raped me?'

'What?'

'He raped me. He held me down and forced himself inside me, even though I begged him not to.' She drops her eyes. 'He raped me.'

I open my mouth to say something, but my throat has closed so nothing comes out. My belly is cold. I move half a—

'Shit!' My foot slides out from under me as I slip in the blood, '*Nygh*,' I grunt, trying to keep myself upright, but I drop onto my hands, the blood squelches between my fingers and I pitch sideways, I can't stop – I fall onto the dead man. I touch his cold chest, and my face is so close I could kiss him.

'Ben,' Mia grabs my arm and pulls me off him, making my knee pop like a can of Pringles being opened. Pain shoots through my leg. 'Agh!' I pull my hand up, and my fingertips are livid with his blood; it's smeared up my legs and on my chest and—

'Oh fuck,' Mia grabs the little bin and sticks it under my chin as I vomit everything I have ever consumed. Ever.

–

'Are you done?' she asks, when I'm finally quiet. I nod, and she takes the liner out of the bin, ties it tight, and places it on the lino, under the window.

'I'm sorry,' I tell her but she shrugs it away.

'We don't have time for this, Ben.'

'I just—'

'We can go over everything later, then I'll tell you what happened, but right now our lives are at stake – *both* of our lives, because you're covered in his blood now.'

I look down at myself. I look like I'm out of some crazy serial killer movie.

'So…' she continues, her voice a little softer. 'We both need to clean up this mess and go. We're not safe here; any minute someone could come.'

'Why would anyone come up here?'

'The guy on reception saw you, and…' A grimace runs across her face, making her lips tighten. '…the room… it isn't paid, not for the whole night, anyway.'

'Until when?'

'I don't know. He paid.'

'Oh Christ, Mia.' The sleaze of it all hits me in the chest.

'Please, Ben, the blame game has to wait. The clock's ticking.'

'So we clear up the room, and make it look like a hit man killed him?'

'Yes.'

'And you're fine with his wife and kids believing that?'

'A wife and kids you've imagined for him,' she snaps, and then drops her voice to little more than a whisper. 'Ben, if we're found here, this will destroy our lives, you do see that, don't you? It will kill my dad, and your mum will be the talk of that bloody gossip-factory of a village she lives in. And it will ruin my career.'

'Your career?' As I say it, I hear the sneer in my voice.

She screws her face up, like she's sucked a crate full of lemons. 'You don't get to have a fucking conscience tonight; you can have the luxury of having one tomorrow okay? Then you can fucking bask in the self-righteous glow of not having killed a man.'

'Christ, Mia, you can't order me not to be human.'

'Yes I can, that is exactly what I can do, because tomorrow you can salve your humanity; you can make amends because you haven't killed someone. I can't do that. I can never do that again. I killed that man there and I have to live with that. Do you understand, Ben – I have to fucking *live* with that – but right this second I can't wallow in guilt, because I have to do every fucking thing I can to make us safe.'

'Us?'

'Yes of course *us*, who the hell do you think I'm doing this for?'

'I…' but I dry up. Maybe, when you come down to it, and there is nothing else left, this is love – fighting tooth and claw for your family; that's true love.

'He's dead, Ben. It's horrible but it's happened. He can't be saved, but I'm not willing to throw our lives under the bus too.'

'But you said it was an accident.'

'Yes, that's what I said, and it's the truth, but who's going to believe me? This isn't even a she said/he said situation, because he's dead. I can tell my version of what happened, but I can't back it up. There's no proof – and even you don't really believe me.'

'It isn't that I don't believe you, I do. It's just...' my words fall away, because I know that I'm not getting the whole story. There is so much more to this, but it's buried deep, and I'm afraid it will be truly ugly.

'It doesn't matter anyway; all that matters is that I won't allow our lives to be ruined by this. I'm going to clean this place up, go home, and hope the police never connect him to me.' She looks at the dead man with a mixture of sadness and malice. 'I'd like your help with this, but if you can't deal with it, then go. It's your decision.' Her eyes bore into mine, challenging me to help or get out. But it isn't fair to make me decide like this.

'What was his name?' I ask her.

'I don't know,' she says, annoyed.

'How did you end up here with him?'

'Christ, Ben, not now,' she spits.

'I will help, but first I have to know what happened.'

'Why?' she asks with what feels like despair. 'Why the fuck does it matter?'

In response, all I can do is look around the sordid little room. 'Why were you here?'

'He brought me.'

'Did he force you to come?'

'He...' She starts to shake a little as she tries to keep it together. 'He raped me. He held me down and... I fought and pushed him off. He fell backwards and hit his head. It was an accident, a one in a million thing, just the exact angle – otherwise he might have killed me.'

49

'Did you know him before tonight?'

'No.'

She says *no*, but it doesn't feel like the whole truth; there's something that jars when she says it, but I don't know what. 'He picked you up tonight? Where?'

She sighs, annoyed at the time being wasted, and then answers. 'I was at a bar. There was a leaving drink for someone in accounts and I went, just for half an hour – at least, that was the plan. I nursed a drink for a while, said hello to some people, but I was feeling like I wanted to leave as soon as I could... until this guy said hello and we started talking. He bought me another drink. He was fun and... he invited me here.' She dips her head, pauses for a few seconds. I feel a single bead of sweat travel down my spine. She's leaving out the most important things about meeting him. How she recognised the desire in his eyes, how the scent of him excited her, how she saw the strength in his arms and shoulders and imagined him holding her, how she thought about him hard in her hand and about how he'd feel inside her. She doesn't share any of that with me. Instead, she merely says:

'I knew what he invited me for...' and she reaches her hand out to mine, an offering of peace and solace, but I can't take it. Instead, I pull away.

'He didn't force you to come here?' I ask.

'No.'

'You've met him before?'

'No.'

'But he works at your firm?'

'No, he was just at the same bar – it was a coincidence.'

I hear her answer and a part of me thinks, *good, it happened out of the blue, it wasn't planned...* but another part hardens, and thinks she's admitting only as much as she has to; pretending that it wasn't a long-standing affair, in an attempt to cushion the blow. It's what I'd do. It's what I've done.

'So, you've never met him before tonight?'

'No. I told you, I met him for the first time tonight. We talked in the bar, I drank more than I should and...'

...and he was handsome and sexy. I finish her sentence in my head.

'He got the room and...'

'You screwed.'

'No!' Her eyes flare. 'It wasn't... it moved faster than I thought and... he wanted more than I was willing to give. I said no, I changed my mind, but...'

I wait for her to finish her thought, and I marvel at how calm I am. I think it must be like when you can see an avalanche rolling towards you; you know there's nowhere to go, that all you can do is let it bury you alive. Maybe you get lucky and a rescue party digs you out before you die – or maybe you don't. I don't know if I feel lucky.

'He said...' Her voice falters, and I wonder if she's actually hearing his voice in her head, the timbre and pitch of it. Maybe he had an accent. I don't know, I'll never hear it. Nobody will again.

'He said he'd already paid for the room, and the drinks, and I owed him a good time,' Mia says in a monotone. 'He pushed me down and held my arms and—'

'You were already naked?' I ask.

'Not completely but...' She stops. She curls her fingers into a fist and her nails cut into the soft flesh of her palm. 'I was giving him a blowjob. I thought that would be enough...' She pauses. The avalanche has buried me. 'But he wanted more and... and... he forced me, Ben. He

51

raped me. I was just trying to stop him; I didn't mean to kill him. You believe me, don't you?'

I don't reply immediately, instead there is a moment where I weigh the evidence. I see hope and despair dance in her eyes as she watches me, and finally I have to tell her: 'Yes... I believe you.'

'Thank you.' She takes my hand and squeezes it so hard I think my fingers will break. 'I just want this night to end and to be safe. I want to go home, Ben.'

'We will, Mia, don't worry.' I look across at the dead man lying in his blood, and I can see the imaginary family I made for him. They stand around him, looking at me, imploring me to choose them – but I can't. I choose my wife. The ghosts of Claire and Harry and Lilly turn to dust and fall away.

'We're in this together.' I tell Mia, and she lets out a sigh, and sort of smiles.

Mia

I think he wants a hug, but I can't give him that at the moment. I have to put aside every thought except: *what do we do with the body to keep us safe and out of prison?* All I can offer Ben is a quick smile, and then I must turn back to our problem. I open the bag he's brought for me. I pull out rags, towels, rubbish bags, cleaning products... I pull the bag inside out, but I can't see the two most important things.

'Did you remember the knife and the hammer?' I ask, and he winces.

'Yes, I...' He pulls at two of the towels, and I see that they've been turned into makeshift cloth envelopes. He rips tape off them, and unwraps the knife and hammer.

'There,' he tells me, as his hands shake. In the past I have loved his soft and sentimental side, but now it's a liability. It's obvious that I can't have him in the room when I actually use the hammer, he will freak out, so I need to get him out of the way.

'I think I should clean in here…' I tell him with as much lightness as I can get into my voice, '…and you clean the bathroom.'

'Okay,' he agrees.

'And you need a shower,' I tell him and he looks down at himself. I think he'd forgotten that he's covered in the dead man's blood. 'You need to get out of those clothes.'

I watch him, as he slides the joggers off and drops them to the floor, then the hoody and the T-shirt. But as he takes off his underpants, he turns away from me, which is a little painful. I've seen him naked a hundred thousand times, there's never been a problem, but tonight something's changed. I can see he's embarrassed by the grey in his chest hair, the pot of his belly, and most of all that his penis is shrivelled and surrounded by grey hair. It's because he's seen the dead man and compared himself to him. Idiot. I know Ben would like some reassurance, and I could try to make him confident again, but that's too exhausting right now – and Ben can't be my priority. I can't be sidetracked by his insecurity.

He finishes undressing, and holds his clothes in his hands, like he's a new prisoner waiting to be told his cell number.

'Did you bring a change of clothes for yourself?' I ask.

'No.'

'Then you need to rinse those in the bathroom and get the blood out.'

He nods.

'When we get home you can take them off in the garage and we'll burn them. You mustn't wear them into the house.'

'I don't—'

'Ben, we can't get away with this if we take any evidence home. Think. We take nothing from here away with us, nothing that can tie us to the body, and we clean away any trace of us from this room. If we leave something here, the police will find it – do you understand?'

He nods. I feel bad that I'm haranguing him, but this is life and death.

'Go and rinse your clothes, and then start to clean the bathroom, okay?'

'If we're caught—' he starts.

'If the shit hits the fan I'll tell the truth. I killed him and you just came to help.'

'I'll still be an accomplice after the fact. I can still be arrested.'

'Yes, I suppose you can. So, thank you.'

'I…' He starts to say something, and I can tell by his puppy-dog eyes that he's going to say *I love you*. And I know he does, but what use is love in this mess? What I want is cunning and grit, and some fucking elbow grease – I don't want a love-struck idiot.

'We need to get this done, Ben.'

He nods slowly and soulfully.

'Us two against the world,' I tell him.

'I'll clean the bathroom.' He grabs a handful of towels, some gloves and bleach, and turns away.

As soon as he's gone I find the hammer, and the carving knife, and start to gaffer-tape heavy-duty rubbish bags together.

I shower first, watching the water turn red, then pink, until it's clear. It doesn't take long to wash the blood away; Lady Macbeth had it wrong.

Next, I rinse my clothes and wring them out. I get them as dry as I can, before I put them back on. They feel a little slimy and cold, but my body heat will dry them better than anything else. I also don't want to be naked any longer. I'm not comfortable, I don't want to see myself. I dress, and then I start to clean the room.

Jesus Christ, it stings. Even through the marigold gloves, my fingertips burn with the bleach. I pour or spray it everywhere – in the shower, all across the wall, over the toilet and onto the sink and taps.

I don't even know that Mia or the dead man used the toilet. This isn't one of those hotels where they put a paper seal across the bowl to prove it's fresh and clean for new clients, and the toilet paper roll isn't folded into an arrowhead to show it's a new one. In fact, I think this is probably the best clean this bathroom's had in years.

I get to the mirror; it's still a little fogged up by the shower. So I take off my marigolds and with my pointy finger, I draw on it. I draw Mia. Then I draw me. I draw us, I draw the Kingdoms: the two of us in our old flat. It's an homage to one of the first panels I ever drew of us; we're dancing in our living room and we're both shouting '*We're never gonna stop!*'

That was the old Mia and Ben Kingdom, in those early years when we really didn't stop. We danced and sang and played music – one time our neighbours actually broke into our flat and turned off the power to make us stop. God, I bet it was horrible to live next door to us. But we were so happy and so bloody alive; it was the Kingdoms against the world back then, and we raged and we burned; we were young, and we thought we could bend the world to our will.

On the mirror, under us dancing, I write:

'*Can we please stop now — I've lost all feeling in my legs.*'

And I start to laugh, at the contrast of what we might say now and how we used to be when we were young and shiny and new… but that dies away as I see that my reflection is perfectly superimposed over my drawing. The *new* me, the forty-year-old me, looks like a ghost, or even a zombie version of myself — insubstantial, empty, and beaten down by life. It's frightening, and I punch—

'*Agh.*' My knuckle splits open and blood smears the cracked glass. Pain spikes through my fist, and up my arm, to explode in my head. That was so stupid. Why did I do it? What the hell is wrong with me?

'What did you do?' Mia calls from the bedroom and then comes in. She's naked, and in her hand is the hammer, and the head of it is wet. I look across at the mirror, scared she'll see the drawing of us, but the mirror looks more like a cobweb, as the shatter-print from my punch has radiated out through it. Seven years of bad luck.

'You idiot,' she says. I frown and drop my head. 'Your DNA will be in the glass fragments.'

'I'll clean it.'

'No, you can't clean it! There's no way you could get all the blood and skin out of the cracks. For fuck's sake, Ben.' She is so angry. 'You'll need to get it off the wall and bag it up. We need to get rid of it. Fuck — it's like you want to get caught. Use this,' and she hands me the hammer. 'I'm done with it. But wash it first,' she says and then leaves.

I look at the hammer in my hand. It's hard to hold, as the swelling is already coming up. My knuckle is tightening and the blood's coagulating; soon it'll scab over. I look at the hammer; the head's red and sticky. I shudder involuntarily, trying to not think about how she's used it. I drop it in the sink and pour bleach on it, which runs pink into the drain.

I pick it up and shake the last drops off it, then I slide the claw end into the crack between wall and mirror. Of course she's right; it needs to come down. I wouldn't be sure to get all traces of my DNA out, even if I splashed a gallon of bleach into the cracks and grooves… so here goes. I rip the claw through the glass. Is it only seven years bad luck, or is it more when you really defile a mirror? I'm turning this one into a trillion shards as I scrape it off the wall, making it ruck and twist and shatter.

'You have to make less noise,' Mia hisses, as she appears behind me.

'I can't do it any quieter.'

She looks at me, and I feel like I've been roasted on a spit over a fire. Then she closes her eyes. I think for a second she's praying and then her mouth twists into a grimace.

'Fuck me, fuck me hard,' she yells. 'Oh yes… Oh yes…' and she slams her hand onto the tile again and again as she moans.

'Yes, I'm going to fuck you.' I shout as I rip the claw through the glass and together we moan and groan, to cover the sound of the breaking glass.

When it's done, and the sink is full of a city of splinters, Mia stops mid-moan, and turns away, back to the bedroom. She doesn't give me another glance, but the air around her is black. Neither of us have come.

57

I walk back into the bedroom and I want to cry. I'm shaking all over. I hated making those sounds – like I was an animal rutting – but that was all I could think of to cover the noise of the glass breaking. But I feel so dirty now. They should be the sounds of love and joy and… *Fuck*. I'm so tired, I just want this to be over so we can go home.

I look down at the three heavy-duty waste bags I've gaffer-taped together – all layered up so nothing will leak through – a home-made body bag. I bet there isn't a design for that on Etsy. I've placed it close to the lake of blood, which has thickened and dried even more. The next job is to get the body into it. Of course, that would be easier with the both of us in here, but that's too risky. I don't want Ben seeing the dead man's face, not now it isn't as handsome as it was. So I'll have to do it alone.

I kneel down, low enough so I can grip his arm, and lean into his shoulder. This is going to be brute force and ignorance. With a grunt, I push with all my might at the lump of meat. I don't think it's gonna work – but then, slowly, there's a slurping sound as the skin pulls away from the floor and the congealing blood, and the body rolls once, and then over onto the plastic sheet.

'*Fuuuuuuuuuuck!*' The sweat runs down my face, stinging my eyes. I have a greater respect for Sumo wrestlers than I ever did before. I look down and see that my knees are bloody; they remind me of the ingrained dirt on a child's knees.

I think about my little sister, Juliette, who used to get into real scrapes at school, and would always come home with ripped shirts and covered in dirt. She was such a tomboy. She looked up to me, and often wanted to hang out with my friends and me, but the older I got, the less I'd let her tag along. Then one day I told her to leave me alone and get lost, so she went off in a huff. Two boys, from the year above me at school, found her crying in the old bus shelter and grabbed her. They tried to touch her up, one got his hand into her knickers, but she screamed and they ran off.

When I got home that night she told me what they did, and the next day I got her to point one of them out to me. He was with his friends, and I stormed over, and with my compass, I stabbed him in the hand and screamed at him.

'If you ever try and touch my sister again, or any other little kid, I will stab you in the fucking eyes, you pervert.' It was loud enough that the whole school heard.

Oh my god. I had totally forgotten that happened, as though I'd erased it from my memory to stop myself remembering the rage. Have I always been this full of anger? The violence from back then, and from tonight, scares me. I don't want to be that person; I don't want this anger in my belly, like acid, burning me from the inside out. I want to leave it to someone else to deal with, I want to have Ben hold me and… but I can't. That's just running away from the problem, because this anger is inside me all the time, and has been my whole life. That's why I wanted to get into law and fight for people's rights. I can't wait for someone to help me, I have to do this myself, without falling apart. I have to control the anger, to tame it and use it. I close my eyes.

Calm down, Mia. I tell myself. *Calm the fuck down.*

I'm okay. I can do this. I take his arms and fold them across his chest. He looks like an angel. I stand up and use my ruined dress to wipe the blood off me, then throw it on top of the body. It covers his face, which makes him easier to deal with. I fold the plastic over and around him, trying to wrap him like a parcel. I pull the edges tight, then I layer in strips of gaffer tape to hold them down. Once the body's wrapped in the plastic, I take the gaffer and slowly start to loop it around, like I'm encasing an ancient Egyptian mummy, before placing it in its sarcophagus. After about five minutes of looping the tape, I'm happy with what I've done. It shouldn't leak. It's tight, like a cocoon.

Now, I have to clean the floor. Thank goodness it's lino, though I guess it's the only way the hotel staff could clean up the rooms after every hour-long booking. I hate to think about the bodily fluids that get squirted over this floor every single day. Yuk. I scour it with as much energy as I can muster. I have to clean away every single particle of blood. I squirt bleach everywhere; I feel its sting, but it feels good. Proves it's working – cleaning, purifying.

Ben

I use the towels to make parcels of gla—

'Argh!' As I pick them up, the glass shards stick through, slicing my hands in a dozen places. *Christ*, I'll have to manoeuvre them into the Adidas bag with something like a stick. I'm so annoyed with myself; it was such a dumb thing to do, punching the glass like that, but it was the drawing and the memories it shook up in my head.

I look around. There's still a lot of cleaning to do, so I get back to it. In fact, I'm pretty thorough and methodical – very different to normal life – as I imagine the room cut into squares, and then I attack it like a grid, making sure I scrub every single centimetre, disinfecting each square completely before moving onto the next. I just put my head down and go, go, go! Until it's done.

The last thing to do is get the Adidas bag and move the glass shards into it. I cut myself about twenty times doing that and then, using my sleeve, I close the door for the last time and go back into the bedroom.

Wow. I'm amazed at the change in here; the lake of blood is gone, and in its place is a cocoon. It isn't silk, but shiny black plastic and gaffer tape. For a mad second, I wonder if the man in there could gestate for a few days, and crawl out as a butterfly. Wouldn't it be nice to think like that, or to believe in a heaven where all the bitterness of life is replaced with sweetness. But I know that it's just all wishful thinking and conscience-salving crap. The man is dead. There is no soul to float on to somewhere else. His body will just rot until nothing is left, and there is no one to remember him, end of story. That is the gospel according to Ben.

I look at Mia. She's naked, and I can see all the bruises now, purple against the paleness of her skin. As well as her arms, they're on her thighs, shoulders and neck. Around her throat they're vivid; they actually look like a hand-print, where fingers have dug deep. All over her thighs, her skin looks broken and grazed.

'Did he do that?' A cold fury creeps into my voice.

Mia doesn't answer me. She doesn't need to; of course he did. It hurts, it physically hurts to see her like this, to see what that man has done to her, and to know that I can't do a thing to make it better. I'm deeply angry, but at the same time so impotent. She already took care of it – she killed him. And what would I have done? Would I have fought for her? Would I have attacked him? Would I have made him pay? I doubt it. I'd have called the police, but even the chance to make that weak response has gone, because the bastard's dead.

'Mia?' I say. She doesn't answer, or even look at me. Instead, she opens another bin bag and dumps the cleaning cloths into it, then the sprays, bleach and towels.

The clothes I brought for her are in a pile on the floor. She puts on the leggings, not caring about underwear, then the black T-shirt and hoody. The utilitarian black clothes erase any femininity. She pulls up the hood and it covers her hair, and now as she stands before me, she looks like a little boy. Thin and small, she could be any waif or stray, out in the night.

'I'm sorry, I must have forgotten to bring you knickers,' I say, but then realise I haven't seen the underwear she must have worn this evening. I look around for them, but she realises what I'm doing and quickly grabs panties and a bra from the floor and throws them into the bin bag. For some reason, she doesn't want me to see them, but I have a quick glimpse of them. They look small and delicate, like silk. Huh! It's a long time since I've seen her in anything other than well-worn M&S knickers.

She doesn't catch my eye as she ties up the bin bag; I think it's so that I can't look in and see the underwear, but then there's a second of panic and she opens the bag again and pulls her bra back out to recover something from inside. I can't be sure, but I think she pulls a folded photograph from the bra cup. I think it was the photo that was missing from her purse, the only thing she'd taken from her regular life when she went out tonight.

And then something hits me: the dress and the underwear. A figure-hugging dress and sexy lingerie – she may not have known this man before tonight, but it was not really a spur of the moment decision to come here with someone. She went out tonight with the express intention of finding a man to sleep with – that's why she was dressed like this. It was planned, the betrayal was planned; she had gone out tonight, looking for someone.

'Everything cleaned in the bathroom?' she asks as she reties the bin bag, a false lightness in her voice.

'Yeah, I…' For a second I want to tell her that I saw her take the photo from the bin bag and I know what it was and what it meant; but I'm really not sure I have the energy for any kind of confrontation now. From somewhere, a real bone-crushing sadness washes over me. I want to be held and comforted but there's no one to do that. I only have Mia in the whole world and… I think I lost her tonight. I think we lost each other. Or maybe we were already lost. If this man hadn't died tonight, would she have come home and just carried on with our life? Would her night of passion have been yet another secret weighing down on our marriage? How different would it all have ended up? Would our marriage have lasted another twenty years? I don't know. I don't know what happens after tonight, and maybe I shouldn't think about it – I guess that way madness lies.

'Are you okay in those clothes? Are they still wet?' she asks. 'It'll be bloody cold outside.'

'A bit damp but I'll live.' I say and see her grimace slightly. It was a poor choice of words. 'I'm ready,' I tell her.

She nods, but I can't tell if it's in answer to me, or she's just reassuring herself that everything's done. Can we move on, I wonder – I mean, physically – is it safe to leave this room? Mentally and emotionally, who the hell knows? This feels like it'll be at least ten years of therapy.

The dead man's clothes are folded on a chair. She goes through them, checking the pockets and retrieving his wallet and keys. She puts them in her big hoody pocket, and when she's sure there's nothing left, the clothes go into the last bin bag.

'That's it,' she says in little more than a whisper.

'Now what?'

She gives me a watery smile. 'The body. We have to move it.'

'But you said we were leaving it here.'

'No. I'm sorry. I've rethought that.' She doesn't meet my eye.

'So what the hell are we doing with it?'

'You need to be calm, Ben.'

'I am calm, Mia,' I say, even though it's clear that I'm a very long way from calm. 'You said we were making it look like a professional hit.'

'Professional killers don't claw mirrors off the wall.'

'I…' I completely dry up.

'Look.' She grabs her sleeve and with it, opens the window and lets the sounds of the night in. Then she takes the little liner bag of my sick and holds it out of the window.

'What are you doing?'

She moves the bag slightly, lining it up with something below, and then drops the bag out of the window.

'What the hell, Mia?' I jump at her, clawing at empty air as the bag drops.

'Don't touch the window, you idiot,' she hisses. 'Look down without touching anything.'

I crane my head out and look down. I can see that there's an enclosed square on this side of the building, and directly below the window is a large skip-sized rubbish bin. I can see the small bag of sick nestling in the centre of the rubbish, directly below.

'We do the same with the body,' she says. 'We can't walk through reception with all these bags, so we drop them into the bin down there. Easy.'

'You had this planned all along?' I feel like an idiot.

'No… maybe I'd considered it, but now there's no option because of the mirror. Think about it, Ben; we've cleaned every bit of evidence from this room, no one can see that we were here, or that a crime's been committed, except for one thing. The biggest fucking clue there could ever be – a body – because as soon as the cleaner comes in and finds it, the police get called and the forensics team come in. And what happens then?' Her eyes blaze at me, daring me to say what's in my head.

'They find a print, or a hair, or a drop of blood – something we missed, and we get caught,' I say.

'Of course they'll find something. We aren't professional cleaners and Mr Muscle has his limitations. But if we get rid of the body, then people come in and clean, and someone will replace the mirror, and by tomorrow night, customers will come in and fuck and cum and slide their filthy hands over the walls, and layer after layer of other people gets smeared over this cesspit of a room.'

'Covering up that we were ever here.'

'And that a man was killed here.' She folds her arms over her chest. We stand in silence.

'But we can't get the body out of the window,' I say.

'Yes we can, we have to – and we have to do it right now.'

Chapter Five

Ben

I crane my neck out and look down. We're three floors up, so I can't judge the exact size of the bin from here. The guy was quite tall, he might not fit, or we could miss the bin completely and slam him into the concrete. Either way, if we're caught dropping the body out of the window, then that's it – we'll go to prison for murder. No jury would believe his death was an accident, not after we wrapped him up and threw him out of the window. I pull my head back inside.

'Jesus, Mia, this is too much. I shouldn't have listened to you, I should've called the police right from the start and let them deal with this; they know what to do and they can read the evidence. They would have looked at your bruises and—'

'No. I am not being prodded and poked by anyone, I am not having my victimhood graded and assessed. I don't have to prove it was self-defence, I know what it was. I've already fought for my life once tonight, I'm not going to fight again. This ends now. I get to walk away from this nightmare. I will not let it poison my whole life.'

'A man's dead.'

66

'And a woman is alive, and she wants to live. I want to live, Ben.'

'But Mia—'

'But nothing,' she cuts me dead. 'We are moving the body, unless you're too afraid to help me,' she says it with such venom, that I feel myself shrink away from her. 'All you have to do is help me get him out of the window. Then you can go, run home, get into bed, pull the covers over your head... I'll do the rest.'

I feel my cheeks reddening. 'It isn't about me running away.'

'Of course it is; this is all about you wanting to run.'

'Well I bloody don't want to go to prison.'

'And this is the only way to make sure.' Her face is beet red. 'If we don't want to get locked up for the rest of our lives, we need to hide the body.'

'By dropping it into the rubbish skip?'

'Yes, it's perfect.'

'And what if we drop the body into the rubbish, and tomorrow or the next day it goes to the landfill and gets tipped in and buried? That could happen. It might never be found.'

'Then we're the luckiest couple alive.'

'What the hell are you thinking, Mia? I know he was a bastard, but his family need to know what happened to him, he can't just vani—'

'He raped me.'

'His kids are innocent.'

'Innocent!' She laughs, like the idea is crazy. 'If you want them to stay innocent, then hide the fact that their dad was a rapist. These kids – if they even exist – have lost enough already.'

'But what if they're real, and they've lost their dad and don't know what happened to him, what if they just wait and wait for him to come home? I don't think I could live with that. I don't think you could either.' For a second her lips convulse, like her empathy has kicked back in and she imagines the kids sitting on the doorstep waiting for their dad; but then she hardens again.

'Okay Ben, I'll do you a deal. If the body isn't found in two weeks, we'll call in an anonymous tip to the police, telling them how to find it. Agreed?' She holds out her hand to me, like we're gonna shake on it, like it's some merger or contract negotiation.

I think for a moment. 'Okay, yes that's good.' I take her hand. It's cold, so I squeeze it, trying to push some warmth into her. It makes her smile again – it's only a thin-lipped half-smile – but it warms my heart a little.

'Clyde?' she asks, and for a second I think she means the orangutan in that Clint Eastwood film, but then I get it.

'Bonnie?' I say, and she squeezes my hand back, just for a second, but it's enough. Stronger than a pinkie swear, or blood oath, or even wedding vows… we're in this together and there's no going back.

'Bonnie and Clyde lived to a ripe old age, didn't they?' I ask.

She wrinkles her nose. 'Yeah. I mean, I'm pretty sure they did.'

'Yeah.' I promise myself I will never look at their Wikipedia page. 'So, what do we do?'

She takes a deep breath and then plucks the black bin liner up off the floor, the one with all the cleaning stuff in it, and with all the flair of a street magician, she drops it out of the window. There is a rustle of the plastic catching in the air, and then the soft *thwup* of it landing in the giant bin, nestling in the soft bed of leftovers and used condoms.

'Now we drop the body out.'

'Okay,' I say, as I remember the last scene of the film with Warren Beatty as Clyde and Faye Dunaway as Bonnie, both dying in a hail of bullets. I think I may have just made a pact with the devil.

Mia

I bend down and grab the cocooned body at the head end, about where the shoulders are. Ben makes a deflating sound, like a wrinkled old balloon giving up its last gasp of air, and then he freezes.

'What?' I say, feeling a little frustrated at how slow he's being.

'You took his wallet.'

'So?'

'You looked inside. What's his name?'

Fuck. I clench my jaw so tight it hurts. 'We don't have time for this, Ben.'

'His name?' he asks and looks all soulful, like some sickening teenage singer-songwriter on YouTube, whining about loneliness and how hard it is to talk to people and find love. 'What was his name?'

'Theo,' I say with as level a voice as I can. 'Theo the fucking rapist.'

Ben looks blankly back at me. I have no idea what he wants from this navel-gazing, not when we're so close to leaving this purgatory. Then he shakes his head, like he's made some kind of internal calculation.

'Okay then, we'll drop Theo out of the window,' he says with absolutely no emotion in his voice and he smiles

69

at me. It's just the briefest of smiles but it seems to say, *I've got your back.* I give a half-smile in return; he can have a full smile when we're safely home.

'On three,' and we both bend down to grab separate ends of the cocoon.

'Try and keep a flat back and lift with your—'

'I know how to fucking lift something,' I snap at him.

'I just…' he frowns. 'Okay, ready, set, *lift*.'

'Oh my god…' I feel every muscle strain, and that's with Ben taking most of the weight. '*Jesus fuck*…' I hiss as we lift the body as high as we can, but there's no way we can get it up to the window.

'Christ,' Ben says through clenched teeth and drops the body with a meaty thud. My heart's in my mouth for a second, but the bag doesn't split open.

'We can't lift it high enough,' he says.

'We could swing him,' I suggest.

'I doubt we can.'

'We have to try, at least.'

He shakes his head sullenly, like a teenager that's been asked to pick his clothes off the bedroom floor. 'I don't—'

'Please… let's try.'

'Okay,' and he grits his teeth and bends his back for one momentous effort. I dip down too, and we grab the body again. 'Up on three, and then…' and he counts and we strain. I use every ounce of strength I have to lift the body. There is no way I can swing it up to the window, but Ben grunts like Rafa Nadal and swings the body back and—

'NYARGH!' It's like a caber toss in the Highland games, as Ben gets his shoulders into it and launches the body at the window.

'Fuck!' I didn't know he was going to let go so quickly, so it's dragged out of my hands, throwing it off course and making it spin. It hits the window and is suspended in mid-air for a second… and then momentum sends it through and past the moment of no return. Ben leaps forward, in case it gets stuck, but the body twists out into the air and pitches forward and tumbles down.

I hold my breath, suddenly scared that it'll hit the building as it falls. Christ, this is so risky – so stupid – and all my confidence and bravado just goes up in smoke. I'd pray, if I thought there was any goddess out there to pray to.

We both look down, as the body tumbles through the night, and hits the metal bin with a sickening *THWACK* – part snap of bone and part tear of flesh. It sounds as loud as a gunshot and it makes my stomach churn. Ben looks like he could be sick again. I think it was the sound of the man's neck breaking. Whatever it was, the body has pitched into the bin, but even from here, I can tell that the bag has ripped open and I see Theo's head, nestled in the soiled linens and food waste below. He looks up, his eyes open and—

'Oh hell,' Ben groans. 'Look at him, look at his face.' But I don't need to see the face to know it's no longer handsome. Beside me, I feel Ben shrink away, but I can't let him wallow in pity, because that's the way we get caught.

'It wasn't perfect, but he's where we wanted him to be,' I say.

'We almost tore his head off.'

'He's already dead, you can't kill someone twice.'

'Mia—'

'Ben, he's down there. We're winning.'

71

'Winning?'

'Okay, that's a poor choice of words. But you know what I mean; we've done what we needed to do. We got him out of the room, now we can leave too.'

'We can go? Home?'

'Almost,' I tell him and watch his shoulders sag a little. 'Let's wipe down the window and close it. Use your hoodie sleeve, then check anything we might have touched in the last few seconds. We should have kept a cloth with us, but it doesn't matter. Let's get out of here. We use the stairs and we go straight out past reception. Don't look at anyone, just go.'

'I don't know that I can even walk down stairs.'

'You can,' I tell him, 'you're amazing.' I give him just a little more carrot and stick because we have to get out of here and leave this behind us. I try and smile, though I think it might look more like a rictus grin, but I'm trying. Lord, how I'm trying.

'Come on, let's go.' I tell him and he nods, and for a second we just stand there, collecting our strength. We wipe down the window and then we head to the door.

Ben

She looks out into the hallway, her head bobbing from left to right, before she risks moving out, onto the sticky carpet and silently heading to the stairs. I pause on the threshold, frozen to the spot. I watch her, walking like a ninja, into the shadows of the stairwell and I reach back to close the door, but at the last moment I remember not to touch it with my hand, and instead pull it shut with my foot. The lock clicks, almost silently, and I'm left in No Man's Land. I offer up some kind of prayer or hope or wish-on-a-star, and then I scuttle after her.

On the ground floor, she's holding the door to the reception area and looking nervously through the little rectangle of glass. 'Hoods up,' she says over her shoulder, and draws her own up, like a monk doing penance.

'Ben... thank you,' she says and it actually sounds heartfelt. I don't know what to say in reply, but it doesn't much matter, as she immediately pushes through the reception doors and marches across the small lobby, not looking left or right, and I know she won't look back at me. She hurries and I follow, head bowed and shoulders up. I feel the tension in them, and the pain that stitches through my spine, but I keep going; I swim in her wake. And as she reaches the door to the outside, she doesn't even pause, but pushes through it, and is gone. I'm shaking; I expect a shout from the tired-looking Ali on reception. I hear him in my head, '*Stop!*' he yells. '*I'm calling the police!*' But in reality there's nothing. As I get to the door, I can't help myself; I look back... The reception desk is empty; there's no one to see us go. We got lucky. I breathe. I hadn't realised that I'd been holding my breath all this time. I reach out to push the door and—

'Not with your hand,' Mia tells me through the glass. She uses the pocket in her hoody to open the door for me, and I step through it, back into the night. The cold stings my cheek like a whip-crack, and my damp clothes leech all warmth out of my skin. *Jesus*. I shiver. Mia closes her eyes and it looks like she blows a kiss into the air. I can hardly believe it, but I think we made it, we actually made it.

'Let's go home,' I say and look ahead to where Earl's Court tube is, just a few minutes' walk away. *Goddamn*, I need a bath and a coffee. And a full English breakfast; I'm suddenly ravenous. I want to celebrate that I'm free and that I'm alive. I turn and take a step towards nirvana, towards the lights.

'You can go, Ben,' I hear from behind me. 'I just need to...' she says, and I start to dread her next words.

'Go on home,' she says it kindly, like she's persuading a child to go to bed, but it still cuts at me. And then she turns away, walks around the side of the hotel, and disappears.

And I'm free. Hallelujah. I've done my duty – I came when she needed me, I did all I could to help her, and now I can run home to the safety and security of... I look out, towards the all-night cafés and the tube station that leads home. Every fibre in my being says *go – run – go now*, but like an idiot I just stand gawking at the hole she left. This isn't over, and my debt isn't paid... and the ties that bind us might be weaker, but they aren't broken. It was that kiss that she blew into the air, it makes me realise how bound together we still are. In that moment she was the woman I married twenty years ago, blowing kisses to her flower girls, and I can't walk out on her, even after tonight and all that's happened over the last few years. I haven't always kept my promises to her, but I have never stopped loving her.

I sigh (because I am shit-scared of what might happen next) and then I follow where she went, like I'm Alice and she's the white rabbit, even though I know she's got myxomatosis. I still follow.

Mia

I step through an alleyway, and it feels like I've gone back in time about a hundred years. I'm in the square at the back of the hotel, though actually it's more like a ghetto of hotels. There are at least five of them that back onto this single courtyard. Once, they would have been fine town houses, but they aren't family homes now; they've all been converted into little hotels. If they were fancy I'd call them *boutique*, but none of these are fancy. They're shitholes for quick fucks and poor refugees on state benefits, with the odd New Zealand student thrown into the mix. I shouldn't be here, this is so far from my normal life, but here I am, fighting to get back home again.

The square itself doesn't have any lights, but enough bleeds in from the hotels for me to see what I'm doing. I think there's enough light to find a dead body. I step into the middle of the square. Under my feet I feel the ground become uneven, made up of old worn bricks where the mortar has crumbled over decades. The council don't re-do the surface like they do on the pavements of the main roads, so I have to be careful how I walk. It smells of food waste and piss and even though I can't see any, I know there are rats here. From behind me I hear Ben. I'm sort of glad he's followed me, I didn't want to do this alone.

'I thought we were done with this when we dropped the body out the window,' he whispers as he scurries up beside me. He's like a meerkat; his head's constantly twitching all around – left, right, back, front – over and over again.

'Calm down, Ben.'

'We aren't supposed to be back here, someone could come out of one of these doors at any moment and find us.'

'If they do, we just say we were looking for a place for a quickie, or to smoke a joint or something. Nobody will care, it's London, and most of the staff in these hotels will be illegal. They'll be more scared of us than we are of them, they won't want to make a fuss.'

'When the hell did you get this cynical?' he asks, with the most judgemental voice, like the idea of assuming everyone's illegal is worse than killing someone.

'It's just realistic, Ben. This is what—'

Bottles clank nearby, and a door squeals, opening and spraying a fan of light across the square; it moves fast, like a searchlight in the blitz. I jump forward, my hand grabbing Ben's cock and my lips attaching to his mouth like a hand-held Dyson. From somewhere to my right, there's a throaty chuckle and then the light recedes and we're thrown into shadow once more. Ben's cock is hard in my hand, I let it go and step back. I see the look of hurt that creases his face but there's no time for *that* – no time for any *us* bullshit.

'Okay, let's be quick. We have to re-seal the bag so his face doesn't show.' I pause. 'I'll climb into the bin and re-bag his head. Get it?'

He looks at me for a minute and I can see the clock-work chugging in his head, like a pound-shop Enigma machine. 'You're right,' he finally says. 'We do need to cover his face.'

'Come on, then.' And we walk to the skip that we dropped the body into. It's bigger than I thought it was from the room. The body of the bin is metal, and there's a lid that hangs down and can be locked for when it's full. The whole thing's on wheels, that look more like they should be on the Mars Rover; huge inflated tyres that turn 360 degrees. Ben sees an upturned fruit box and drags it over, so I can stand on it and look over the lip of the bin.

'Shit…' Theo's face is even worse than I thought.

'What?' Ben scrambles up alongside me. I hear his gasp of shock. The dead man's head hit the metal lip as he fell from our window. His neck's snapped and his jaw's broken, unhinged at one side, and cocked at an unnatural angle so it shows what I did upstairs.

'The teeth,' Ben says with horror in his voice. 'Where are they?'

I step back down off the crate, and gather my thoughts. Ben stays up there, but I know what he's thinking. He thinks the jaw was already broken before it hit the side of the bin; he thinks I broke it when I removed the teeth upstairs. He's right – that's exactly what happened. I see the disgust and pain in his face. He steps away from me.

'You…'

'Yes. I took out his teeth so dental records can't be used to identify him.' I use my lawyer voice on him, the calm professional one I keep for saying truly awful things to people.

'I know what you must think of me,' I say, even though I actually don't know how deep his disappointment might go. 'But this is what needs to be done if we're going to get away with this. I had to do it, and… I did it for us.'

'Us.' He repeats the word like it's foreign or something.

'I had to.' I repeat, because I honestly think it's true. We both stand silent for a few moments, and I wonder what's happening in his head.

'What did you do with the teeth?' he finally asks me.

'Here.' I pat the pocket of my hoody.

'Show me.'

'You don't—'

'Yes, I do.'

Slowly I twist my fingers into my pocket and draw out a baggy of white and red shards. I feel the shame burn me – I don't like what I have done, but I know that I had to do it. I want Ben to understand that; I need to wipe away the horror on his face.

'When they find the body it'll take them much longer to identify it. The longer it takes, the safer we are,' I tell him.

'But...' and I can see the question form in his mind even before he asks it, but he can't stop himself now. He has to ask: '...what else... what else did you do?'

I feel my heart stop for a second. I think this will be it. No amount of love or shared history will paper over the cracks of the hole I'm about to make in our marriage. He will think me a monster... and I might agree with him. I take a deep breath and try and keep my voice level. My eyes lock on his.

'I cut the tips off his fingers,' I say, then I cross my arms, like a child daring their parent to punish them for something the kid thinks is petty. I dare him to judge me. It feels a little juvenile but I can't help it. He looks at me, no emotion on his face, and then he just turns and walks away.

'Ben,' I say and I know it's me but I don't recognise my voice. It sounds old and tired and desperate. But he doesn't turn around, he just keeps on walking into the shadows and is gone.

'I'm sorry,' I mumble. He can't possibly hear me, but it's true; I am so bloody sorry. I truly don't think there was any option; the body had to leave the room and we have to make it hard to ID, but I didn't want to kill Ben's feelings for me. I didn't want to hurt him like this, and I didn't want to be left all alone. Now there is nobody in the world who can— *oh*.

He doesn't say a word as he walks back towards me. He doesn't have a white charger but he looks like a hero to me. I go towards him; I'm going to hug him but he side-steps me, deftly climbs onto the edge of the bin, and vaults inside.

'Ben, what the hell are you doing?'

'His face needs to be covered, you're right, so the bag has to be sealed. I'll do it, you be lookout.'

I want to cry; I think maybe a couple of tears do escape. I don't deserve him. 'The gaffer tape's in one of the black bags,' I say at just above a whisper. 'The one with his clothes in, I think, and there are more bin liners in there too.' I crouch down in the shadow of the skip and look out for anyone else in the square. From the street I can still hear traffic, and there is the occasional sound from the hotels, but nobody comes out here.

'Ben,' I whisper, but he doesn't answer. He probably can't hear me over the rustle of the rubbish. I crouch down and start to sing to myself, something to take the fear away.

Ben

I almost carried on walking, but then I hit the main road and found I just couldn't go through with it, because she's right; there will be time enough for recriminations and fights tomorrow. Tonight is about survival, and the only way we can do that is to work together. What she did has scared me – scared the shit out of me – it was so callous and brutal, but she's still Mia. She's still the woman I married and love, so I had to come back. And the real truth is that, while I may not have met some stranger at a bar, and gone to a hotel for sex, I still haven't upheld my vows. I haven't been honest with her, so I must take some of the blame for what's happened tonight. We're both responsible for her finding herself here, in this horrible mess – searching for intimacy in the wrong place, with the wrong man. When we finally get out of this, get back to the safety of our home, I will have to confess and tell her what I've done. Maybe when everything's out in the open, we can find a way to work through this. I hope so.

Though right here, right now, I'm regretting choosing to play the hero and jumping into this skip. I think we should have drawn straws or done *rock, paper, scissors* for the joy of wading through this foul-smelling filth. It's disgusting in here, and there's barely enough light to see anything clearly. It's wet, in an oozy bin-juice way; all rot and decay and entropy – the three unknown brothers of the seven deadly dwarves.

Outside I hear her singing to herself – a Nirvana song – but in here it smells a lot worse than teen spirit. I reach into the mass of rotting vegetation and detritus, as I see a murky shape that looks like a bag full of dead man's clothes, and I hope it's exactly that.

Inside the bag I find the gaffer tape and roll of black plastic bags. I open a bag, get it over his head and onto his shoulders. I pull out a strip of gaffer tape – it sounds so loud in here – and I wrap it around his shoulders and neck. *It's just a task, just a job I have to do.* I go around and around, until I'm sure the bag's staying put, and then I put the tape back in the black bag and pull it, and the body, down to the bottom of the bin. I submerge Theo under a hundred half-eaten meals, paper, condoms, plastic bottles and assorted crap.

As I do that, my old Adidas bag floats up to the top. It's good to see it again; I love that old bag. I remember buying it when I was first moving to uni, so I've had it longer than I've known Mia. I used it for my kit when I used to play squash and then—

Oh shit. Oh shit.

I go completely cold and start to shake.

I was leaving, going home, I thought this was over but… *oh god*. I stretch out my fingers and grip the zip on the bag, and I open it slowly. It's too dark to see inside, so I tip it over, and the glass and towels topple out into the mush and mulch in the bin.

'For fuck's sake, Ben, what the hell are you doing?' I hear Mia hiss, but I take no notice, and finish tipping the glass out, into the belly of the bin. I stand up as best I can, holding my old Adidas bag, now empty.

'Is there anyone watching?' I whisper. 'Is it safe for me to come out?'

'I think so.'

'Can you give me a hand?'

She steps onto the upturned fruit box, looks over the lip and down into the bin. She wrinkles her nose at the stench I've stirred up, but offers her hand to me anyway. I take it, and put my foot on the metal and, *shit*, I wrench my shoulder getting up over the lip and tumble off the top and fall. *Christ*, my knee hits the concrete and pops so loud, I think a bomb's gone off.

'I am going to have to go to the doctor's tomorrow,' I groan as pain surges up my leg.

'What have you… why the hell did you grab the Adidas bag?' she asks angrily. 'We're supposed to be leaving it, we're supposed to be leaving with nothing but the clothes we're wearing, so why the hell…' Her question washes away as she looks at me. I think I must look as pale as a ghost. I hand the bag to her.

'Look inside,' I tell her.

'Why? What do you—' but her voice is strangled as she opens it and reads what it says inside.

'Jesus Christ,' she spits. 'Our bloody name and address.'

'The police would have been straight round.'

She nods, her eyes wide. 'It would have buried us.'

'So I had to bring it out of the bin. I couldn't leave it,' I say.

'No… no, you're right, you couldn't.'

'But that's the problem, isn't it? We were going to leave it. We weren't careful enough.'

'But we've got it now.'

'But what if there's something else?' I say. 'We aren't robots, we're just humans, and we don't think of everything. We probably left evidence.'

'That's why I said not to bring anything – nothing that links back to our everyday lives.'

'But I didn't think about the bag.'

'But you remembered before it was too late, it's okay.'

'*Okay*,' I shrug. 'Okay.'

'You saved us,' she tells me and then she smiles. 'Let's go home,' she says, and I take a step forward and my leg gives way.

'Are you hurt?' She grabs my arm.

'I— hell…' I go down onto my haunches. I can feel the knee bone grating against something and it sets fire to my whole leg.

'Can I…' She goes to help me stand up and then pulls away violently. 'My god, you stink!'

'Lynx Africa?'

'You smell like—'

'I went swimming in a hotel bin?'

'Yeah. Yeah, I guess that's exactly what you smell like.' She laughs for the first time tonight. 'Thanks,' she says and then her eyes blaze, as I can see she's thought of something. 'You sit down and massage your knee, I need to move this bin.'

'What?' I ask. 'Aren't we done?'

'Last thing.'

'It better had be. What are you doing?'

'Look around,' and she points to all the doors that open up into this square. 'I think that all these hotels share the same bins; they're probably provided by one company.'

'I guess… I mean it makes sense, it would be so much cheaper to deal with one drop-off and pick-up,' I say.

'Exactly, and they all look the same, so if we swap this bin with another one then, even if they find the body, they won't know which hotel it came from.'

'That's— that's really smart,' I tell her and she smiles.

'Actually…' I start, as I've remembered something, and I limp back towards the main road.

'Are you leaving?' she asks as she sees me head off – and she sounds disappointed. For the first time it actually sounds like she wants me to be here with her.

'No, I'm not going, but it's just that when we came in here I thought…' I don't finish my sentence, as I can see that I was right. There's a slim passageway, even smaller than the alley from the street into this square. It's mostly hidden between two hotel doors. There's no way a truck, or even a car, would get down there, but one of the bins would fit. I head down it and find myself in another square, just like this one. More hotels back onto it, and of course, the same bins line the walls.

'Perfect,' I congratulate myself and then limp back to Mia. She's frowning in the centre of the first square. Without telling her what I'm doing, I grab the side of our bin and pull it away from the wall. The Mars Rover wheels are actually pretty good, and it's easier to steer than a supermarket trolley. As I swing it out and trundle it away, the grating sound of the wheels makes me wince, but it isn't loud enough to raise any suspicions… or to raise the dead. I steer it over to the slim passageway. I push it through as quickly as I can and pull out an almost identical-looking bin, and wheel that back to our hotel.

'Done,' I say. And without a word she turns and walks away leaving me standing there, holding the bag. The bag that almost sank us.

Mia

I walk away so Ben can't see that I'm shaking so bloody hard, and I don't know why. I mean, we've done it, we got rid of the body and left the hotel unseen and—

I can't stop shaking, and I feel that there's a black cloud of doom hanging over my head, about to unleash the mother of all storms. It might be that I've just watched too many movies – because in the films it always happens like this; the heroes think they're home and dry, that their plan's worked, and then it all turns to shit. The police arrive, or gangsters, or in *The Sound of Music* it's the Nazis, armed to the teeth. That's what the movies do – they lull you into a false sense of security, then they flip it, to turn up the suspense and excitement. That's why I can't breathe now, as I walk away from Ben. I don't want him to see how freaked out I am – because of the damned Adidas bag. I thought I was so smart, that I'd got every angle covered, but I hadn't. I forgot the bag came from home. I guess that I'm not as good a criminal as I thought I'd be. That's why I'm expecting the Nazis to turn up at any second. That's why I'm shaking.

I head through the alleyway and out onto the street. I walk slowly and try to look confident, even though my legs feel wobbly.

'Mia?' Ben says from behind me and suddenly a hand is on my shoulder and I freak out.

'Don't fucking touch me!' My hands ball into fists without me telling them to. I want to lash out – my fight or flight response wants me to kill him.

'Mia.'

'I'm sorry, but we need to keep going, we aren't far enough away yet. And keep your head down,' I tell him and I turn and keep walking. *Keep walking.* One foot in front of the other – that's all I have to do – and I keep that up for a couple of minutes, until I see a little square with a grassy area and a statue in the centre. I expect the shadows are full of drunks and junkies, but it's an ideal place to stop and take a breath. I head straight there, and only stop when I'm on the grass. I consider taking my shoes and socks off, feeling the grass and the earth between my toes, but then I think about dog shit and hypodermic needles, and decide to keep them on. I know Ben's behind me, even though I don't look back. I just trust that he's following me – I don't need to look.

'Mia.'

I turn to him. I think we're free now. 'Thanks for coming when I called you.'

Ben doesn't speak. I know he fears that this is the end. In little ways, he's always been insecure in our marriage; he's always thought that unless I'm publicly declaring my love, or pulling him on top of me, that I'm leaving him or getting tired of him. And I can see that fear in him now, sitting on his shoulder and whispering in his ear.

'Mia, can we go home, and maybe put tonight behind us?' he asks.

'Do you mean that we forget about what happened?'

'Not forget but...' tears well in the corners of his eyes, and he swats them away. 'I just want to go back to how it was. Can we?'

'Ben I would love that, I just...' but I can't finish, because everything has been swept away by one agonising thought. I feel my vision swim a little, and I sway on the spot. I feel a quake run through me, my limbs shake and I am so cold in my bones and in my belly.

'What's wrong?'

'The Nazis have arrived,' I tell him.

'What?'

I slowly check my pockets, keeping calm – I need to make sure.

'What's the matter, Mia? For god's sake, tell me!' He's worried; he can see the horror that's creeping through me. First I pull out the room key from my hoody pouch, then the dead man's wallet; I feel for the bag of teeth and his fingertips.

'It's not here,' I mutter as I start to burn.

'What's not?'

'The phone.'

'Your work phone?'

'No, his phone, Theo's phone.'

'Did he have one?'

'Earlier, he made a call and... shit... Ben, he had a phone.'

'Okay, he had a phone, but I don't get why it's important.'

'Where is it?'

'Well I don't know but I guess...' and I see the penny drop, as his eyes widen. 'It must be back in the room.'

Chapter Six

Mia

'We need to go back,' I tell him, even though the thought of it makes me feel queasy.

'You said it was over,' he says, sounding like a scared kid.

'I know I did, but it isn't. I'm sorry.'

'But we're out.' He opens his arms to show that we're free.

'The phone's inside.'

'But how would we even get back in the hotel?'

'I've still got the room keycard,' I hold it up, like a Wonka golden ticket. 'The receptionist didn't see us come out, so he still thinks the room's occupied. It won't get cleaned until the morning now.' I say it with complete faith, but we both know it's just a guess.

'But we're safe,' he says plaintively. 'We can go home.'

Christ, I wish that was true. 'Ben, if we don't go and get the phone, then everything we've done is for nothing. If they find it—'

'Then the cleaner will sell it for a few quid.'

'Maybe, but are you willing to risk everything on that? What if the cleaner gives it to the manager? In the morning his family will start calling and if anyone answers the phone… we're dead.'

'But the battery might die; it might never ring.'

'You'd gamble our lives on the battery life of a phone… Really?'

He doesn't reply; his brow knits together and I can see him scrolling through the choices in his head, desperate to find something that will work, but I know he won't find anything. There isn't another option.

'Help me get the phone?' I ask, plain and simple. 'Help me one last time.' I give him my best goofy smile. 'We just need to run in, find it and get out. You can be lookout, we can do it, there's nobody there now. This is the easy part! Us against the world, remember?'

He looks pained, like it was unfair of me to use his wedding vow against him. 'I just… I don't think… I can't help you, I can't be a part of this anymore.' He shakes his head without looking at me.

I feel a cord encircle my heart and start to squeeze. I didn't expect him to turn me down.

'I'm sorry,' he says as he turns and walks away.

'Ben?' I call, and he stops. I see his breath drift up in the cold air, but he doesn't turn back to me. I think I could beg him to stay… but my dignity has already been shredded tonight. Instead of trying to get him back, I say: 'Go home. I love you.'

With a deep sigh, he turns back to me. He looks tired and old, like he's aged fifty years in the last hour. I know I have to let him go, it isn't fair to put him through more of this horror.

'I'm sorry, I just—' he starts but I wave his words away.

'Don't you dare be sorry. It was good of you to… I mean thanks, just thanks, for coming to help.' I smile with all the warmth I can muster, and then I turn and walk back to the hotel.

I climb the steps, up to the main entrance, and look in through the panes of the revolving door. We were lucky when we left, as the reception desk was empty, but now the tall receptionist is back. I hover there, like a hummingbird, unsure what to do and where to go. I just rock back and forth between heel and toe, as I hope and pray he'll leave again. Pray – how stupid. Hope – almost as stupid. I just watch and wait, ignoring the cold that bites at me, and the fears that gnaw at me. He has to go to the toilet at some point, so I wait and watch and rock back and forth.

Ben

I follow Mia at a distance, watch her climb the stairs, and see her hesitate on the top step. My fingers are numb and my clothes are still wet, so my teeth chatter with the cold. My knee is screaming. I should go home. She said it herself, I've done enough – more than enough – what more can she expect of me? I can't keep running after her, I mean, she kept the truth from me, about getting rid of the body, so that I'd do what she wanted. She played me, and I can't forgive that. I'm not her monkey. I'm going to go, leave her – but I feel this pain in my chest like there's a rubber band stretched between us, and as we move apart, it's ripping my heart in two. I can't go. I can't.

I can see she's at the top of the steps waiting, so some-body must be at the reception desk. Maybe it's Ali, with all the weight of the world on his shoulders. Mia must be waiting for him to move away before she goes inside, but that could take ages.

'Damn,' I mutter to myself.

Then, all of a sudden I'm moving, but not towards her. I'm moving away, going around the side of the hotel and back into the alleyway. I limp through it, as quickly as I can, and into the square behind the hotel. Once I'm there, I count from the road, one… two… three… four… and that must be the back door of the Lampton. It's darker now. None of these hotels are fancy enough to offer twenty-four-hour room service, so they are mostly dark, just a few jags of light between curtains and window.

I head to the Lampton back door, assuming it must lead into a small kitchen area. That would make sense, so that all the waste can be pulled out and taken through to the skips outside and dumped there. Slowly, I walk across to the rear door of the Lampton, and peer through the windows. They're dark and filthy. On the inside of the glass there seems to be a layer of chicken wire – which is all pretty low-tech cheap security, and fits in with the general vibe of the hotel. I touch the door, pushing at it, in the hope that it might be unlocked, but it doesn't budge.

I turn and trot into the middle of the square. I know there are loose bricks here. I bend down and stretch my fingers into the ground, trying to burrow into the dirt and soil, feeling the broken bits of slab come up, and trying not to think about the creepy-crawlies underneath. It only takes a few seconds, and I manage to lever three good-sized bricks up. I pull back my arm and, with all my might, launch them at the windows.

There's a terrific crash as the glass shatters. Dogs start barking and lights come on all around the square. One catches me in its beam, like a prison searchlight. I jump sideways, into the shadows, and crawl behind a skip. From there I can see into the Lampton kitchen, as a light turns on inside, and I hear a mutter of some foreign language I don't know.

My heart's racing. I have never done anything like this before; even when I was on anti-war protests I never threw anything. If there was ever any trouble I ran away. I stop breathing, as Ali throws opens the back door and steps out. He shouts something I don't understand, and then he steps into the square.

Christ. He's holding a huge knife, long, sharp and vicious-looking. The tiredness in his eyes has gone; now they glitter with fury. I push myself down further behind the bins and cower. He kicks at the closest one and it clatters into three others, setting the dogs off again. I still have no idea what direction they're in, as the frantic barking bounces off the walls, seeming to come from everywhere at once – like ricocheting bullets of mongrel fury.

Ali hisses something, I assume in his native language, and turns to examine the windows. He's so close to where I'm squatting, that I could reach out and touch his foot. His knife is freaking me out. Then he turns and goes back to the Lampton to examine the damage. He pushes his fingertips into the broken glass of the window, and just the faintest touch makes more of it collapse and fall to the ground, shattering on the bricks. Then he pushes at the mesh behind the glass, which seems to be intact. He seems pleased that nobody's actually broken into the hotel. He spits on the ground, and then heads back inside – without locking the door behind him – and disappears somewhere into the bowels of the hotel.

'Damn.' I wish he'd locked the door. I really do, because then I'd have no choice, no chance to go inside and find her. If all has gone well, she will have been able to run into the hotel the moment Ali left reception, sprinted up to the room, found the phone quickly, and beetled back down the stairs and out into the night. Right now she's probably walking towards Earl's Court tube and freedom. Probably… if everything went to plan… if… *Damn*. Nothing has gone to plan so far tonight – so I have to go inside and make sure she's safe. I have to find her again.

I stay low, scuttle like a crab to the kitchen door, and push inside. The floor is stone or a slate tile. As soon as step onto it, I hear my footsteps echoing through the room and out into the rest of the hotel. I stop and hold my breath, sure that the tall man with the giant knife will have heard me. I hold my breath… one Mississippi… two Mississippi… three Mississippi… but there is nothing. He can't have heard me. With my heart beating wildly, I slip my shoes off. In my socks, I pad through the kitchen and into the hallway. I can see light at the end of it; I guess it's the office and then the reception area beyond that. I stand still, wondering what to do. I have never broken into anywhere before, and then I hear someone coming. I almost go back into the kitchen, which would have been suicide, but at the last second I see that there's another door off to the left and I gamble on it being empty as I rush in. It's a cupboard, full of cleaning materials, but there's just enough room for me to squeeze inside. I close the door, leaving a crack open that I put my eye against to see through. I make it just in time, as Ali storms past, with his arms full of broken up cardboard boxes. I suppose he's going to put them up over the windows to keep the cold air out; but that means there's no chance to go back – I can only go forward, to look for Mia.

I count to fifty, before I open the cupboard door. I can hear Ali nailing the cardboard in place. I don't know how long I've got, but I hope it's enough time. I head off, through the hallway and past the office and reception. I cross the lobby and up the stairs again: first floor, then second and third. I step out of the stairwell; in my socks the carpet feels even stickier. I need to be quick, out on the landing there are CCTV cameras, so again I bow my head and look down to the swirl of filthy carpet at my feet. Ali must still be dealing with the broken glass, I should have time left – ten minutes, maybe, but that's all.

I'm at the door to 303. I tap on it softly, not wanting to disturb anyone in the adjacent rooms. I wait, but there's no response. Maybe she's gone already. I hope so, but I have to know for sure. I tap again… no reply. I do it for a third time, this time louder and I hiss: 'It's me.' But there's still nothing from inside the room. Can I go? One last try. I knock our song – the song we first danced to twenty-something years ago, *Keep it Comin' Love* by KC and the Sunshine Band. It isn't an easy song to tap, but as I finish the chorus, the door cracks open and there is a rush of bleach smell that's so cloying it makes me gag.

'It's me, let me in,' I whisper. The door opens a little further and I slide inside, pulling it closed behind me. Mia stands there. 'What happened?' I ask, as I see tears streaming down her face. She looks like death.

'I can't find it.' Her voice is brittle. I look past her, and see that she's ransacked the room; everything we'd been so careful to leave in its right place has been pulled out. The bed is skewed and all the bedding has been stripped and rolled into a ball. The little table's on its side, the chair lies on the bed and the rubbish bin looks like it's been thrown against the wall.

'It isn't bloody here,' she says. 'I don't know where it is and I don't know what to do. Help me.' There's such desperation in her voice that I can't do anything except take her into my arms and have her fold into me.

I hold her, like she's air, and I'm the only thing keeping her from dissipating. I want to tell her that I love her... but that's crazy talk tonight.

Mia

I see how the smell of bleach affects him as he comes through the door, his eyes even start to water and I don't think it's tears of sadness and I damn well know it's not tears of joy. I'm glad to see him – no, that isn't right; the feeling goes so much deeper. I honestly thought I was going to go out of my mind in here. I'm at my wits' end. I let him hug me.

'I can't find it,' I tell him in a strangled voice, trying to keep the sobs and tears inside, but not succeeding.

'You don't know the thing's even here,' he says, and it isn't unkind or bitchy, but I still shove my hands into his chest and push him away from me.

'I know it is – don't tell me I don't know! It's here, it has to be, I just can't find it... Ben, don't tell me I'm wrong – help me.'

For a second he looks annoyed, frustrated with me, his lip curls like Nicolas Cage doing angry, fat Elvis... but then he softens, like the Hulk turning back to Bruce Banner, and he's just Ben again.

'Of course, let's search for the phone together. Okay?'

And he holds out his hand. I look at it, the formality of the gesture, and I almost laugh, but I don't. Instead, I take it and shake it. I am so sad that I've pushed us to this – I'm scared for tomorrow.

'Ben—' I start, and I'm not sure what I was going to say but that doesn't matter as it's all washed away by the sound that swamps the room and fills the inside of my head.

DA DA-DA DAH DA, DA DA-DA DAH

It's a really annoying Star Wars ring tone; it seems to bounce around the room, coming from every surface, nook and cranny.

'Where is it?' Ben asks, his head darting this way and that.

'I think…' I start, but actually I have no idea where it's coming from.

'The chair,' he suddenly says.

'I looked and it's not—'

But he digs his fingers down into the sides of it and wriggles under the covered plastic seat. Christ, I hate to think about what's down there and what you could catch by touching it.

'Here!' With the tips of his fingers, he pulls out a slim phone. It's still ringing and the screen is lit up: *Alex calling*.

'Do I answer it?' Ben asks, but I'm frozen. I don't know what to do. So we do nothing and both of us just stare at the electronic rectangle until it stops ringing.

'It was wedged down under the seat. I don't think anybody would have found it,' he says.

'Unless it rang.'

'Yeah – unless it rang.' He hands it to me. I take it, just holding it with my fingertips like it's a bomb or something and—

The phone buzzes as a text comes in.

Where you? Can't still be going, she won't be able to walk for a week. Shall I pick you up at hotel?

I feel the cold burn up my body as I read it. Ben steps behind me, his head craning over my shoulder, trying to see what it says, but I hide it away from him. I flick the ringer off.

'What does it say?' he asks. He tries to make it nonchalant but I can see there's a glint of something in his eye and he senses a shift; there's a change in the story.

'Can I?' He puts his hand out, it's open and in no way aggressive, but he wants to see the phone, and I know he has the right to see it, but I can't allow that – he can't see it. I'm thinking this was a mistake, a huge error that will catch me in a net, and it's my own stupid fault. I should have done what Ben said and run. I should have trusted and hoped, even bloody prayed, that the phone would never be found. But I didn't. I put my head back into the lion's mouth and… *oh Christ*.

'Okay, we've got the phone,' I say and try to force the commanding tone back into my voice. 'Let's go, we should be fine now,' but I can hear how thin it all sounds – like I'm some corrupt politician caught with his fingers in the sweetie jar. *I am not a crook.*

'I want to read the text.' Ben says with an edge to his voice that was not there before. 'Can I…' He stretches out his hand. 'I want to read the text, Mia.'

'Let's get away first and then—'

He tries to snatch it. 'Let me see,' he demands.

'For fuck's sake, Ben.' I step back, smacking his hand away.

96

'What did it say? What the hell aren't you telling me?'

'Nothing.'

But he doesn't believe that, and I don't blame him. I actually think he might try to take the phone by force. 'Mia, you have to—'

Shrill ringing cuts through the hotel room and smashes the wall of anger between us. Fear turns us both around, to look at the hotel telephone that was on the desk and now sits on the floor. It's ringing.

'Maybe we should answer that,' Ben says, and he starts to move towards it.

'No.' I snap at him. And we both just watch the telephone ring, holding our breath – like that will have any fucking influence on what happens – but neither of us can move or look away.

It makes one last insistent bleat and dies.

'It's probably reception, maybe that's time, and they're just kicking you out,' Ben says, trying to keep us both calm.

'Or they want more money for the extra time.'

'Well that's—'

'Loads of cash, which we don't have,' I say and Ben shakes his head, realising at last what a problem this could be. 'And we can't afford to have them see us and take our names and address, and we especially can't have them call the police.'

'I hadn't thought of that,' he sounds sarcastic.

'No, thinking isn't your strong suit.'

'Says the bloody genius who got herself in such a mess that she needed the idiot to come and rescue her.'

'Rescue? Like hell! All you've done is bitch and whine. And by the way, this is not a rescue – I'm not some fucking damsel in distress.'

'Okay I get it, so what the hell is the plan?' he snaps angrily.

'I say we put the room back together, wipe it down and leave. Unless your megamind has a better idea?'

'Maybe not screwing—'

Knock knock knock.

The pit of my stomach drops through the floor. There's someone at the door.

Ben

I see her freeze, like a spell has turned her to ice. Ever so quietly, I step next to her and slip my hand around hers... *Christ*, her fingers are cold and she's shaking, like an electric current runs through her. I'm not sure I'm any better. We hold our breath, each of us wondering if the person outside heard us arguing... if they didn't, then maybe they'll leave and—

The electronic lock clicks, and the door starts to open.

'Hey, you can't come in here, we're not dressed,' Mia yells and the door pulls back instantly, banging shut.

'I am sorry, so sorry, I thought maybe there was illness or you had left. I call on telephone and no one pick up,' a voice calls through the inch and a half of wood. His accent is quite thick, but his English is good. It must be Ali.

'There was urgent call, it was Mister Alex for his brother. Are you there, Mister Theo?'

I open my mouth to answer but Mia hits my arm and looks like she wants to kill me.

'Of course he's here but he's a bit tied up at the moment. We're having personal time, and it's two a.m. So please get lost.'

'The room was only booked for—'

'I know that, but we're spending longer than we planned. Don't worry, you'll get the extra money – but in the morning. Now leave us alone.'

'I am sorry… very sorry,' Ali says through the door, and we hear him walk away.

'Christ, you're scary.' I tell her, though I think she was amazing under all that pressure. I can see she's pumped up on adrenaline; her eyes look wild. I feel an overwhelming desire to kiss her, and lean across to—

'What the hell are you doing?' She jumps away from me. I feel like she slapped my face and poured cold water on me, all in the same second.

'I just—'

'For fuck's sake, Ben, this is no time for a quick snog; this is getting serious. The staff know Theo. His brother knows he should have left by now, and he's called his phone and got no response. Now he's had the receptionist come up and been turned away without talking to him.'

'Well, you wouldn't let me pretend to be Theo.'

'No, because you would have blown everything.'

'Why?'

'Because you have no idea what he sounds like.'

'Well… what does he sound like? If they come again I can pretend to be him.'

'You— I don't… I can't tell you. I don't remember his voice.'

'Well, it wasn't his voice that you wanted.' I know how mean it sounds, but I can't stop myself from saying it. Mia looks disappointed in me.

'Ben, we can do all this later, but there's no time now. If we get caught we will go to prison, or this bastard's brother slits our throats.' The image of us both dead flashes through my mind.

99

'You're right,' I tell her.

'I know I am.' She pauses. 'So, what we need to do now is to put this room back together, without leaving fingerprints, and then go.'

I nod, and using my elbows, or with my hands still in my pockets, I start to rebuild the room. I let her make the bed while I replace the table and chair and bin. There isn't much to put back, really. I look around the spartan little room. *Am I missing anything?* There's nothing else here except the wardrobe.

'Did you check the wardrobe?' I ask.

'No need, we didn't use it; the only thing I saw him with was the phone.'

'But maybe you didn't see everything.' I cast my mind back to when I got here, and realise I haven't seen a coat, not for either of them. 'It's cold outside, like really cold,' I say.

'I noticed.'

'So where's his coat?'

'He didn't have one.'

'Are you sure?'

'Positive.'

'It took you a while to remember the phone.'

She glowers at me, and her jaw tightens. 'We didn't use the wardrobe.'

'I just want to…' I look at the mirrored wardrobe, and for some reason my Spidey sense tingles. I can immediately see why it's positioned where it is. From the bed, a couple can see themselves in the act of making love, except this isn't a room for lovemaking; it's a room for screwing. I don't think love comes into the equation here.

'Let me just check it, and then we can go.'

'Fine,' she shrugs and I use my hoody as makeshift gloves and reach out to the doorknob. I pull. I expect to see an empty wardrobe with some cheap metal or plastic hangers. I do not expect to have my world thrown upside down, but that's what happens, as the door swings open, and all the air is kicked out of my body.

'Oh my god.'

'What?' Mia hears the shock in my voice and pushes me to one side so she can see past me. She gasps, and I feel both of our hearts skip a beat as we look inside the wardrobe. There, pointing through one-way glass, made to look like a mirror from the outside, is a video camera with a blinking red light on the top. It's pointing directly at the bed.

Chapter Seven

Ben

The light blinks on the top of the camera and I can't tear my eyes away from it. *Recording – recording – recording –* it flashes, as I look down the barrel of its lens, with no comprehension of why it's here, but I do know what it means: that everything has changed. Everything.

Behind me I hear a groan and turn to see Mia as she curls into a ball on the floor. 'Mia,' I say, soft and insistent, but there's no reply, not a flicker of recognition – she's lost. I kneel down beside her.

'Did you know about this?' I ask, even though I know it's a stupid question, as I can see she's in total shock. She obviously had no idea the camera was here. I lean forward and slowly put my hand onto her shoulder. She doesn't flinch, which is good but then again, she doesn't make any movement at all.

'Have you got any idea why the camera's in there?' I ask, but there's no reply – which is the worst response she could have made. I want her to be sarcastic. I want her to make some caustic comment about how stupid I am but she doesn't; she just lies there, shaking.

'Okay,' I whisper and stroke her hair – just once – and then I stand up. I can see she isn't up to this now and

I'm going to have to step up. Okay, okay... I can do this. 'We're going to be fine,' I tell her and then, with a heavy heart, turn back to the blinking camera.

So the sixty-four-million-dollar, jackpot-rollover question: why is there a hidden camera in the wardrobe and who put it there? *Oh Christ...* I just thought about the next logical question: is the camera merely recording, or is it also broadcasting live? If anyone is watching this, then Mia and I will be going to prison for a very long time.

I step forward slowly, like I'm approaching a wild animal. I open both wardrobe doors and look in. The camera is expensive and professional, the kind a news crew might have. It's mounted on a sturdy looking tripod, and next to it is a small plastic stool. Sitting on that is a laptop. It looks like the camera's linked to the computer. If that's the case, it could be making a back-up on the computer hard drive, and broadcasting the film. My hand is shaking. I lean inside the wardrobe to get a closer look at the camera. I turn it around on the tripod and I can see the small monitor screen that sticks out. The recording has been going for four hours. I can see that it records onto a large SD card – maybe 256 GB. I take a deep breath and push the red button. The light on top stops blinking.

I hold my breath as I slide the laptop around so I can see the screen, and look at the open software; it's recording a back-up onto the laptop and... *thank god*, I breathe again. There's no software that's sending the signal out of the room. It looks completely self-contained to me, so that means somebody started the camera, presumably before Mia and Theo got here. Then after they've left, someone will come back and retrieve the laptop and SD card. But why? What is this all about?

I look back into the room, as if I'm the camera. The first obvious thing is that it's filming the bed. Is this some kind of honey trap? Like in a spy novel, where a shitty hotel is used to snare politicians – get them filmed with a prostitute pissing on them – and then they're owned forever. But why would that involve Mia? How is she important enough for this? Does she know some kind of industrial or commercial secret? But she can't, not Mia. How the hell could she be the target of a sting? It makes no sense. No damned sense at all. But what else can it be? If this was the guy's home it might just be so he can watch it again, but this is a public hotel, this means some serious planning.

'Mia…' I turn away from the camera, and kneel down next to her. She hasn't moved an inch and I'm starting to feel a little scared for her.

'Mia,' I say softly, with a kind of sing-song quality, trying to make this as light as I can. 'Mia, the camera filmed you with this guy. You were set up, but it's okay, as it wasn't sending the film out live.' I pause. 'Do you understand?' I ask, but she's dead to the world.

'Mia we have the copies, nobody's seen this, but we need to work out what happened. Why you were filmed?' Still no reply.

'Have you worked on something that might make you a target? Is there some patent you've seen that would warrant all of this?' But she's still mute. 'Has anyone approached you and asked for information, or offered you any money or…?' Or what?

I sit back on my heels and think about what I just said. This has been planned, so could be a big operation – shit, at any second, police or spooks could smash the door down. I am starting to feel all this tighten, like a noose around my neck. It must be something to do with her patent work; she must have seen something or talked to someone on the brink of some massive discovery.

'Mia, come on, what have you worked on recently? Anything that could be so secret?' Still nothing. 'Why did the guy bring you to this hotel? He must have known about the camera, so you were the target – he was going to blackmail you, but what for? What did he want?' But she just lies there like a rag doll, broken.

'Mia!' I grab her shoulders and shake her hard. 'Snap out of this.' She looks up at me but her eyes are swimmy, like she can't fully focus. 'Mia, do you have any idea what's going on?'

But she just looks vacantly at me. Christ, I'm scared this is some serious shit, either with the government or a criminal gang. I don't know if it's prison for years, or we're going to be thrown into wet concrete and used to build a bridge. I can feel my heart pounding like a train. I have to think this through, because Mia isn't going to; she isn't responding to anything, so it's up to me now. Oh god – it's up to me.

'Okay Mia, rest a little longer,' I tell her, using the kind of voice you save for kids and old people. 'It's good that we came back, because now we know what's been happening and we found the camera, which is great.' I say, trying to make it upbeat. I can do this.

I approach the camera like it's an unexploded bomb. I find the SD card slot, press it in and the little square of incriminating plastic pops out. I put it in my pocket, zipping it up so I won't lose it. Now I'm going to erase the back-up from the laptop and… *huh!* I stop dead. On the top of the laptop is a sticker that I hadn't noticed before.

It reads: 'studslovemums.com' and underneath that, it says *'the guys who love to fuck the mums'*.

I grab the laptop. It's still unlocked so I can use it, except that this crappy hotel hasn't got guest wifi. All the computer can find is a weak signal from some place called Poke My Bowl, which I guess is a local restaurant. I open the browser and type in 'studslovemums.com'. It is painfully slow but it finally opens the website. *Oh my god* – this isn't about Mia's job. The site reads:

> Real women getting fucked on hidden cameras – the best amateur porn.
>
> Join now for £24.99. Bathroom cams, hotel cams, spy cams – this is the premium horny hot wife site. Is your wife on here?

I look over at Mia and I feel a tsunami of tiredness, shame, guilt and just plain wretchedness hit me. This isn't about extortion, but abuse on such a basic, primal level, just because she's a woman – an attractive older woman – who still wants to be held and found desirable. That's all.

I look at the photographs of the women on the home page, they aren't porn stars, they're just normal. Middle-aged women, housewives, mothers – all shapes and sizes, but what they have in common is that they want to enjoy their sexuality. The women are beautiful but the site is ugly. It's all stolen pleasure and enjoyment; there's no consent, and that is hideous. And the poster boys for the ugliness are pictured in the centre of the page, Alex and Theo – *'the studs that love the mums'*. And… oh my god, I look at Mia. 'They're…'

'Twins?' Ben says with amazement, and I force my eyes to the screen and there... I see him, Theo, and he's alive again and smiling, his eyes twinkling once more. He's more than merely good-looking, he's Hollywood handsome; with his perfect jawline (not now), twinkling eyes (not now) and easy charm... *not now*. Of course, women are attracted to him, and lonely women wouldn't be able to resist him. I remember his laugh, big and hearty, full of life. I saw how he looked at me, held my gaze, and I saw how he wanted me, wanted my body. At least, I thought that was what I saw, but maybe all I saw was what I wanted to see. But it hardly matters now – I killed him.

I look at the other man, his brother Alex. His twin. They're identical, at least fully clothed they are. Only their tattoos show any difference, and I finally understand what happened tonight – the simple mistake that ended in a man's death.

I am such an idiot, I think, as I read the page and look at the pictures of the women on there. Normal women. They're naked and excited – they moan, they touch themselves and they touch the two men. There's no covering up, and no hiding; everything is on show because these women thought they were safe. Safe enough to open themselves up, to enjoy the power of their bodies and the lust of these hot young men. But none of them know the hateful darkness that lay behind the twinkling eyes and heady charm. These women thought they were free to be themselves, but they were betrayed.

I read the words on the screen, and feel my skin crawl: milf, gilf, amateurs, desperate housewives, swingers, creampie, breeding, squirting, mature, granny... I feel sick to my stomach, but I can't stop looking. I lean across Ben, to the laptop, where there is a preview film – edited highlights, I would guess – and I hit play. I feel Ben squirm beside me. I don't think he wants to watch, but tough luck. I need to see, even if it is hell itself.

I steel myself, and together we watch the man I killed have sex with nine or ten women – just thirty seconds of each – during which they scream and moan, and orgasm.

'Jesus Christ,' Ben says beside me.

I feel so angry; none of these women know that they're starring in a show, that their pleasure is just an entertainment for pathetic men all over the world. Men who will watch them with their hands wrapped around their cocks and masturbate, imagining it's them, and not the young virile twins, that these women give themselves to. It's a vile stolen intimacy. These women have no idea their sexuality will be abused, stolen and shared with any man who wants to see them. Bastards… bastards… bastards.

The film ends and I'm trembling. I close my eyes and in the dark I'm like a child. Anybody can find this on the internet, and these bastards can blackmail me and threaten to send it to someone I love. I won't have my dad see this – see me like this – or my sister, or my friends, or my colleagues. I won't. I won't.

–

This isn't the first time I've had sex that's had nothing to do with love, or passion, and wasn't even with somebody I liked. Once, when I was nineteen, I was at a wedding and I was too smashed to say no. I didn't even get undressed, neither did he – just pulled his pants down, pushed mine to one side and fucked me. It was really quick. It wasn't unpleasant, and the booze took the edge off. He wasn't a really bad guy, he was more of an opportunist – it could have been a lot worse. It was private. There are no photos. I remember it happened, but it isn't *out there*, in the world for anyone to see.

I once had sex because I was scared to say no. It was with the flatmate of a friend, and I was staying with her for one night. The man was angry and scary, and I actually thought he might hurt me if I didn't go along with it – I didn't know, back then, that I could fight back. That time was nasty, and the next day I took the morning-after pill and broke all contact with my friend. She should have protected me; I think she might even have used me as a human shield, or maybe she even fed me to the lions to save herself. Either way, we have not been in contact since. I don't know or even care what happened to her, I really don't want to know. She was not a good sister.

I gave a guy with a stutter a blowjob once – I think I was trying to be like Mother Teresa and do good – not that I think Mother Teresa used to give blowjobs to help people. But he was sweet about it and didn't spread it around. It did nothing to help his stammer though.

And then I met Ben. He wasn't a virgin but he probably should have been. There was a girl in the first year – Fifi or Fluffy or something stupid – they'd gone out for a few months and she'd not even started his training. He hadn't gone down on her, had no idea what/where or why a clit was, and they'd done missionary and that was it. So, he was my sexual project. He thought I was very worldly and exotic – but I wasn't really. I hadn't had much experience, but I'd read a lot, and I knew what I wanted – and I told him. The sex was lovely and freely given and mutually enjoyed… for a long, long time. Fifteen years or so, until—

'Oh god…' I curl into a ball again.

Mia… Mia… snap out of it… I hear Ben call to me and I think I can feel him shaking me, pulling at my shoulders but it's not me. He sounds like he's a thousand miles away and I'm just a broken toy on the floor. I can't feel my body. It's just like… just like the day she died. The day all this started, I guess, the real day our marriage failed. The day our daughter died and…

Rosie.

–

I was away, on a business trip, when he called. I'd known something was wrong – he sounded so cold on the phone, and clammed up when I asked what it was, but I knew. Deep down I knew something awful had happened. I didn't even pack; I left everything except my passport and the clothes I was wearing and went to the airport. I paid a fortune for a ticket on the first plane out, and I sat on it with my nails embedded in the plastic seat rests. It was two hours of hell, and as we touched down I was out of my seat and down the aisle to wait by the door, so I'd be the first person off the plane. I didn't care what the crew said to me or the threats they made; I ignored them all and they let me off first. I sprinted through passport control and into arrivals, and I saw him standing there… alone. *Alone.*

I just knew she was dead.

I loved Ben. I had loved him all my adult life – so many happy years. The passion had dwindled over time and been replaced by something just as good: the family.

Our family was beautiful and vibrant… but when Rosie died, it died too. The family was broken and our marriage began to slip away. We tried to rekindle the passion, tried to have sex but it was awkward and full of emotional pain. We went away – to Lisbon where we had been so happy many times – but while we were there we couldn't even hold hands in the street, and we stopped hugging and even talking about what really mattered. We were lost to each other. I don't think either one of us could stop thinking about Rosie – so our marriage just slipped out of focus. We were both absent – off with the fairies, or in some private hell we'd made for ourselves. Our marriage wasn't working and our shared closeness just slowly evaporated. We were still together on some level: we went out to eat and see films and plays; we still had friends and had our history; we had memories, but there was nothing new being made. No new love was being formed, and a marriage can't survive on the past alone.

We started to hide from each other, in work or the news and crap on Facebook. We could get passionate, but it would be about Brexit, or Trump, or the pandemic – but not ourselves, not about our marriage or about *us*. There was no sense of renewal, no moving forward with our lives. We were stuck and floundering. There was a hole in *us*. For me it became an ache, like a bad tooth, and it spread slowly through my whole body. Not loneliness exactly – though I was so bloody lonely – and not just a need to be touched, though that was very real too, but the sense that I was petrifying, turning to stone, my life was bleeding away. How pathetic that sounds now, such a frail and poor excuse for where I've found myself tonight – a killer fighting for my life. I am sorry, Ben. I am sorry, Rosie. I am so sorry, Mia.

Ben

I can't do anything for her. She just lies, unmoving, curled in a ball. We need to get away from here as fast as possible, so I have to leave her and turn to the computer. We need to find out about this site and what it does – what this means. A part of me wants to just grab the laptop and run, but are there other nasty surprises? I need to log onto the site. I haven't seen it before, but I have looked at others like it. I watch porn sometimes – no, that's not true. I watch it a lot, and I feel guilty about it, but I don't stop. I seek out 'regular' women in porn, I can't imagine myself with some pneumatic Barbie doll, but I do watch porn about swingers, wives next door and… hell, I am such a hypocrite.

I call myself a feminist, and I've stood alongside women on marches and demos. I try to support them, say they have to get equal pay and women-only shortlists and so on, and yet the next day I will watch them, or someone just like them, have sex with their son's friend, or pay their rent with their bodies, or meet a guy in a bar and go home with them. I will watch their loneliness exploited to salve my own. I make myself sick.

'I'm sorry, Mia, this is all my fault,' I tell her sadly and she stirs and moves onto all fours.

'Mia, are you okay?'

She looks at me, uncomprehending for a second and then she swings her arm and slaps me hard in the face.

'Fuck you, Ben.'

Mia

I can actually see the outline of my hand on his cheek, all red from where I hit him. He looks surprised and hurt, like a little baby whose doting mother just called him a bastard. Boo-fucking-hoo.

'I don't—' He starts, but I cut him off.

'Of course you don't. You think the whole world revolves around you, that you own me and my life; that I am here just as a reaction to you.'

'No, that isn't fair.'

'Then why the hell say sorry? Do you think that's why I'm out on the prowl, rolling on my back for any fucking tomcat that wants some; because you don't screw me anymore?'

'I—'

'Fuck you, Ben. I have made this mess all on my own, I own it, in all its fucking craziness, and all its misery and pain. You don't get to say *sorry* for making this happen, that isn't on you.'

I turn away from him. My whole body burns with anger and shame and guilt and – Rosie. God damn, it's bad enough that I have to deal with the rapist twins but I am swamped by my grief all over again. I feel beaten down. It feels like I've been in this room for weeks, maybe even months. Maybe I died here, and this is my purgatory.

But at least I'm not here alone. I mustn't forget that, when I needed him, Ben came to help. He followed me into hell. And I have to remember that I loved him and… that we're both sorry; that we're both such sorry fucks.

'Ben, I—' I turn back to him, I'm going to apologise for slapping him, but he's doing something weird, and then he jumps up on the bed.

'What the hell?'

I'm thinking about the preview film we just watched. Some of the videos were shot here, in this very room – I recognise the bed and the curtains – but other scenes weren't. There must be other rooms they use, other scenarios for securing their victims. But there was something I saw in the films that were shot here: they weren't only shot from behind the mirror, they were shot from above, too. There's another camera. There's a camera in the ceiling.

I stand on the bed, and yes, I know, I'm sure this is spreading my DNA around but… but… I stretch up as high as I can and— yes, there's a camera in the light above the bed. I have to stretch up to reach. It feels like I'm tearing myself in two, but I can just get enough leverage to – *ugh* – pull it off the ceiling. With a jerk, the cable snaps, bringing a puff of plaster down with it. Mia looks up at me for a moment, and there is a look of absolute horror on her face.

'There's a second camera above the bed,' I tell her. 'I don't know where the footage goes, it didn't feed into the laptop.'

I follow the cables, the snaky little bastards, down from the ceiling, along the wall, then down along the skirting board and behind the bed where there's a small box, and inside I find a digital recorder. I pull it out of the wall. It's got two SD card slots. I take both cards and put them in my pocket, zipping them in.

'Did you get it?' she asks in a voice that fears the worst.

'I did but… There might be hidden mics, too. I'll find them.' I tell her, jumping up and lurching over to the wardrobe. I start to dismantle everything inside the evil Narnia. After a few seconds I find some wires and pull them up. They're built into the floor and in the wall, even wallpapered over, so they must have been here some time. I trace them up to the bed where two high-powered mics are hidden. This is a really professional set-up. I pull the mics out of the wall, drop them on the floor and stomp them to shit. When they're completely trashed, I pick up the pieces and drop them out of the window, watching them spiral in the air before they thud into the skip below. I turn to say something to Mia but I don't even get to open my mouth as, out of the blue, she puts her arms out and around my back and pulls me to her, as she embraces me and rests her head on my shoulder.

'Thank you,' she breathes.

I stand awkwardly for a moment, not quite sure what to do with my arms. But then, with a sigh, I put my arms around her and pull her close to me and... the years just melt away.

–

We're back in our first flat, holding each other so close that neither of us knows where one begins and the other ends. It was the first place that we ever lived together. It was cheap because there was a really low ceiling in the bedroom, and Mia couldn't put on high heels without her head hitting it. The stairs were so narrow and shallow that her dad couldn't get up them and, when he stayed with us, he had to sleep on a blow-up mattress on the living room floor. Those early months were the best. It was a great flat. We had huge windows that looked out onto a really trendy street that was always buzzing and, at Christmas, the lights were exactly level with our window. One year Saturn – with all its rings – was right outside and flashed a red and blue and white light into our living room that was hypnotic. In that space-glow, we put on music and danced. We even made love on the carpet, with the curtains open so the man in the moon and the twins on Saturn could see us. It snowed one night and we leaned out of the window, naked, and caught the flakes on our tongues. It was so beautiful.

During the day we would sit in the window and watch the people go by. We saw Kevin Rowland of Dexys Midnight Runners one day, and I swear I saw Kylie but Mia didn't and said it was just wishful thinking as she was my freebie. Other times we'd watch the Ben's Cookies shop over the road and wait for the sample lady to appear – usually about one p.m. for the lunch crowd. As soon as we saw her, we'd run down and grab everything we could get. Mia always went for peanut butter and I'd grab the fruit and nut and we'd eat them in the street. Most of the time we were still in our pyjamas, but we didn't care. I couldn't do that now. When did I start to care what other people thought of me?

I loved that flat, and back then we were such a great team. We did everything together and we knew the other so well, we were like two halves of the same being – at least I thought we were. Was I wrong, was I always wrong? No. No, I wasn't, and maybe the roots of our love are still there and still strong. Maybe they just need some tender care. Tonight, here in this awful death room, I hold her close to me, for the first time in months, and I wonder if this could be a new beginning. Maybe we could have our love back again. I'd like to try.

'Mia, after this is over, and we finally get home, do you think we could start again? *Us*, I mean, now that all the secrets are out in the open?'

'All the secrets?'

'Yes. I love you, Mia. I don't care about tonight.'

'All the secrets?'

'They don't matter, we can get away and start again.'

She looks at me, and then tilts her head, like a dog might. 'So you know my awful secret, what I did, and you forgive me?'

'Of course. I love you,' I tell her.

'That's very magnanimous of you. So, is there anything you want to confess to me?'

'Me? No… nothing.'

'Oh, good.' She pulls me tight into her. For a moment I forget all of this and just lean into her, but she puts her lips up to my ear and she says one word. Just one word, and my blood turns cold. I shrink away from her as she repeats the word she whispered.

'Ella.'

Mia

'Why did you say you had no secret to confess?' I ask, as I step out of our clinch. He opens his mouth to answer, but there are no words; his lips just wobble in and out, like a goldfish. 'You let me lay myself bare,' I say.

'I…' But that's all that comes out of his mouth. I know this isn't the biggest crime of the night, but right now I am so upset that he lied to my face like that.

'I know about Ella,' I tell him. 'I have done for a long time.'

'You never said.'

'No. I'd hoped you'd do that.'

'I should have – I know that. I'm sorry.' He drops his head and curls his neck, like he's awaiting the guillotine.

Fuck, I find that so annoying. I want to smack him and yell *posture*, like I'm some sadistic nineteenth-century ballet madam. But that isn't his major crime.

'When you talked about her, you were really mean. You said she was a wannabe Sloane Ranger and had no empathy for writers.'

'I know,' he says with obvious discomfort.

'Well, did you say it to put me off the scent?'

'No.'

'So, what? Was she stupid but that didn't matter because she was really pretty?'

'No. I mean, she wasn't ugly – it wasn't about what she looked like.'

'Was it just that she was young?' I ask and he drops his face away. I assume it's embarrassment, but I don't care about him being embarrassed.

'How did you find out about her?' he asks and the question makes me laugh, but it isn't a joyful laugh.

The reason I know about the two of them is because she sent him a picture. A naked picture, like these fucking kids do nowadays – these idiot kids who don't sag anywhere, or have dimples of cellulite on their arses. These kids who shave their pits and their bushes so they look like bloody children. And she was so stupid that she sent it to an email we both share – at least, I think she was stupid, maybe she wanted me to know? Perhaps the idea was to taunt me with her perfect tits and her flat stomach. But I bet he didn't send her one of him, not with his grey pubic hair, and the little pot belly, and the thinning hair, and the desperation in his eyes.

'So… tell me all about it, tell me about *your* affair.' I see the colour drain out of his face as he thinks about where to start, and what to say. It pleases me, and I know that's wrong, but at last I get to feel like I'm on the higher moral ground, even if it's only for a few minutes. Then we have to get out of here, before we're caught in the net.

Ben

'Ella and I...' I don't look at Mia. '...we slept together three times.'

'When?' she asks. I take a deep breath.

'The first time was about three years ago, when I went to a book launch party for one of their A-list clients. She had borrowed an apartment from a friend who was away, we went there and there was a drunken...' I start to say it was just a fumble, that it could have been anyone – but that sounds like it's going to turn into an excuse, and that's cowardice. I went to bed with my agent's assistant, no excuses or stories or lies.

'Second time: there was that trip to Dublin, to meet my publisher over there and... we shared a hotel room.' I steal a glance at her, but I can't see her face as she's turned away from me. It feels like I imagine a Catholic confession to be, where the priest listens but you can't see him.

'And the last time was eighteen months ago, after a meeting, and we had a quickie in a car park.' I feel ashamed; I burn like the sun. 'It was very juvenile – I think I got off on the fact that it was risky. It was stupid and we never did it again.'

She doesn't say anything.

'I'm...' The word *sorry* dies on my lips. What good does saying it do? I'm *sorry* that it happened; I'm even more sorry that she knows that it did. I'm sorry... I'm just sorry.

She's still turned away from me. A priest would give me a penance and forgive me. I don't think Mia will.

'Three times?' I turn to him and hold his gaze.

'Three,' he repeats.

'Why did you stop?' I see a flash of fear in his face. 'Why did you stop?' I ask again.

'She was too young,' he responds but it's more like a question than an answer. He wants to know what will placate me, make me stop asking him questions. But I won't stop until I get the truth.

'Was it you who stopped the affair?' I ask and try to imbue my voice with as much nonchalance as possible.

'I wouldn't call it an affair… but yes, I ended it.'

'Even though she said you could *do her* anywhere?' I try and make the question light – like a puff of wind.

'Anywhere?' he repeats like a parrot sick with bird flu.

I smile. '*Anywhere*' – she'd written it under the photo she sent, the one with the pert little breasts.

'You fucked her in the car park – was it bent over the hood?' I ask, and he doesn't say anything, but I know that was what they did. It was what we did on our third wedding anniversary; it was always such a fantasy of his, so I gave him a special treat. Though I think it's weird that we waited for three years of marriage yet they did it on their third date… *date*… everything's so bloody fast these days. And again I see the flash of fear in his eyes and I wonder… I wonder.

'Did you use condoms?' I ask and he blushes, so deep and scarlet that I know the truth, and I feel my heart start to pound.

'I thought she used…' He doesn't finish.

'Did she…' and now it's me that can't finish my question, as I feel my toes and fingers go cold. 'Why did you end it, Ben?'

'I just…' I can see his eyes pleading with me to let it go.

'Why?'

'She…'

Oh god. I feel like a car's about to hit me at a hundred miles an hour.

'Tell me, Ben.'

'She was… we had…' He can't say it; the fucking coward.

'Abortion.' I have to say it while he says nothing, just looks angst-ridden and sad. In the past I would have taken him in my arms and soothed him – *there there, you're okay* – but not anymore. Now I'm distanced from him, like I'm the camera in the wardrobe now, my light blinking on and off, recording everything and yet touched by nothing. The camera doesn't care that the woman killed the man, it doesn't plead or ask for mercy. It just bears witness, as I do now. I can't intervene for the child; it's gone – was never here; there was only the potential for life… and even that was snuffed out a year and a half ago. About the same time I first started thinking of taking a lover. *Huh.*

'Her parents, have you ever met them?' I ask.

'I…' He turns back to me and looks bemused. '…her mum. I met her once, at a launch for some cookbook I did an illustration for.'

'How old?'

'I don't—'

'Higher or lower.'

'Mia.'

'Higher or lower. Fucking answer me, Ben. At least give me that.'

'The same, I'd guess she's the same age as us.'

Us. Bastard. I throw a punch at his head, a real live actual punch. It isn't very good, though. It hits too high and too much to the right, kind of bouncing off his temple and hurts my hand more than it hurts him.

'What the hell, Mia?' he says, all hurt.

'A child, Ben… you threw a life away.'

'Since when are you so pro-life?'

'I… I…' and of course I'm not. That stupid Ella had every right to do what she did. It's her body, and she can make all kinds of dumb decisions – like sleeping with my idiot husband – but he can't. Ben isn't free to make those kinds of decisions, because he has a wife. And I know that I'm a much worse hypocrite than he is. I know what I did tonight, but that doesn't stop me feeling hurt and angry. And it doesn't stop him being a bastard.

'I would do anything to make this right.' He says. I should tell him to do a billion push-ups, but I am tired, so tired. And this is a distraction from what we need to be doing – as what really matters, right this second, is dealing with this damn video camera and the bro—

Zyurch zyurch – a phone rings again.

Ben

We both freeze, as Theo's mobile sounds from inside Mia's hoody pouch. She lifts it out, and this time doesn't try and hide it from me, as I move to stand next to her and we both stare at the home screen. On it is a picture of Theo with a woman and two children. They're at some park somewhere and look so happy.

'I guess that's Claire and Lilly and Harry,' I say, as Mia declines the call. Then she takes the sim card out of the phone. Her fingers are shaking as she manoeuvres the little plastic square out.

'We have to go,' she says. 'We leave all of this – the plan still works. There's no body—'

'No.'

'Jesus Christ, Ben, that man's brother will come here any minute.'

'No, he'll talk to Ali, and he'll tell him that Theo's busy with you. Alex won't come until morning.'

'It's almost three a.m. It's already bloody morning.'

'This isn't about the police now, this is bigger and scarier, Mia. This is proper crime – pornography, prostitution and rape – maybe extortion, too. These men are criminals, but we've got proof against them, the film of Theo attacking you, you saying no and fighting him off. We've got proof that you acted in self-defence. We don't need to be afraid anymore.'

'That would be great if we hadn't disposed of the body.'

'We can prove you were frightened, and felt it was the only way – that's the truth, isn't it?'

'I smashed the teeth out of his head with a hammer and I cut his fingertips off. Does that sound like a frightened woman to you?'

'I…' *Christ*, this is a mess… because she's right, we can't go to the police – not now; we're in too far.

'Yes… I guess you're right,' I tell her despondently.

'We have to run and hope they can't find us,' she says.

'But…' and I finally work out what has been nagging at me ever since I saw the film on the laptop. The camera angles – all the shots except one are in a room – the camera focussed on the bed. But there is a shot at the start, in the hallway and— 'Oh hell.'

'What?'

'Alex and Theo – they can access the CCTV, they use it in their films.'

'Oh god,' she wobbles and almost falls – she under-stands the new danger.

'There's CCTV all over this place. Right now we're hiding our faces but when you first arrived here… in that dress…'

'I…' Panic flashes across her face as she replays the memories in her mind. Going through what she did – and I see the answer in her eyes, as she realises that I'm right. 'I wasn't trying to hide anything when I arrived here, I looked directly into the camera.'

'There's face recognition software, they'll use it, they'll search, and eventually they'll find you.'

She nods grimly. 'What do we do?'

'There's only one thing we can do: we need to wipe all the CCTV tapes for tonight.'

'But how? How the hell do we do that, Ben?'

'My guess is that the CCTV is connected to the office behind reception. It'll go into a computer and be stored there. They probably wipe it every week or it would get too much. I'll go into the office and erase it.'

'What about me?'

'We need a diversion.'

'What sort?'

'You need to burn the hotel down.'

Chapter Eight

03.00 a.m.

Ben

I push at the window. There's a safety catch on it, but I slide it out carefully so the frame can swing open all the way. I look down, keeping my hands clear of the glass and metal. Fingerprints will still bury us.

'Don't be such a bloody idiot,' I hear from behind me, but I don't look back, instead I look down at the skip below. It's the one we put there from the other hotel, so I roughly know what's in it. On top is a layer of cardboard boxes, some broken-up, others still intact. Below them are what seemed to be black bags of rubbish, and food waste from the kitchen.

If I hang from the window, and let myself drop into the bin, I should be okay. I reckon it's two and a half storeys – what's that in feet? I guess about thirty to thirty-five feet. It's the kind of drop a professional stuntman does every day of the week, and they hardly ever get crippled – so a professional cartoonist should find it a breeze.

'Please don't,' she says, as I pull the chair from the desk and slide it under the window.

'You know what to do,' I say but don't look at her. I'm pretty sure I'll chicken out if I do.

'Ben,' she says in the kind of voice you use with a naughty dog that's too big to grab, but I ignore it, and step onto the chair and grab the window frame.

'I'm gonna leave fingerprints here – please clean them off,' I tell her, then I lever myself out.

'Ben please don't, we can find another way.'

But I'm not listening to her, as I look down and try to slow my racing heart. I take a deep breath and think about Tom Daley, the diver. I need to be straight in the air, like a pencil… I can do this.

I turn back to look at Mia, one last time before I jump and… *Christ*, she looks ten years older than she did an hour ago. I smile at her. I can't think of anything to say that isn't stupid, so I don't say anything. Instead I hold onto the lower sill and let myself unfold, sliding down the glass, then when I'm fully stretched I just open my hands and— *oh shiiiiiiiiiiitttttttttttttttt*.

I fall – it isn't pretty. I immediately panic and start to wheel my arms – so much for Tom Daley's beautiful pencil. I can feel I'm drifting. The image of Theo's shattered jaw flashes in my mind and I feel myself twist. *Hell*. Upstairs, there seemed to be no wind, but now I feel it whip around me. *Shit. Shit. Shit.* I try and keep straight, but my back corkscrews and my arms flail. It feels like it takes forever but it's only a fraction of a second and—

THWACK. The air is forced out of my lungs as I hit the rubbish. There's a tearing sound – I think it's my knee again, but it's only a bag splitting open. The cardboard buckles and breaks beneath me, I lose balance and smash into the metal of the bin wall. My knee screams, I'm winded, but I think I'm fine. *Christ*, my heart is beating so fast.

In the rubbish, I stretch and flex everything. It all seems good – except the god-awful stench I'm enveloped in. I've stirred up every rotting piece of crap in here. It is truly disgusting – but I'm fine. It worked.

I look up, and I can see her craning out of the window. Even from here I see the concern in her pale face. It certainly beats the contempt I've seen creep across it at times tonight. It's clear that she doesn't think I'm up to this, that I'll bend under the stress and that physically I'll crack. I probably would have said the same thing yesterday, but after seeing that camera in the wardrobe, and that awful film – I'm not letting this beat us. I won't let them harm her anymore. And, let's be honest about this, I am trying to make amends for Ella.

I give Mia a goofy kind of wave and then try to stand, which makes me wince, but it's nothing serious. I grab the outside lip of the skip, and with a grunt, I haul myself up and out of it. I don't really have much upper-body strength, but I can just about get my foot up onto a ridge on the metal and jump over. I land awkwardly on the tarmac. I've cut my leg, maybe on an old tin can, but I've got so much adrenaline pumping through me that I can't feel it. I could probably lose an arm or a leg and not feel anything for a couple of hours. Is that good? I'm not sure.

I look around. The square's completely dark now; there are no lights anywhere. I keep low and kind of lope, like a wolf, towards the main road. I have a job to do.

Mia

I watch his dark shape, as it crosses the square, and then passes through the archway and is gone. For a little while I watch the shadow where he disappeared. *Hell*, I don't like leaving this to him, I don't like not being in control. My life has gone to shit in one evening, but at least I was on top of it. I'd got rid of the body and cleaned the room – I was almost home. But finding the camera, and seeing that film, has thrown me. I'm only just keeping myself from melting into a puddle of despair. I need to snap out of it. I need to get back in charge and not leave it to Ben. I know he means well, and he's doing his best, but when it comes down to fighting for survival, I think he's too good a man to do what needs to be done. And tonight I've learned that I won't let anything get in my way. I need to shake off the fucking funk of seeing the film, stop thinking about what might have happened and get back to how I – how *we* – get away from all this. I have to put aside the fear of my dad seeing the video and my career burning, and I have to stop thinking about Ben and Ella and the abortion. *Fuck!* There is too much shit in my head tonight. *Get back in the game, Mia, clear your head and start fighting*, I tell myself.

Ben will be back in the square soon, and I have to get on with the next part of the plan – his plan, god help us. So, this room needs to be cleaned up *again*. I need to wipe down the windows – damn I wish we still had bleach – and make sure our fingerprints have been wiped away. At least we still have the crappy hotel towels. I need to re-make the bed, put back the desk and chair, and make sure that nothing we've touched still has our prints on it. Christ, this night doesn't end. I get to work.

Ben

I keep my face turned down as I walk. My bad knee makes me limp a little, which is good, makes me look even more unloved, unwanted and invisible. I see the convenience store again, the one with the roses outside, but this time I'm not tempted to buy any.

As I go inside, the brightness of the overhead lights hurts my eyes after the darkness outside. I guess they're pumped up to stop shoplifting, and for better results on CCTV – shit, I drop my head even further and flick my eyes up, looking for the cameras. I see two of them, one directly behind the shopkeeper, and another to his right giving a clear view of the cash register. I can see the guy behind the counter has sat up straight, and he follows me with his eyes as I walk towards him. In the street I was invisible, but in here I'm a threat, a shoplifter or maybe worse; maybe I've got a weapon in my hoody and I'm here to rob him. I can see those thoughts shift through him, and his hand snakes under the counter. I guess there's a panic button there.

'Cheapest half bottle of vodka,' I say, purposefully stopping myself saying *please*. He folds himself backwards in a weird shape, trying to keep his eyes on me and get the bottle at the same time. It looks really uncomfortable, so I take my hands out of my hoody pocket and hold them up so he can see them. He grunts something that could have been *thanks*, and turns and grabs the bottle – though he still does it with as much speed as he can. I wonder how many times a knife has been pulled on him.

He says something I can't make out, as he puts it on the counter, but he keeps his hand on the bottle, thinking I might grab it and run.

'Where's it from?' I ask as I don't recognise the language written on the bottle.

'Eight pounds,' he says, eyes glued to me.

'And a lighter.'

'Nine, fifty.'

I put a ten-pound note on the counter. He gives me the change, the bottle, and the lighter in a brown paper bag. He watches me, like a hawk, all the way out of the shop.

In the street outside, I unscrew the cap and take a sip. It burns as it goes down, and I think it might actually be white spirit. Perfect for what I want it for, but it makes me feel afraid for all the drunks who buy this cheap crap. But I can't let those thoughts in; I'm on a mission. I wish I had a watch. I wish I had my bloody phone so I could Google this and make sure I really do know how to make a Molotov cocktail.

I need to get back. I think I've been about ten minutes, so it's time to signal to Mia, then we can get the final part of the plan together.

Mia

I'm in the hotel hallway, on the floor below, and I'm tucked tight against the wall in the dark of the shadows, hoping to be invisible to the CCTV camera at the end. I wish I had a Rennie, I've got wicked heartburn. At least that proves I still have a heart, and I'm not the tin man after all – I'm just that prissy wimp Dorothy, desperate to go home – back to boring old black-and-white Kansas. I never understood why Dorothy wanted to go back to the shitty life she had, when Oz looked so interesting. I'd have stayed, got myself a flying monkey slave, and been a celebrity – at least for a while. I have no delusion that home is best. Of course it's better than the Lampton Hotel, but that isn't saying anything; anywhere and everywhere is better than this shithole.

I look down at Theo's phone – though I guess without a sim card it's just a glorified clock. I have ninety seconds.

I should use it to call this off – stop Ben from doing what he's doing – but I won't, because I've lost all sense of morality now. Back in the room, when he said we had to burn the building down, the image flicked though my mind of the hotel burning and the receptionist screaming and dying – and I didn't care. Christ, I am a monster.

They say that once you've killed one person, the second is much easier – though that might be from an Agatha Christie book rather than actual psychological research, so I'm not sure I'd give it that much credence; but I'm pretty sure I'd kill again to keep myself safe. And that scares the shit out of me. I don't know what my moral boundaries are anymore. I don't know how far I've fallen tonight, how deep down I am. If I get out of this, I really do have to double my direct debit to Amnesty International – at least double. Maybe I should give to a donkey sanctuary too.

I look down; time's almost up. My fingers hover over the glass, ready to break it. Ten seconds. I hold my breath. Five – four – three – two—

Ben

I'm standing on the front step of the hotel, looking through the revolving door into the lobby. I can see Ali on the reception desk; he's hunched over the counter and could be asleep, I can't tell. He doesn't look healthy. Night work must take its toll. I'm pretty sure the nocturnal life wouldn't suit me. After staying up just tonight, my tummy feels rotten; I wish I had some Imodium.

In my right hand is the half bottle of vodka, though now there's a strip of cloth, soaked in spirit, pushed into the neck. The vodka has sloshed up my arm a little way and the smell makes me nauseous – actually, it isn't just the alcohol that makes me queasy; there's a heady cocktail of sweat, bin juice and booze that wafts off my body. I'm disgusting. At least I am physically. Emotionally I think I might even be worse, after all I'm about to burn dow—

WOOOOAAAHHHHHHHHHH –
WOOOOAAAHHHHHHHHHHH

The blare of the fire alarm makes me jump. She's done it. I see Ali jump up, like a bunny with ten thousand volts shot up his arse, and run into the back office. It's go time.

I push through the revolving door and into the lobby, rushing over to reception. I vault the counter, like I'm nineteen again. I can see into the back office, and Ali's at the desk, looking at the computer screen. He's pulled up the map of censors and fire alarms and can see that it was the alarm on the second floor that was tripped. He pulls up the CCTV cameras to see if there's actually a fire and… there. He's accessed the hallway camera and he can see that there's nothing. He hits the button to stop the fire alarm, and then rolls through the other CCTV cameras. I can see exactly how the CCTV cameras operate – and that was the plan all along. Now I know exactly what I need to do.

'False alarm?' I say and Ali turns around in his chair. His first response is incomprehension – he has no idea why a homeless guy is there, but that turns to fear; like the guy in the convenience store, he thinks I'm going to pull a knife on him.

'My friend, you—'

But I raise my hand, stopping him dead, because he sees the vodka bottle, and the twisted rag hanging from it. He knows what it is, and what it can do. For a second I wonder if he's been in a situation where he's seen them used before, maybe he's even seen the blankets of flame that spill from them, consuming all in their path. His eyes widen.

'No, no,' he yells but I hold my lighter to the cloth, which bursts into flame, and I toss the bottle into the lobby.

Whoosh, the crappy curtains turn to flame – the Lampton obviously didn't invest in fire-retardant fabrics. I'm not surprised; I don't see customer safety as being a high priority at this establishment.

'You crazy—' Ali yells, as his anger flares and he screams something at me that I don't understand. He gets up, his fists balled and I think he could do me real damage, as his eyes burn like the curtains and sofa in reception – but he has no time for me, as he leaps into action and grabs a fire extinguisher from the floor behind the desk and runs past me. I hear him throw the counter open and then there's a squirt of foam. I have bought myself some time, but I have no idea how long it will be. And once the fire is out, I think Ali will want to beat me to a pulp.

I quickly slide into his chair and open the CCTV links. I delete the night's footage from all cameras; it only takes a few seconds. Can it be that easy? I hear a final whoosh of extinguisher foam. I should run, but I hesitate… nothing tonight has been simple. In our room upstairs there were multiple back-ups and… *hell*… I hiss and crawl under the desk. This is going to get me killed, I think – but I can't stop.

There it is. Under the desk I see a cable that snakes out of the back of the computer, and into a removable drive on the floor. I reach over and rip it out. Then, with all my strength, I throw the plastic and metal brick down on the floor to smash it to pieces.

'Jesus Christ,' I yell as the hard drive bounces and almost takes my head off. It bounces twice before skittering into the wall where it stops.

The bloody thing still looks completely intact, so I jump on it and kick it, stomping it into the floor until it splinters and cracks open. I think I killed it. I look through the doorway. The fire is out, and I can see Ali stamping out the final embers from the charred curtains. I have only seconds left, before he turns his attention back to me. I can just get past him, and out onto the street. I don't think he'll chase after me. I have to go now, I have to—

'What the hell are you doing?' A woman appears in the office doorway, blocking my view of Ali and my escape. She looks like she's in her forties, petite with black hair pulled tight into a ponytail. Her face is gaunt. She looks like she doesn't get enough sleep and smokes way too many cigarettes. She's dressed in the same black shirt, plain black trousers and burgundy jacket as Ali, but she doesn't have a name tag. She must be a manager or something. I could knock her down, push her away. I could hurt her in an attempt to run. I could...

'Who are you,' she demands, and I think she sounds Eastern European, but I'm terrible with accents. I back away and shrink my head down into my hoody, like a tortoise pulling back into his shell. I can already see that I'm not getting away from this. If it was just Ali, I would have been able to skip past him, but I hadn't reckoned on a second person, and I just can't see myself going through her. No matter what's happened tonight, I'm not hitting a woman.

I wait and watch, hoping she'll let me go, but Ali appears at her side and he looks angry. He waves the fire extinguisher in the air, like he'll use it to batter me if I try to escape.

'Who is this?' she asks Ali.

'He started the fire.'

'Why?' she asks.

'I have no idea, he might be crazy.'

'Are you the manager here?' I ask the woman.

'I am Nadia, the night manager.' She turns to Ali. 'Call the owner.'

'No… I mean, I really don't think you want to do that.' I try to sound confident, even though I'm feeling quite sick inside.

'Nadia, what do I do?' Ali asks her.

'I know what happens in room 303,' I say, and I see panic in both their eyes. Ali looks away, I think he's ashamed, but Nadia holds my gaze.

'That room is off bounds to us, we don't—'

'But you know what happens in there, don't you?'

'We are not part of that, we do not help them,' Nadia insists.

'You might not help them, but you take money to look the other way, don't you? You're as bad as they—'

Ali's eyes flare, and he moans with a guttural and angry grunt. 'We do not take their money,' he tells me through gritted teeth. 'We work here, we are paid to run hotel, not to help those men.'

'But you know what they do in there. You know they film the women they take in there.'

Both Ali and Nadia look away from me and drop their heads, but I'm not letting them off that easy.

'They rape those women,' I say.

'No,' Nadia squares up to me, her chin tight. 'They not force the women, I see them when they arrive here. They

135

come because they want to – it is their choice. They swear that to us. I see these women. I would not allow what you say – no violence.' Tears well in the corner of her eyes. 'No rape.'

'Maybe the women agree to come here, but none of them know the cameras are there,' I say and Nadia jumps back, like she's been scorched; she looks distressed, the tears in her eyes suddenly break through and course down her cheeks, giving her raccoon eyes and mascara tracks that run down her face. She looks to Ali; he doesn't have tears in his eyes but he still seems distressed; they both look like they've been hit by lightning. Slowly, all the anger drains out of them and they slump down.

The woman says something. It's little more than a mumble under her breath, and I don't understand it, but then I hear the cadence of it, the rhythm of it, and I realise that it's a prayer of some kind. I don't know if she's praying for herself, or me, or the women she's seen come and go in that room. Then Ali raises his head and reaches out to put his hand onto my shoulder, not in a threatening way, but in a bond of friendship. Up close, he looks younger than I thought, he could be as young as mid-twenties. His skin is smooth but his eyes are those of someone who has seen a lifetime of suffering, and in his hairline I see scar tissue, tight and angry-looking. I look closer and see that it loops across his scalp and down his neck and disappears into his collar. I wonder how far it stretches. It could be from a fire, or a beating – or even from torture.

'You should go, my friend,' he tells me. 'Mr Alex will come soon. You will not want to be here when he does…' He pauses and I see fear jag through his eyes. 'He is a bad man.' His fingers grip my shoulder for a moment and I get the impression that *bad* doesn't go anywhere close to describing Alex.

'Thank you.' I tell him as I reach my hand onto his shoulder and squeeze it briefly. 'I wanted to destroy all the CCTV footage, so my wife couldn't be identified from tonight, did I get it all?' I ask. Nadia screws up her face for a second, weighing up the threat, and then opens the bottom drawer of the desk and fishes out a second back-up drive.

'You should break this too, just to be certain.' She drops it on the floor so I can stamp on it. I give it hell – it feels really good to smash it to shit.

'Thank you,' I tell them.

'The film in the room?' Ali asks, and he sounds scared. 'You have it?'

'I've taken it… and Theo will be gone for a while.' Both of them jump at the mention of his name. I can see he scares them too, though perhaps not as much as his brother Alex does.

'He will come and ask us to describe you,' Nadia says. 'I like your red hair and beard,' and for the first time there is a glint in her eye that is not fear.

'Thank you.' I turn to leave, but Ali grabs my arm.

'There are devils on your track; they will hunt you. Run and do not look back.'

'What about you, will you be blamed for what I've done?'

'Not more than normal,' Nadia says with a defiance that makes me feel scared for them.

'I can't let you get in trouble for me,' I say.

'Not for you,' Ali says, and there is a flicker of a friendly smile on his face, but then that is swept away. 'Now go.'

'Thanks,' and I leave. I walk quickly through into the lobby. The smoke from the burned sofa and curtains is in the air and tries to choke me. It's acrid and bitter, and tastes like charcoal. I am going to need to wash my mouth with soap to get this nastiness out. Then I'm going to need to scrub my whole body to try and get clean from tonight.

I can see the revolving doors that lead to freedom. I am so close, so close. Through the glass I see Mia. My heart starts to beat faster as I get near to her. I put out my hand, and almost touch the cold glass, but at the last second I use my elbow – Jesus, did I touch the glass earlier? I put my hand into my hoody pocket and use that to wipe at the glass – mostly just smearing the layer of filth and germs on the handles – then I push hard at the door and it swings. I step into that little bubble of air in the revolving door, like an airlock on a space ship. Are we going to do this? Are we going to get away to restart our lives? Are we finally safe from this nightmare?

Mia was right that we did have to do this, we had to erase all the evidence. She was right all along to do what she did, and I shouldn't waste a single thought on a man I know to be a rapist and pornographer, or his family who live on the money from abusing women. Mia was right to hide the body – we can't have our lives ruined by these abusers, we had to do this.

Christ, the rush of endorphins is giving me such a high. We won. I look at my wife ahead of me, as she stumbles down the steps; I see the bone-numbing ache of tiredness in her, the tension from what she has just been through and… and… I want to hold her and kiss her. I want to tell her we can start again. We have both betrayed the other – me with Ella and her with Theo – but that's behind us now. We have told the truth.

What do they say: *the truth will set us free*? Well, it has and it can. I want our marriage to work. We should go away, a holiday, some sun… We can start again. It can work.

I grab her hand and we look into each other's eyes. I think there are equal parts fear and hope for both of us. I want to kiss her, but not yet, we shouldn't yet, not here. Instead I pull at her hand and we run, like on that TV show, where the kids run through the wheat field – *Little House on the Prairie*? We run like that, hand-in-hand, like newlyweds. We run down to the end of the road and then round the corner – to get away from the hotel – away from the devil that's coming. We run until our lungs burn – or at least until *my* lungs burn; I expect Mia could run all the way home, but I'm in terrible shape. So I have to stop when we get a few streets away, and pant heavily as I try and say, 'I love you'.

'Don't.'

'But… we did it. We're free.'

'No. You might be free but—'

'What? Why?'

She pauses… and in that pause, my heart stops. 'I lied to you,' she says.

'What?'

'All of this; it's a lie, it's been a lie from the start, and you have to know the truth. I have to tell you what I've done.'

'I don't—'

'Ben, this isn't over.'

Chapter Nine

Mia

Everything freezes for a second. I watch Ben's face as it morphs through confusion, anger, betrayal and good old-fashioned bewilderment. I expect him to explode, but he just stares at me, with his mouth open, as he tries to make sense of it all.

'Mia, what are you saying. Why isn't this over, why can't we go home?'

I try to smile, though I think it must look truly pathetic, judging by the look of concern I get back from him. What I'm about to say makes me feel sick, but it's time that the truth was told. But I can't do it right now – not here. I need to sit down, and I need caffeine. *Christ*, I need a coffee.

'Not on the street, come on,' I tell him and turn away. I trudge forward, so tired that I drag my feet like a zombie, but it's about all I can do. I remember seeing an all-night café by the tube station, and I head there. I must have something to wake me up before we talk – before I tell Ben the truth. I march, as fast as I can.

'Mia, stop, please.'

'I need a coffee, come on.'

I walk, hoody up and head down. I can't believe how much bloody chewing gum there is on the pavement, it's disgusting. The streets are filthy; there's crap everywhere, and the pavement slabs are broken into a trillion pieces. When I was a kid we'd play a game where you couldn't step on a crack in the pavement or you'd break your back – nowadays that's impossible; everyone in London would be paraplegic today.

I get to the corner. Which way? I don't know, I'm lost. I feel like I'm underwater, or my head's been encased in bubble-wrap. I need a coffee so much. I need to wake the hell up.

'Ben, where's the tube?' I ask. He points, in what feels like the direction we just came from, but I'm all turned around and have no idea where anything is anymore. 'Okay,' I trudge off again. He follows in my wake.

Just as I feel like I'm about to drop, I finally smell the bitter, heady notes of strong coffee. I could weep. I want to feel the hot liquid in my mouth and sliding down my throat, but more than that, I want to hold a viciously hot cup and feel the heat seep into my fingers. My hands are as cold as ice.

'There,' he says and points. It's the café I saw before, and the lights are on. I rush over to it and put my hand on the glass of the door, not caring about leaving juicy fingerprints, and push inside. Oh my god, it's lovely and warm in here. Behind me, I just know that Ben's glasses have steamed up.

'Anywhere you want, love.' A voice comes from some-where in the air around us, but I don't see anyone.

'Okay,' I call back and make a beeline for a table right at the back, and sit down. My lower back and legs finally relax – god, that feels good. Ben sits down next to me and grabs a serviette off the table and starts to polish his glasses. He doesn't make eye contact but I can see a twitch in his jaw as his dark thoughts tumble and turn in his head.

Okay, it's show time. I take a deep breath. 'I was lying,' I start.

'There's no table service,' the voice from nowhere booms again, like God, but with a Welsh accent. 'Not this time of night; it's just me working, so you have to order at the counter.'

'Right, okay,' I call back.

'Menu's on the table, the specials are Valentine's bubble and venison meatballs,' he pauses, maybe for dramatic effect. 'Do you want drinks?' And finally he appears from behind a display case full of puddings. Tall and in his mid-fifties, sporting an incredible salt and pepper quiff, he looks like he should have been a rocker in *Quadrophenia*, or an if-Elvis-had-lived-past-forty-two impersonator. He makes me smile.

We went to a fancy dress party as Elvis once – I was young, hip-swinging, sex-on-a-stick Elvis, and Ben was Vegas, burger-in-the-hand, biggest Elvis. There was a karaoke machine and we dueted *Wooden Heart* and *In the Ghetto*. That was a great night.

'So what'll it be?' Elvis asks.

'Can you do a latte?'

'I can do anything, love,' and he flashes me a cheeky wink.

'Great, then a latte for me and…' I look at Ben who's glazed over, staring into the distance, not thinking about drinks but trying to keep it together as his brain goes crazy, thinking about what the lies might be. He looks totally miserable. 'Two lattes,' I call over.

'I'll get going on them, while you look at the menus,' and Elvis turns on something that grinds the coffee, and he vanishes again.

I open the menu and hold it so we can both see. 'Do you know what you want?'

'To know what your lies are,' Ben hisses.

'Let's get food first. We can—'

'Bubble,' he says, cutting me dead. 'Not the Valentine's bubble, the regular bubble,' he pauses while his eyes scan the options. 'With two poached eggs and bacon.'

'Classic choice,' I say, with what I hope is a smile, and go up to the counter. As I get there, Elvis appears, as if by magic.

'So, what's it to be, love?'

I order the bubble, eggs and bacon for Ben and I have bubble, beans and sausage. 'Not the Valentine bubble – just normal bubble.' I tell him and he looks disappointed.

'Where did all the love go?' he mutters under his breath.

'And two rounds of toast – one brown and one white – and I'll take the coffees.'

'I can bring them over.'

'I'll wait for them,' I say, and he shrugs and steams some milk. I wait at the counter. I'm scared – not of Ben, but of what I'm doing to our lives and our marriage. I wish I didn't have to tell him the truth, but I do. I owe it to him, and to me I guess; tonight has already uncovered too many lies.

'There you go.' Elvis bangs two mugs down on the counter, the froth tall, swaying slightly, like a perfect soufflé. I can actually feel my mouth start to water as I look at them – like I'm Pavlov's caffeine-junkie pooch.

'Careful, they're really hot,' Elvis warns, but I don't care. My hands are so cold they could go into a bonfire. As I walk back with our coffees, they both slop some burning foam onto my fingers, and it feels good.

I put the drinks down on the table, and can see that Ben's not just lost in thought, but working on a cartoon. He's opened up a paper napkin and is drawing on that. I sit down and sip my coffee for a few seconds before he sits upright and slides the napkin over to me.

In the centre are two horses being ridden by knights in tarnished armour, and to the side of each horse is a large cat on a chain. The two knights look angrily at each other and both have the same speech bubble: 'We can't both be the hero of this story.' And underneath the drawing, the caption reads: *Lions led by Don Quixotes.*

'It's funny,' I say. Then my eyes are pulled towards two smaller figures I hadn't noticed at first. They stand in the background with their arms out like windmills. One of them is naked with blood on his head – Theo – and the other one has long hair; I assume it's supposed to be Ella.

'You didn't laugh,' he says.

'Inside I did.'

'I suppose it's kind of a niche joke.' He looks down at his coffee. 'There's a shape in the foam, like an old woman in the snow.'

I look at both the coffees. I think they might have been love-hearts when I began walking over, but now mine looks more like an octopus fighting a shark. It's like clouds in the sky, forming faces that come and go, as our brains desperately try to make something out of random shapes. That's how Rorschach tests work, assess the light and dark in our minds, asking our brains to see either butterflies or dead bodies. Tonight it's all dead bodies.

'It's good,' he says after a sip of his coffee. 'I didn't expect it to be.'

'You can get a good coffee anywhere these days. Even McDonald's makes good coffee.'

'Brave new world, amen,' he says with a tired sigh. Together we sit and sip quietly, enjoying the religious experience of caffeine sweeping away our sins.

'So, tell me.' Ben eventually breaks the silence. 'What did you lie about?'

'I didn't…' I say, as the caffeine starts to raise me back from the dead. 'I didn't meet Theo like I said. Tonight was… it was all messed up.'

'You—'

'Ketchup's on the table, do you want any other sauce?' Elvis calls over, as he walks up holding two enormous plates of food.

'I'm okay,' Ben mumbles as he picks a knife and fork out of the pot on the table in front of us.

Elvis lays the food down and is gone. My stomach rumbles. I take a deep breath and look at Ben. He looks old – older than he is in my head anyway. I think in my mind I've trapped him in aspic, forever twenty-two and alive with possibility, not aging, while I sag and droop and make compromise after compromise. Tonight, until this moment, I haven't really looked at him – not properly, anyway. I've been afraid of seeing the disappointment in his eyes that I know, sure as fuck, will be there. Just like I know that the cracks in our *love* and *marriage* and *happy-ever-after*, are so deep and wide, like massive chasms, and they will reduce us to dust. I see everything crumbling, and I can't bear it.

He used to idolise me. He'd look at me with adoration and love. He thought I was so cool, and I bloody *was*, and I made him cool too. Without me he wouldn't have become a cartoonist, he wouldn't have trusted that he was funny. I mean, he liked fucking Genesis when I met him, and not cool prog-rock Peter Gabriel Genesis, but crappy Phil Collins Genesis. I gave him the confidence to come out of that cocoon and be a butterfly... but that was a long time ago.

The Ella thing had— shit, I don't even know how that had affected me. The years have taken their toll on us both; we've failed to become the people we'd imagined we'd be when we first met. Ben took the job in advertising and stopped drawing for *Time Out*, and I let the legal aid work go and settled into corporate law, with the lunches and trips and *gifts*. Both whoring out our talents to the highest bidder – which in my case was really quite high – but the days of being proud of who I am have long gone. Maybe that's how you end up in a hotel room with a man you hardly know.

'Maybe...' Ben starts. 'Maybe we eat first and talk after?'

'Perfect,' I say looking down at the plate as he grabs the ketchup and with a smack on the glass bottle, splodges the tomato sugary goodness onto his plate, and starts to eat. I dig my fork into the bubble – oh my god, it's buttery and peppery and delicious. We both tuck into the food like animals, shovelling it into our mouths until every last morsel is gone.

Ben

The food's good. It's stopped me feeling so light-headed, I'm almost back to normal again. I use the last piece of toast to mop up the final smear of bubble. The plate is completely clean – I just hope it wasn't my last meal. I close my eyes for a moment, preparing myself for this new onslaught of terrible news from Mia. I love her, I always have; I need to remind myself of that. *Whatever she tells me, remember that I love her.*

'Okay, I'm ready,' I tell her. And under the table I cross my fingers. She takes a deep breath and begins.

'We didn't meet by accident.'

Breathe Ben… Breathe… 'You're having an affair,' I say.

'No, no, not an affair. I actually hadn't seen him before tonight.'

'So it's just casual sex? Are you on some app like Tinder – swipe right for a quick nameless hook-up?'

'No.'

'Then what? Jesus Christ, Mia, I'm not playing twenty bloody questions.' I smack my hand down on the table, hard. Coffee spills and plates clatter.

'Are you okay over there?' Elvis yells.

'We're fine,' I shout back at him.

'I need to hear it from the lady,' he answers; his voice is level, but there's an edge to it. I'm sure he's used to dealing with a lot of late night fights.

'I'm okay, just a silly disagreement. The breakfast was lovely,' Mia calls like a true diplomat.

'Lovely,' I echo and then hiss at her. 'So what is it? Match.com? Don't tell me it was a blind date.'

'I… Ben… I…' she stumbles.

'Christ, Mia, you said he raped you. What happened?'

'I never wanted you to know.'

'But we're past that now, tonight all the secrets have to come out, no matter how ugly they are. So tell me.'

She stares at me for a moment and there is such aching sadness in her eyes, but then she looks back down to her plate.

'I booked him. It was all pre-arranged,' she says, not looking up.

'I don't understand.'

'By the hour, I booked him. I paid him.'

'For what?'

'Don't make me say it, Ben.'

'Because I don't—'

'For sex! I paid him for sex!' she yells, so loudly the bloody chef must have heard.

'He's a prostitute?'

'I prefer male escort.'

There's a part of me that wants to laugh, because this just isn't real, this is crazy. I can't imagine my wife paying to meet a stranger; it makes no sense. She's beautiful.

'Why, Mia? Tell me why.'

'I wanted to be in charge.'

'What do you mean?'

'If I was paying, it would put me in charge. I would decide what happened, and I thought that would make it safer.' She winces slightly, at the memory of what had happened.

'I didn't want an affair, I didn't want conversation, I didn't want to flirt with someone – I'm not looking for the excitement of the hunt, and I'm not just desperate.' She pauses. 'It was business.'

'Business? I don't understand. Was this the first time?'

'Yes… with him.'

I hear her slight hesitation and feel the squirm in my guts – *with him* – so is that the *truth* that must be spoken?

That there are others? Has she been doing this for a long time? Does she regularly meet strangers for sex?

'Why him? How did you find him?'

'He was recommended to me.'

'Who by?'

I see some internal struggle creep across her face; she doesn't want to tell me that, for some reason.

'Tell me, Mia. Who the hell recommended you see a rent boy?'

'Sandi… Sandi gave me his name, and he isn't a rent boy.'

'How the hell did she know him?'

'I don't know how she first met him, but she said he was clean and healthy – that he was safe, he had tests and certificates and…' She drops her eyes from mine. 'She said he was discreet and… and she said I would be in charge.'

'Well, that was a bloody mistake. Jesus Christ, Mia, why would you trust Sandi on anything? How could you bring a prostitute into our marriage?'

'How could you bring Ella into it? And you met her three times and got her pregnant, so do not take the fucking moral high ground with me.'

'At least she's still alive.'

Mia slams her fists on the table.

'Is there a problem?' Elvis calls out.

'No, no problem.' Mia calls back, then hisses to me. 'Is there a problem?'

I drink the last of my coffee, as my flash of anger fades away. 'You booked him?'

'Yes,' she says, all matter-of-fact.

'And he suggested meeting at the hotel. Obviously because of the cameras,' I say, and she turns red. 'You said he raped you?'

'I… I changed my mind halfway through. I asked him to stop and he wouldn't. That's rape. I didn't lie about that.'

'Why did you ask him to stop?' I ask and immediately wish I hadn't.

She looks so sad for a moment and her eyes cloud over like a thunderstorm has broken behind them.

'He was rougher than I wanted. I asked him to be gentler, but he wasn't. He said women liked it when he took control. He slapped me and said I had to do whatever he asked. I told him to stop, told him it was done, finished, that I'd still pay him the full amount. I thought all he would care about was the money, but he said I'd booked the best and he would give me what I really wanted… even if I didn't know it myself. He said I'd thank him for it afterwards.' She pauses. 'He pushed me down and used his knees to…' Her voice cracks. '…and he put his hands around my throat. He said I'd like it more. *More intense if you can't breathe*, he said, and I tried to scream but I was choking and he was…'

I remember the marks on her neck… I feel my jaw tighten so hard I think it might snap.

'…I thought he might kill me. I tried to push him off, but he just tightened his fingers on my throat. I didn't have the strength in my arms to do anything, but I got my foot up… I put it against his shoulder and I kicked, I kicked as hard as I could and he let go of my neck. He fell backwards.'

The café is totally silent. The world is totally silent.

I recall the moment I walked into that room, saw him lying there, with his life-blood spilled all around, and I'd felt sorry for him. I'd worried about his family, the wife and kids I created for him, his parents, uncles, aunts, nieces and nephews. I imagined a man loved by his community – but now I know the truth. He was a thug and a bully; he preyed on vulnerable women for money and perverse thrills. I hate him. For what he did to Mia, and for how this night has poisoned both our lives. I had thought that I was the lonely one in our marriage, that I was the one who'd been abandoned, left vulnerable to stupid fantasies; but I'd not realised it was a two-way street. There I was, feeling unloved and untouched, and at the same time Mia felt the same way… *Jesus*…

We sit, in the silence of the café, and then I walk my fingers across the table and squeeze her hand.

'I'm sorry that I pushed you int—'

'No Ben,' she practically spits at me.

'I don't—'

'This isn't because of you. Don't think your dick is magic and can solve my problems.'

'I didn't—'

'You bloody well did! You think I'm sad and desperate – longing for the touch of anyone, because you've rejected me. Well, forget that bullshit. This isn't about being desperate for a man. I'm not that sad. I'm not any kind of sad.'

And she gets up and goes to pay the bill, leaving me at the table, back to feeling confused and angry. I don't know what to say.

When she comes back she doesn't sit, but stands, her hands wedged deep in her hoody pocket and her back bowed. I look up at her.

'So, is that what you wanted to tell me? Is that why we came here, to this culinary institute?' I hear the sarcastic whine in my voice but I'm unable to do anything to stop it.

'No. No that isn't what I have to tell you – not everything,' she says, and I see the pulse in her neck get bigger and faster.

'Tonight, meeting him…' She takes a second to calm herself. Under the table I feel my hands curling into fists and the nails begin to cut into the flesh of my palms. 'It wasn't the first time.'

'Oth-others?' I stammer slightly. 'There have been others?'

'One, one other.'

'An affair?'

'No… no, I wish it was.'

I feel that like a kick to the stomach. I think she must be trying to hurt me because of Ella, but then another thought hits me, one that makes me feel cold. 'Do you mean it was the same as tonight?'

'Yes,' she says and I see her jaw set and a steel come into her eyes. 'He was another male escort.'

'When?'

'Maybe a few weeks ago, perhaps a month.'

'You paid… the same agency?'

'It's not exactly an agency, I wasn't booking a fucking babysitter,' she says angrily.

'You didn't meet there?' I ask. 'In the same hotel?'

She bites her lip – I see the flash of scarlet – and there are tears in her eyes. She looks frightened.

'The cameras,' I say with dread.

'There's no record of tonight, not now but…' She can't finish her thought; it's too difficult.

'Other nights.'

'One other night… It was the same room, so I guess it could have been taped.'

'But not with Theo?'

'No... but I didn't know that.'

'I don't understand how... oh shit,' I suddenly get what she's saying. 'You thought the men were the same...'

She can't speak; she can only nod her head. Her eyes are huge with worry.

'...because they look the same. The first time you met the brother, Alex.'

Mia

I feel ashamed by this and I don't honestly know how much I can tell Ben. Sandi had recommended Alex to me and told me that he would understand my wanting to be in charge, and he did. More than that, he seemed to get off on it too, not just me being on top but I called the shots on everything. He did what I wanted and it was good. It was so good, like I was the guy and he was the girl and... And I thought I was booking him again, but I didn't know there were two of them. And even though they look the same they are not the same man at all. Theo was disgusted that a woman would take charge – he got angry and rough. But how do I tell that to my husband?

'They looked identical Ben. It was only when I saw Theo naked and realised that the tattoos were different that I knew. I panicked and tried to back out and that's when it turned nasty.'

'Christ, this is such a mess,' he says.

'Yes, yes it is, and it might be a bigger problem than it was before. I don't know for sure that they filmed the first session with Alex, but what if they did?'

'Oh my god, Alex knows you met with Theo tonight and if they did film you last time, they can show that to the police or—'

'He can use it to find me, and kill me himself.'

'Christ...' He looks ill, and his skin is so pale it's trans-lucent. 'This isn't over Mia... in fact it's more dangerous than ever. *Oh my god*. This is a link, a direct link to you, to us.'

'I know. That's why I'm scared, Ben.'

'Okay, okay. A direct link,' he says and I can see his brain is whirring fast. 'How did you pay them?'

'Cash. They can't trace me through money.'

'Was it online – the booking?'

'Online and... I had to give a phone number in case there was a cancellation.'

'What number?' he asks.

'I... I bought a phone.'

'A throwaway, a sex phone – you bought it so you can arrange to meet men.'

'Okay,' I snap at him. 'You can burn me for a witch later. Yes, I have this,' I pull my pay-as-you-go phone out of my pocket and wave it in the air. 'I tried to be careful – more than you did with Ella. I tried to keep this away from our marriage... but I didn't know they were filming. I didn't know the danger I'd put us in.'

'So that was how you called home tonight.' I see his fists ball as anger grips him. 'What the hell do you want from me now, Mia?'

'I want... I had to tell... you have to know what might happen – these people have film of me, maybe I can be identified from it. I don't know, but if they do find me, find *us*; we will either go to prison or we end up dead.'

'So, what do we do?' he slams his fists on the table, and Elvis comes out from behind the counter with a rolling pin that he whacks into one hand.

'Lady, are you okay?'

'This doesn't concern you,' Ben yells at him.

'Shut your mouth.' He levels the rolling pin at Ben like he'll cave his head in with it. 'I'm talking to the lady.' He turns to me. 'Do you need me to call someone?' he asks gently.

I smile as broadly as I can. 'Thank you so much for the offer, but no, it's okay, we're fine. We're just having an argument, but I'm in no danger here. We'll go.'

'Are you sure?' Elvis asks with a frown.

'I am – but it's really good to know there are still gentlemen in the world.'

Elvis nods his head to me, but his eyes are still thunderous as he looks at Ben.

'Thanks,' I say as I head over to the door.

'Hey,' Elvis calls out and then he comes around the counter with a box of lollipops – like you might offer a kid – and he shakes it. 'Want one?' he asks, offering me the box. I smile, and reach over to take a raspberry one.

'Good choice,' he says and walks away without offering one to Ben; instead, he whispers as he passes him, 'I got your number, guy.'

I smile as I open the door and head out.

The cold hits me as we emerge onto the pavement and I watch my breath spiral away into the dark. I stand for a few seconds, crunching through the lollipop, and then I drop the stick down the drain cover into the sewer.

Ben

'Come on,' she says and starts to walk. I think she's heading to the tube but just before she gets there, she takes a sharp right into an alleyway and it leads into a little green area, like a private garden for the houses on the mews. She walks into the centre of the little area and pulls Theo's phone out of her hoody pocket, then takes the sim card and puts it back into the phone. As soon as she snaps it in place, the phone starts to ring.

'Who is it?' I ask and she shows me the front of the phone. I can see that it's Alex, and he's trying to FaceTime.

'We can't do that,' I say anxiously.

'I've got this.' Mia answers the call in audio only. She puts it onto speakerphone so I can hear.

'Theo, what the fuck—' Even though Alex's voice is tinny from the little speaker I can hear the violence in it.

'It's not Theo,' Mia says with as much strength and confidence as she can muster.

'Who the fuck is this?'

'Doesn't matter.'

'You're that bitch he was meeting tonight – you're that Julie?'

'Yes, you're right, and I have the recording from tonight. I was both shocked and upset to find a camera had been filming me.'

'Jesus Christ, what did the fucking idiot do? Pose for it? Or did he offer you a copy to take home and show your cuckold husband? Bloody idiot.'

'It doesn't matter how it happened, but I found the camera, and I've viewed the site, so I know what you're doing with the films.'

'What can I say – it's art.'

Mia scowls. I know she wants to rant and rave at this bastard, but she reels it in; she has to keep calm with the guy.

'I really don't think you can call what you do any kind of *art*.'

'Eye of the beholder and all that crap, I guess.' We hear him take a drink of something, and it sounds like he's gargling with it.

'Well, I do not want to be associated with your *art*, I'm sure that doesn't surprise you, and I'm guessing that you won't be shocked to hear that I want the film from last time.'

'Hah!' He snorts with laughter. 'There's no way you get that film, sweetheart. Your amazing debut is going up on the site on Saturday and you are gonna have a lot of fans.'

'Do that, and you will not see your brother again. You have my word on that.'

Alex laughs, but this time there's a dirty anger to it. 'Forget it, bitch, you're not made for blackmail, and you're sure as fuck not gonna do a thing to my brother except open your legs for him again… and me. You'd like us both together. You might not want to admit that to yourself, but you would.'

'At this moment my husband has a knife to his throat.' Mia pauses to let that sink in. The phone's quiet – so quiet I wonder if he's still there.

'Alex, I am going to offer you a one-time deal, and I really think you'd better take it or… is your mother still alive?'

There's no reply.

'Well, if your mother is still with us, she'll be very unhappy at having to bury one of her sons… and if she's dead, she'll turn in her grave and rain down pestilence and plague on you, for letting him die when you had it in your power to save him.'

'Get to the fucking point,' Alex snarls.

'I want the film, or he's dead, and you're in prison. You have thirty seconds to decide.'

He spits. 'I'll erase it… let my brother go.'

'I want the SD card and I want the laptop and I want to see your eyes when you tell me there are no other copies.'

'My eyes?'

'They are the windows to the soul, Alex, I want to see them when you swear to me you will never show that film to another living soul.'

'You are fucking kidding me! What do you think you are – some kick-ass human lie-detector?'

'That's right.'

Alex laughs, high and clear, and genuinely like he hasn't got a care in the world. 'Where we meeting, lover?'

'Putney Bridge, by the little park on the water there: Bishop's Park. There's a monument, to the International Brigade.'

'I know it.'

'How soon can you be there?' she asks.

Alex chuckles. 'Half an hour or so, can you wait that long for a real man?'

'Just you… nobody else, or you don't see your brother again.'

'That—' Alex starts to say something, but Mia ends the call. She immediately turns the phone off and pulls out the sim card. She stuffs them both into her hoody. Her hands are shaking.

'You know you can't trust him,' I tell her.

'I know.'

'The film's digital, he'll have back-ups. No matter what he gives you he'll still upload the film. You can't stop him doing that, and once they find the body—'

'So we have to make the most of tonight.'

'But what can we do?'

'Trust me.'

Trust… she's asked for that already tonight, when she wanted me to come to the hotel. I did trust her, I came, but I don't know if that still holds true. *Christ*, that thought makes me so sad.

'Mia, that man isn't an idiot, and he wasn't scared when you threatened to kill Theo; he doesn't think for a second that you will – that you could.'

'He doesn't know me very well, does he?'

'Yes he does. It was an accident with Theo – you aren't a killer, Mia.'

'You don't know what I am, Ben, not now.'

'Fine, okay… you're a killer,' I sigh, annoyed that she answered the call in the first place. 'Why did you even talk to him?'

'I wanted to find out what kind of man he was.'

'And did you?'

'He's arrogant, and he doesn't believe we can hurt him and his disgusting operation. He doesn't take us seriously. But he does love his brother. We can use that.'

'And do what? We don't have Theo, we don't have any kind of leverage; we're amateurs in a serious game.'

'And he thinks we're just going to roll over, that we're too scared to act, but we can surprise him.'

'How?'

'We do the only thing that makes sense. We kill him.'

Chapter Ten

Mia

Ben turns pale. 'K-k… kill?' he stammers.

'Come on,' I say and I turn away and start to walk, back through the little park and onto the main road. I don't look back, but I feel him behind me. I wish I could let him go home, but the plan that's evolving in my head won't work without him. I wish it could, because I'm not sure how Ben will live with himself after he's helped kill a man. That's why I have to protect him as much as I can. I will plot Alex's death and I will be the assassin. I think I could do almost anything now, and I certainly won't squirm over taking *his* life. I feel that justice – maybe not that of the law courts, but natural, *human* justice – is on my side. None of the women he's filmed would want me to suffer for snuffing him out of existence. I can't believe anyone would care – or maybe that's just what I want to think. Perhaps that's how a lot of people justify murder. As Ben is keen to remind me, Theo had Claire, Lilly and Harry and perhaps Alex has those who love him. Maybe. But I find I don't care. I don't feel any sympathy or guilt. After all this is done, I might need to find a therapist – but that's for after I kill him. And after Ben leaves me, because killing a man together will be the final nail in our marriage. But what else can I do, there's no other option. It's either Alex or me tonight. One of us will be dead by morning.

Ben

I can't move. This is insane… Isn't it? This is cold-blooded and pre-meditated. This isn't like before; this is not the same as answering Mia's call and turning up at the hotel to find a dead body. This will be… *murder*… Jesus Christ. It's one thing, to push a man away who's attacking her – that's instinctual – but to plan a man's death… I don't know what to do. There's a part of me that sees the logic and, god help me, but I admire her for it. She's a fighter, and I'm proud of that spirit but to take a man's life isn't right. Or is that just more of me lying to myself? Am I okay with him dying, just as long as I don't have to actually do it myself? I'll just watch Mia kill another man… *Christ*, why did I bring the hammer and knife – how stupid am I?

I should have stopped all this when I first arrived; I should have made her call the police as soon as I saw the body. I should, but we didn't know then, we had no idea what was in the wardrobe and—

'Mia!' I call as she starts speeding up. 'Mia, slow down,' but she doesn't; if anything, she gets a little faster. She's so bloody obstinate when she has an idea in her head. We walk past Brompton cemetery. It's bounded by tall railings, though you can see through them, to the shimmering grey stone sentinels that stand in the grounds, watching over the dead. I feel a shiver, and I don't think it's just the February chill. I've only ever been inside this cemetery once before, to bury an old friend from university. Rat – John – but we all called him Rat because... I've forgotten. *Jesus*, I open my mouth to ask Mia why we called him Rat, but I stop myself. Maybe talking about the dead is not the best thing right now. His funeral must have been at least five years ago, and everyone was there. I suppose that's the thing about dying young; everyone's still around and able to attend, like it's an unofficial school reunion. We all looked shell-shocked; he was the first one of us to die, and it hit us hard.

I stop walking and look through the bars into the cemetery. There are many stone angels inside, and one gravestone's a giant dartboard, which is strange. I wonder if Theo will be buried here? He's even younger than Rat, so there could be hundreds at his funeral – if they find the body, of course.

I turn back to the street and... *Damnit*, Mia's gone. I run forward, heart racing again, and—

There. I see her. I almost run past her, but she's gone inside a twenty-four-hour convenience store. I look through the window. She's at the counter, pointing at something behind the shopkeeper's head. He reaches up and grabs a bottle of cheap whisky and hands it over. I don't get it; she hates whisky, says it tastes like burning soil in her mouth. The lights in the store flicker, and the light they give off makes everything look a dirty brown, like the stained rings you get in old teacups.

I watch her pay for the whisky. It reminds me of when we first got together – she was twenty, but looked a lot younger, and she would buy booze and hope to get asked for ID. When they did ask, she would flirt and cajole and persuade – *It's okay, you can let me off, I'll be careful*. She wanted to see how many men (it was always men) would bend to her will. How many would let someone they thought was underage buy drink without proof. It was most of them. She loved being able to tempt men to break the rules. *Huh*. I hadn't ever thought that before – that she's always been a temptress.

'Let's go,' she snaps at me, as she leaves the shop and hurries on. I catch up with her, and walk alongside.

'You don't like whisky.'

'No… here.' And she pulls a can of Red Bull out from her hoody pocket and tosses it to me.

'We need to be alert,' she says and opens a can for herself. There's a part of me that thinks for a second that she shoplifted them. I don't dwell on it. I pull the ring and hear it snap and hiss.

Mia

OMG, that's good. I can feel the syrupy energy flow through me. I have to stay sharp. I shiver, and don't know if it's the cold or fear. I can feel a bead of sweat run down my back as I shift gears to a jog. It's further than I remembered, and we have to get there before Alex does. If he sees just the two of us arrive, he'll know we don't have his brother, and all this will turn to crap.

I speed up, and feel Ben start to strain beside me. He isn't used to running. I run a lot. People say that exercise gives you pleasure – an endorphin rush – but I've never found that to be true. Quite the opposite; I find exercise boring and it hurts – knees and hips mostly – and I think that's why I like it. *No gain without pain;* that was the mantra of exercise when I was a kid. My mum was always on a diet, always exercising. She had these four-litre jugs filled with sand that she used as weights, and giant rubber bands on the door handles. She never touched butter, and ate cottage cheese, which is gross and shouldn't be allowed to have the word cheese in its name.

'Can you slow down a bit,' Ben asks with a little nasal whine, as he starts to fall behind. I wish I could just run off and leave him… but I can't. Instead, I drop the pace a little. Who runs to their death anyway?

Finally I see the river and the path to the right of it that leads down into the park. 'What's the time?' I ask him.

'I don't…' and he looks around like a clock's going to magically appear in the air. *God*… I don't mean to be so mad with him but he's the only one here and he's so bloody annoying, and we might be dead in an hour.

It's colder here, with the wind blowing off the water. I've been here many times over the years. There used to be a snooker club on the corner and my dad used to play there sometimes with his brother and some old friends. The club was temperance, which seems so old-fashioned now.

The church on the river's edge is historically important, at least my dad always said it was. If I remember rightly, he said that during the civil war there were meetings there and Oliver Cromwell wrote the first British constitution inside… or something like that. My dad showed me the plaques, and told me all the stories, but that was years and years ago now. I've forgotten it – sorry, Dad. I wish he was here now – no that's a lie. I'm glad he isn't here. I don't want him to see what I've become, what one fucked-up night can do to you. He'd be disappointed. I'm letting down all the men in my life tonight.

I stop walking. There's no sound except the river slapping at the brick walls. I look around, searching for any sign that Alex is already here, but there's no car parked anywhere that I can see. I would guess he'd pull up, and leave the car right at the steps down to the park, so he can make a quick getaway if he needs to. That's what I'd do.

'What if he brings a gang with him?' Ben asks.

'Like the Famous Five?' I laugh.

'Seriously Mia, what if four or five nasty blokes turn up?'

I don't answer; instead I turn to the steps and walk down them into the shadows. He's right to be scared; if Alex is smart he'll dig up some muscle from somewhere. Or bring a gun. Either way, we'd be dead. I just hope he's as arrogant as I think he is, and doesn't believe he needs anyone or anything else to deal with us; with Julie and her cuckold.

Down here, at the bottom of the park steps, I'm protected from the cutting wind. It's a beautiful little park that runs along the riverbank. Not much has changed on this side of the bridge, though along the other it's all so different. Huge glass buildings tower over the water, and hundreds of people live there, but it's only rich folk who can afford more than half a million pounds for a glass box suspended over the most famous waterway in the world. It's crazy – criminal, even. So much bloody money for so few people.

I step up on the wall that runs along the edge, and I stand and watch the water ebb and flow, way below me.

Ben

I feel like I want to wet myself; I have never been so scared in my whole life. In contrast, Mia looks calm on top of the wall where she stands like a statue. I don't know what's going on in her head. I feel like I don't know her anymore. The Mia I knew could not consider killing a man – nothing could make that possible – but here she is, ready and willing to snuff out a life.

I watch her. The mouth I have loved for almost half of my life now looks cruel. Her eyes, that have always been so soft and alive with fun and mischief, are now dark and hard. Her hands snake into her hoody and pull out the bottle of whisky. She twists the cap and cracks the seal on the bottle. She takes a slug and grimaces at the burning in her mouth. I don't understand what the hell is going on.

'Mia?' I ask, but she turns away from me and walks along the wall that marks the river's edge.

'Mia.'

'It's okay Ben, just hold it together.' She says over her shoulder, as she just stands there, looking out on the water as it sparkles with the moonlight and the yellow sulphurous streetlights from the opposite banks.

She stands frozen like that, looking out across the water for a while and then suddenly snaps into action.

'Ben, you get into the shadows over there. Remember, you're supposed to have a knife at his brother's throat.'

'But he won't believe we have Theo if he doesn't see him.'

'He will.' She rummages in the pocket of her hoody and pulls something out. 'Here,' she says and holds it up. It reflects dully in the moonlight.

'What is it?'

'It's Theo's ring. It looks like some club or class ring – it's quite distinctive.'

'You… you took it off his body?'

She shrugs.

'Christ, Mia, when did you do that? Were you always planning to lure the brother down here?'

'Don't be bloody stupid.' She jumps off the wall and I actually flinch, backing away from her. 'I don't want to be here any more than you do. There wasn't some grand scheme, for fuck's sake, it's a distinctive ring. I took it after he died – just like I took his wallet and watch – because I didn't want him identified. The longer it takes for the police to ID the body the better. Okay?'

I can see her face, pale and hurt, her mouth stretched over her teeth and slightly quivering. 'What do you think of me – that I don't have a heart? Jesus Ben, I'm still the same person I was yesterday.'

'I know that,' I tell her. 'It's just that I'm freaked out, and nothing makes sense. I'm tired. I'm just really tired, that's all.' And then I look away from her, so she can't see the worry trip across my face as, on some level, I do think she's lost her compassion. I hope she recovers it, but… I don't know how she can do that with so much blood on her hands.

'I know you're tired, we both are.' She steps back up onto the wall, and looks out over the river once more. We listen, straining into the night, waiting for him to come. Quiet. It's quiet as the grave… and then, from the direction of the bridge, we hear the roar of a sports car. I feel my hand shake and Mia stiffens. 'That might be him. Get out of sight and hide,' she hisses.

'But Mia—'

'Quickly,' she says, as a car door slams from some way off, sounding like a gun shot in the night.

'Look, it's good that I took the ring, we can prove we have the brother. Now, hide. Just stay in the shadows and don't come out. I'll do all the talking and, if he demands to see Theo, stay hidden and just say something from the darkness – so he knows you're out there.'

'What do I say?'

'I don't know, something menacing, but for now, just hide.'

There are footsteps, but I can't tell where they're coming from, as they seem to echo from every direction.

Mia

Ben shrinks back into the grey swirl of the trees and is gone. I honestly don't know if he's up to this; he's never been menacing – not for a single second in his entire life – and I don't think he can start now.

The footsteps stop, their echo dies away, and everything's quiet once more. I strain into the night; there's no sound but the water slapping on the walls of the bank, like a drumbeat. Is he going to be alone? I stand tall – no slouching when death's on its way. I stay on the wall, silhouetted against the moon and—

'Ah,' I pull my arm up to shield my eyes, as a powerful beam of light hits me in the face, swallowing everything and making me blind.

'Turn the light off,' I yell, hoping it sounds commanding, but I think it just sounds desperate and scared. 'If you want to see your fucking brother alive, do it!' But the beam doesn't snap off. It runs up and down my body, and then to my left and right and back to my face. I see stars, like in a *Tom and Jerry* cartoon.

'I remember you,' a voice says with a half chuckle.

I can hear him, but I can't see him, not even an outline. I feel a tear on my cheek – fuck him, it's the light in my eye, not fear. I want to wipe it away but I don't. Instead, I let it run down my cheek and spiral into the air to fall onto the stone wall.

'You were on top, you held my wrists down and told me not to move. You did everything and you were quiet, like a mouse, but you liked it – I knew by the way you held me inside you and you shuddered. I think you even cried – you did, didn't you?' He laughs. 'I'm sorry I wasn't free tonight, that I had to send the brother along. I hope he was what you wanted. He can be a little more aggressive than me, but next time I'll look after you myself.'

'There won't be a next time, not now that I know what you do.'

'Ha,' he laughs and steps out of the shadow and… *Christ*. They are so alike; not just their faces but the way they move and the twinkle in their eyes.

'Why did you pick here to meet?' he asks.

'I… it wasn't far from where we were.' I don't tell him about the church – I don't expect his dad brought him here to lecture him on the finer points of Oliver Cromwell as Lord Protector.

'My dad brought us here,' he says, as he turns around and looks through the leafless trees along the riverbank. 'The three of us would walk through the park to Craven Cottage to see Fulham play. That was our team; we had season tickets. We came on the tube, and then through the park with thousands of others. It was a sea of black and white shirts and scarves.'

He waves his arms in the air, mimicking the child he once was. 'And after every game, win or lose, we went for spaghetti and ice cream. They were the best times of my life. Me, my dad and my brother.' I see a tear appear at the corner of his eye and it makes me angry.

'If you're trying to make Theo more human so we can't kill him, then think again. I would relish putting a knife into that fucking rapist's heart.'

'Rapist?' He looks genuinely surprised by that. 'Don't make me laugh.'

'He hurt me – I would enjoy hurting him.'

'I bet you would, darling, I knew you'd be kinky. Do ya like it dangerous, with no safe words?'

'Shut up.'

'Oh come on, Julie, remember, I seen you naked – body and soul. I seen the darkness in that head of yours.'

'You have no idea who I am or what I'm capable of.' I feel my whole body burn with contempt for him. 'Your brother's life is in my hands and I want my film.'

He smiles, with perfectly straight, white teeth. 'Do you have any idea how much porn there is out there, in the big wide world?'

I don't answer – I figure it's a rhetorical question.

'Well, I'll tell you: a new film is posted every minute. It's mostly vanilla – boy and girl, two boys and one girl, lots of girls… I'm sure you know what I mean.' He smiles and his eyes twinkle in the moonlight. He is a handsome devil.

'So what?'

'I'm just saying that this is a big business, and I'm just a businessman, looking for a little spot in an overcrowded market. And I've spotted a space – a little niche, a USP – and I'm providing a much-needed service.'

'So how is it good business to exploit the customer?'

'Customer? You think you're the customer?'

'I paid for your time.'

He smiles, but this time his face isn't handsome; instead, he looks vulpine. 'You want the money back? I will gladly refund your money for tonight with Theo.' He pouts and makes sad eyes. 'You can even have the money back from your night with me.'

170

'I want the film.'

'But you see, with the film you aren't the client, you're the talent.'

'Give me the fucking film,' I snap at him and realise I'm losing all control of the situation. 'Don't patronise me with this businessman shit. You're a pimp, an abuser and—'

'Don't!' he screams, the sinews of his neck suddenly taut and twisted, the moonlight stretching shadows into his eye sockets as the rage deforms his face. 'Don't push me. Where is my brother, you fucking whore?'

'Whore?' I smile. He should not have called me that. 'You are seeing this from entirely the wrong direction Alex. I'm the victim of sexual assault and rape. That is what the police will see when I—'

Alex throws up his hands in mock alarm. 'Oh no, not the police!' Then he laughs and drops his hands. 'Oh my god, I thought you were smart, but you're just a stupid bitch. You are playing this all wrong. There are millions of fuck films out there and your film will be just one of them. It'll be seen by about five thousand men – probably most of them will be Japanese and American businessmen. They're fed up with watching perfectly sculpted, hairless, teenage girls who fake their orgasms. These men want to watch real women with pubic hair and stretch marks and creases and flab – real women who really come and cry and yell and enjoy having a man, enjoy giving themselves to a man. They crave women that actually like sex and want sex. These guys watch women like you, women they can imagine being with, and they wish to god that their own frigid wives were—'

'You arrogant bastard, you actually think you're doing some good in the world, don't you? That you're one of the good guys – supporting lonely men all over the world.'

He laughs. 'I'm not a monster. I help guys get off; I'm just a pornographer who knows his market, and I'm a good lover, but then you know that already, don't you?'

I don't give the bastard an answer to that; even in the dim light I can see how he grins, like he's the cock of the walk. Behind him, in the bushes, Ben must be burning with rage; I can almost feel the waves of heat in the air.

'But who cares about all this crap? Let's cut to the chase, Julie. You invited me down here... Where's my brother?'

'Close.'

Alex narrows his eyes, thinking through his options. 'No. No I don't believe you. He isn't here. You've got nothing to bargain with, bitch. I'm gone.' He starts to turn away from me.

'Really... so you think we're bluffing?'

'Oh yes, I think exactly that.'

'And you're willing to risk Theo's life? You'd make poor Claire a widow, and Lilly and Harry fatherless.'

There's a beat, and then he swings the torch back up and hits me with the beam, blinding me with the intensity of it. 'Where's my fucking brother?' he screams. 'Theo... *Theo!*' He bellows, keeping the light full in my face. His voice is like an explosion, I step back and—

'*Mia!*' Ben yells at me. 'The water!'

Shit. My foot is almost off the slab of stone. I'm tottering on the edge of the wall, half on and half off. Ben bursts out of the bushes like a fucking idiot, and Alex swings around, catching him in the beam of his torch. Ben looks scared, like a chicken about to be eaten by a fox.

'Mia?' Alex turns the beam back on me, as he wags his finger like I'm a naughty schoolgirl. 'Tut tut, that isn't the name you told me.' He puts his hand to his chin. 'Julie must be your fantasy. She must be the girl who can do the things poor Mia only dreams of. Kinky, slutty Julie, who likes to ride a big cock and—'

'You have no idea about what a woman wants,' I tell him.

'You might be surprised; foxes know a lot about the habits of chickens,' Alex grins at me.

'You're a fucking bastard.'

'Yes please to the fucking – but my mum and dad were like a sodding love story, so I'm no bastard.' He grins again and turns back to Ben, the torch beam scanning up and down his body. 'This your cuckold?' he asks me and Ben curls his hands into fists like an idiot. If he tries to fight him, Alex will chew him up and spit him out.

'Ben,' I hiss, warning him. Alex just laughs and looks Ben up and down.

'So you, Mr Knight on a white horse, what's your part in all this?'

Ben stays rooted to the spot as Alex walks around him, weighing him up and tutting with disapproval as he finds him wanting.

'Bit of a chubster, your bloke,' he says to me with a sympathetic pout. 'I can see why you looked elsewhere. It must be like having Moby Dick climbing up on top of you.'

'You piece of—' Ben yells and moves to hit him.

'Ben!' I scream to stop him from lunging at Alex, because that's just what he's trying to provoke.

'I bet it's all over quickly too. Thar she blows!' Alex cackles at his own cleverness, and the torch beam darts between the two of us, making us both cover our eyes with our hands.

'I called Ben to come and help with your brother,' I tell him, my voice steady and cold, trying to intimidate him.

'Yeah, I mean I can't see little Julie being able to take on my brother. I can see you ain't got that kind of strength – except in your thighs, I remember that from when they were wrapped around me.'

Ben makes another move to grab Alex. '*No!*' I yell at him, and he pulls back.

'So,' Alex continues, clearly having fun. 'If your chubby hubby is here, it does beg the question: where is my brother and who's babysitting him?' His grin is savage, like the big bad wolf. 'I think I'm hearing some little white lies from you two. Shame on you both, you don't have Theo and you don't have anything to bargain with, so I am out of—'

'Here's your fucking proof.' I throw the ring at Alex. It hits him in the chest and falls onto the path. He has to take the torch beam off us, and shine it down onto the ground to search for the ring. When the beam catches it, the stone in the centre sparkles red. I can see from his silhouette, from the way he stiffens, that he recognises the ring.

'Pick up the ring and turn the torch off,' I yell. 'Then toss the torch into the river.' *This is our one chance*, I think. We have to take it, while he's off-balance.

Alex doesn't say anything; he merely squats down and gets the ring. He holds it up between his fingers and squints at it. Then he slowly stands and takes the heavy-duty torch and—

'Here!' He slings it right at me. I move as quickly as I can, but it still hits me in the shoulder.

'Mia,' Ben yells as I almost stumble back and fall into the water but I manage to right myself. The torch bounces a long way off me and then tumbles down with a splash into the Thames.

'That hurt,' I say, keeping my voice as level as I can.

'Not as much as I hoped it would,' Alex tells me with a smile. 'Julie, lovely Julie with the sopping wet—'

'Shut your mouth.' Ben steps forward to hit him.

'*No!*' I jump down on to the path, and move between them. I push Ben back towards the shadows.

'Shame,' Alex crows. 'I like a good workout before I negotiate for hostages. And beating a cuck to a pulp is almost as good as fucking the wife,' he tells Ben with a shit-eating grin. I can see that Ben is desperately trying to think of a witty comeback but he's dry. In about an hour he'll have a great cartoon about it. That's if we're still alive.

'Alex, we've got Theo and—' I start.

'The two of you?' he asks, like he's talking to a kid.

'Yeah, the two of us.' Ben answers with a sneer.

'Great, so I can kill you both, find Theo and no harm done.'

Ben steps back; he's scared, and I can see that Alex is getting off on his fear. He's a bully and he likes to make people feel afraid.

'I thought you said you were a businessman?' I say.

'I am, and doing very well, too.'

'So it's stupid to kill us. The police aren't idiots – don't you watch TV? The second they find our bodies, they check where our mobile phones have been and they find the hotel. They check the CCTV and they find me there… with your twin. They look back and they see you both there a lot… they add two and two and they get – you, in prison.'

'They might not find your bodies,' Alex says with a voice dripping with poison.

'Excellent point, though I'm pretty sure a top corporate lawyer disappearing in the middle of the night with her writer husband will warrant an investigation. And there again, the police get the phone records and – Bob's your pervert uncle – Alex is in prison again. It looks like all roads lead to prison... and I'm guessing that's less fun for you pretty boys.'

He starts to say something, but pauses and glares at me, the twinkle in his eyes now a bonfire.

'You make excellent points,' he says, 'So what do you suggest?'

'You brought the film?'

Alex sniggers, like a teenager talking to a grandparent who asks what the internet is. 'There's no actual film, darling, this isn't the 1970s, I can't hand over a reel of sixteen millimetre and have you burn it... this is the digital age.'

'But you can delete the files.'

'I can.' He smiles that vulpine smile again.

'You can say you have – but then post them online a month later.'

Alex shrugs. 'Honestly, babe, it would be a crime against humanity to not share your incredible body with—'

'Shut up about my wife,' Ben shrieks from behind Alex.

'Leave it, Ben.'

'Oh I can tell you two have been married a while – trouble in paradise?'

'This is not about us.'

'Oh, but I think it is. Ben and Mia… Mia and Ben, and I know who wears the trousers, and who wears the tiny little panties. You know, I don't think I'm going to have any trouble finding you two after tonight – finding where you live, and work, and who your friends and family are. And some night, I'll come and visit you both, bring along some of my friends, and we can have a party. I know how Mia likes to enjoy herself, maybe we'll find that Ben likes the same kinds of parties.'

Ben looks like he'll jump at Alex, but that would be so bloody stupid. I hold up my hand and glare. Ben stops, but I can see he's still seething.

'I am so disappointed in you, Alex. Is that what we're back to? Threats that you'll rape us both? I suppose I shouldn't be surprised – we already know you're a rapist – but I didn't realise that you could only think with your dick.'

He snarls at me.

'I just hoped that there was some sense in there too. After all, you say you're a businessman, but that's difficult to see. Maybe that's just you being delusional.' I smile, and I like how angry that makes him. 'But let's see if we can find the businessman inside you after all. Here's the deal: you will not upload the film you have of me. I realise you can always have a copy, but it will not get uploaded to any site in the world. In return, we will return your brother unharmed.' I avoid looking at Ben; I don't want to give the game away.

'We will give you our address, you will give us your address. We will keep an eye on your sites, and if my film is ever uploaded we will go to the police with the details of the hotel and how you operate. We can cause you a lot of trouble and expense, hiring lawyers and all that shit.

I'm a lawyer, by the way, so I know how to make your life hell. Now, isn't losing my film worth not making an enemy of me?'

'Hell, bitch, you make a convincing argument.' Alex nods and smiles, his eyes twinkle again. I don't trust him for a second.

'Let's drink to it,' I say and pull out the bottle of whisky I bought earlier and I take a pull on it. I grimace as it burns my mouth.

'Sure,' he says.

I put the cap back on, and throw the bottle to him. It arcs in the air and I hold my breath. He catches it and untwists the cap. He takes it up to his mouth and chugs half the bottle. 'That's good.' He holds out the bottle to Ben. 'How about you, Ben, my boy, you likey?'

'Fuck you.'

Alex laughs. 'Suit yourself,' and he takes another long pull on the bottle.

I turn and look out at the water again, and as I do so, I open my mouth and let the whisky run down my chin and soak into my hoody. I count to ten and then turn back to see Alex finish the bottle and wipe his mouth.

'I wouldn't have taken you for a whisky drinker,' he says and drops the empty bottle to the ground where it shatters into a million pieces. 'I'd have gone with white wine,' he smiles. 'Or battery acid.'

'I needed something to wake me up,' I tell him. His eyes lock onto mine and don't let go.

'There's no way we can trust him, Mia,' Ben says from behind, but I keep my eyes on Alex.

'Well, Alex?'

'Our little deal you mean – I'll cross my heart and hope to... I... die... hope to die.' He shakes his head and blinks, and for a second he looks a little lost and unsure – as a shadow crosses his face.

'So is it just the two of you that run the company?' I ask, trying to keep him with us.

'Yes, we started it, just the two of us. We got a tech guy that built the actual site and a… an… em… money guy, you know, who does the books.'

'Accountant?'

'Yeah, accountant, but it's our company, just Theo and me.'

'Don't you argue?'

'Us? No, we're close, like one person. The two musketeers…' His eyes glaze over for a second and his head tips forward like he'll fall asleep standing up, but then his head snaps back and his eyes blaze.

'I am… I need…' he stammers.

'It's late, like, four a.m; I think we're all really tired.'

'Yeah… yeah, I guess I'm tired… so I just want… Where's Theo?' He looks back at Ben. 'I need to give him his ring back, he always wears it… I don't get how you got it off him and… oh shit.'

His knees buckle, like a new-born baby giraffe, and he staggers around, desperate to stay on his feet, but his legs are like jelly now. Ben moves to grab him.

'No, Ben.' Instead, I slowly move towards Alex and reach out, like I'm going to stroke a wild animal. I take his hand and steady him.

'Careful,' Ben says, imagining Alex is going to pull a knife on me, but I know he won't. I can see his eyes, they're drifting in and out of focus. Reality is shifting for him.

'You have to be exhausted, my friend,' I tell him, in as calm a voice as I possibly can, and lead him by the hand over to the low wall and sit him down.

'I jus… Theo…' He sounds like a little kid calling for his brother. If I didn't know he was a manipulative rapist bastard, I'd feel sorry for him.

'That's good, Alex.' I pat him on the back and he starts to slump over, his spine collapsing in on itself, as he no longer has the ability to hold himself upright. He folds onto the wall, his head smacking hard on the bricks. It makes me jump. I remember the sound of his brother's head hitting the floor, and I feel nauseous for a moment.

'Alex… Alex?' I click my fingers above his face, but there's no response. His breathing's shallow. Up close, he isn't so much like his brother as I thought; he's leaner and his nose is sharper. His eyes are crueller too, though they're dimming, as his intelligence is seeping out of him – just like the blood that drained from Theo's head. I lean down and whisper into Alex's ear.

'He's dead. Theo's dead. I thought you might have known, might have felt it in the ether. Don't they say that twins know what's happening with the other, that there's some kind of psychic link? But you had no idea – no idea that you're all alone in the world now, that no one else has your face anymore, so maybe you weren't that close after all.' I smile. I'm enjoying this – it's just a pity that he's too far gone to respond. I would like to see his horror, as he realises what's happening.

'You're only half a person, now that Theo's gone, but it doesn't really matter, because you won't outlive him by long – just a few hours.'

Alex makes a kind of gurgling sound, so maybe he can hear me, and understand what I'm telling him. I hope he does, that he knows what I've done – that I've beaten him and his brother. That I've made them both pay for what they've done to me. I hope he knows – and that inside his head he's screaming in agony.

I slip my hand into his pockets, pulling out keys, a phone and a wallet. He does nothing to stop me; his arms fall away like jelly. He drools a little, and there's a shift in his breathing. Maybe he's trying to warn me off but it's little more than a soft growl in the back of his throat.

'Mia?' Ben calls and walks towards me.

'Stay there, Ben,' I warn him and then slip my hands under the body. 'Rot in hell,' I hiss at Alex, and then with all my strength, I flip him – up over the wall.

'*Mia!*' Ben leaps forward, but I grab him and hold him back, as Alex's body hangs in the air, suspended for a moment, and then it falls, twisting and turning, to splash down into the water.

'Mia you can't… you can't.' He tries to push me away. I know he'll jump in and try and save Alex, so I hold on with all my might, my arms snaked around him as he struggles against me; but I don't let go.

'Ben, it has to be like this. We said he had to die. At least this was peaceful.'

'Mia, he's drowning.'

'He's unconscious, he won't even know… trust me, Ben. It's a good way to go – better than he deserves.'

'What did you do?'

'What I had to do,' I say. 'There was no other option. It was him or us.' I say it firmly and I hold Ben's eyes until I feel the fight draw out of him.

'I thought…' he says in a weak voice.

'What? What did you think, Ben?'

'That maybe we could negotiate—'

'We had nothing Ben, we couldn't produce the brother, and as soon as he found out Theo was dead, we were too. He had our real names. This was the only way.'

'I can't—'

'And it was quiet and peaceful, far better than violence.'

'But he had no chance, it was like we...' His voice falls away.

'Like what... like we cheated?' I ask.

'No, I mean not exactly but – it was rigged.'

'We outwitted him, and it saved you from being beaten to death. He threatened to come to our house with a gang and rape us both. Christ, Ben, what did you want, a duel? Do you think he deserved a fair fight?'

'No, not that, but this way he didn't have a chance.'

'No, he didn't, but that's good, because in a fight he would have won. He would have kicked and scratched and clawed, and he might have killed us both. We couldn't take that risk, so I made it easy and clean. I think that's good. And now we're free.'

'Really... free? You think it's done?'

'What... what do you mean? He said the business was only him and Theo and they're both dead.'

'But his computers are still out there somewhere, and the guy that did the website or the dodgy accountant or anybody with access to them – they can just carry on.'

I feel my throat tighten and all that joy at finally feeling safe, seeps away like someone pulled the plug out of a drain. I'm such an idiot, because he's right: this hasn't removed the threat that the first film goes live. We could still lose everything.

'Mia—'

'I can't.' I wave Ben away and walk over to the wall. I stare down into the shifting water below me. I expect to see Alex down there, floating in the oily blackness of the Thames, looking up at me like his brother did from the bin at the foot of the hotel, with his shattered jaw and broken neck, but there's nothing down there. No ghosts.

'What do we do?' I ask the air as I look into the shifting, oozing water below. The two of us stand, lost in thought, for what feels like hours and then Ben breaks the silence.

'We should go to the police.'

'No.'

'Then do we just go home and wait for the knock on the door.'

'Shut up Ben.'

'Then what?'

'I don't know.'

'But what do we—'

'I don't know. I don't bloody know,' I scream at him. He looks back at me, hurt and bewildered, and then all that melts into plain anger.

'Christ this is such a bloody mess. You didn't think anything through; you've killed a man for nothing. Nothing. I don't understand you – I don't know who you are anymore.'

'You don't know who I am?' I snap at him angrily. 'Of course you bloody do, because I've not changed! I've always been willing to fight for what I love, who I love. It's you who's changed. You've lost yourself – your mojo went a long time ago, and you've been trailing in my slipstream for years, without any fucking direction.'

'And whose fault was that? Who begged me to stop writing the strip?'

'I didn't tell you to take a soul-sucking job in fucking advertising.'

'Then, what was I supposed to do?'

'I didn't know and I didn't care. I just couldn't bear to see *us* anymore – not the three of us. I couldn't see the happy Kingdom family in the fucking magazine every week.'

'But I wouldn't—'

'Wouldn't what? Wouldn't have written the jokes? Then what *would* you have done? Would it have become *The Kingdoms in Mourning*? That would have been worse, I couldn't see us sad either – I knew you were going to keep the strip going and… and… I couldn't stand to see the hole where she'd been.'

'Mia, I'm—'

'Don't. Don't say you're sorry, I can't fucking bear it. I am so fed up with your *sorry*.'

'Agh,' Ben kicks out at the brick wall and hurts his foot. He doesn't know what to do when he's angry, doesn't know where to direct it, he never has. It comes out in stupid ways, because he always runs from his dark emotions. But not me, not anymore: I am fucking celebrating my dark spirit. Tonight I have killed two men. I am in control. I look down into the shimmering depths of the river.

'I'm glad he's dead, that they're both dead,' I say, but I can't look at Ben.

'You're glad they're dead? And Claire and Lilly and Harry, what about them?' he asks.

'Shut up about them, for fuck's sake. I did what I had to do and I'm not going to be shamed into feeling guilt by you.' My face is burning as I turn to him, and I see how his jaw clenches and I feel my fingers tighten into fists. I want to fight. I will fight him if I have to. I will fight the whole fucking world.

'I just…' he says. 'I just—'

'You just what?'

But I can already see that any desire to confront me over Alex's death is dying in him. 'I wish…' he starts.

'Kids wish for stuff, Ben, but we're fucking grown-ups. There are no wishes.' Clouds scud across the sky and cover the moon, plunging us into near dark.

'How did you do it?' he asks in a small hurt voice. 'I don't understand what happened. How did you—'

'I drugged him, I put it in the whisky.'

'But you drank some.'

'I didn't swallow.'

His brow furrows, like there's some big question forming in his mind… and I know what it is – and I don't want to answer it.

'But what was it, and where did you get it? I didn't see you buy anything from the shop, and it worked so quickly; you can't buy something like that from a corner shop… it must have been some serious drug… you must have had it with you already.'

'We need to go,' I tell him, desperate for him to stop asking these questions, but he's like a dog with a bone, worrying out the last tiny shreds of meat.

'What did you have on you, that worked so quickly?'

'I…'

'You have to tell me, Mia.'

'Ben.'

'*Tell me.*'

'Rohypnol, I put Rohypnol in the whisky.'

The clouds part and the moon reappears. Ben is so close to working it out.

'Why do you have it? Why do you have anything like that? I don't see why you…'

And then the light in his eyes changes, darkens, as he realises the awful, ugly truth of what I did.

'You… You…' Anger swarms around him. 'You said at the café that you were going to tell me the truth, but it wasn't the truth, was it? It was a partial truth, just enough to get me to go along with you, just enough *truth* to stack up against Ella and me. But nothing like the whole truth.'

'Ben, I—'

'You already had it with you, but it wasn't meant for him.'

'Ben—'

'You came out tonight with it on you, so you either planned to give it to someone—'

'That's ludicrous, Ben, I wasn't going to date rape anyone, how can you even think that?'

'I don't… but that makes the alternative even worse.'

'Ben, forget this, it really doesn't matter. This isn't something to obsess over, you know.'

'Because if you didn't have it with you to use on someone you met at a bar, then I think it means you wanted to use it on someone to get them out of your way.'

'Please Ben, don't.'

'You wanted to put someone to sleep, to leave the coast clear so you could meet your gigolo.'

'Ben, you have it all wrong.'

'But I don't think I do. Tonight, when I woke up, I felt so sick and dizzy, and I couldn't remember how I'd got there. I didn't remember last night — and I still don't. I can't recall anything about it.'

'Ben, please.'

'And you called on the landline, and you said, "Please wake up," but normally I wouldn't have gone to sleep that early. You knew I was asleep and you were worried I wouldn't wake up. How did you know I was asleep?'

'Ben, we're both tired.'

'Oh my god, Mia…' He looks at me like I'm the devil. 'You gave me the Rohypnol, you put me to bed and then you went out, thinking I'd sleep until morning and have no memory of you leaving.'

'Ben.'

'Or was there something more? I put on my best suit – was I meeting you?'

'I don't want to hurt you.'

'I think it's too late for that. I think the harm's done. And… and I think that you've done it before, a month or so ago. I thought I had food poisoning and – that was the night you met Alex – you drugged me then, too.'

'I wanted—'

'Oh my god, you called me to help you tonight, knowing I was unconscious. That's why you called so many times and were so loud; you were trying to wake me up.'

'Please Ben, I—' I try and hold him, I reach out, but he pulls away.

'Jesus Christ, Mia, you talk about these two men and how they abused you, but you did this. You drugged someone that you're supposed to love – and you did it so that you could go out and meet someone you'd paid for sex.'

'Ben, it wasn't like that.'

'Don't lie to me, Mia. How could you do that? The betrayal—'

'Ella.'

'Ella? You say her name like that absolves you of all guilt. Okay, so I had an affair – yes, I am a shitty man, I let us down badly, I know that. But what you did, that's worse, that's the ultimate gaslighting. To turn me off like I'm a bloody robot, so you can go out and get sex—'

'It wasn't sex.'

'Then what the hell was it? It certainly wasn't love. It was one night of sex with someone – and you were desperate for it, because your evil old hubby won't touch you anymore. Is that it?'

'I'm not wicked, Ben.'

'Then what the hell are you? You drugged me, stole my memory, got me out of the way for sex and you end up killing two men. I'm sorry, Mia, but maybe you are a monster.' He looks at me with such intense sadness. 'I can't do this… I can't…' and he turns and starts to walk away.

'Ben… Ben, don't go… I need you… *Ben*, we did it… please don't go…'

But he keeps walking, through the little park and past the angels that are supposed to keep us safe from the demons and devils – but they don't. I watch my husband leave and I beg: *look back, look back, look back…* I pray that he'll stop, turn back and see me… but he doesn't. He keeps on walking, until he gets to the steps that lead up to the bridge, and even then he keeps going. I've lost him. I've frightened him away, and I'm still not safe. Someone else might take over the porn sites, maybe the accountant, or the videographer, or the guy who makes the website. Any of them could find my film, upload it onto the site, and all this will have been for nothing – nothing. I've lost everything.

Chapter Eleven

Mia

I should go – this place is full of danger – but I can't move. I'm stuck, pinned here by the weight of the lives I've ended tonight. Theo and Alex of course, but there's the death of the Kingdoms too, because tonight I've killed our marriage – I've killed *us* – and I am truly sorry for that. I feel damned. And so my eyes stay glued to the twisting water below me. I would guess that his body's already started to float downstream. I can't tell how fast the river moves here, but I expect someone will see him as soon as dawn breaks, and the police will recover the body. The clock's ticking; there's so little time.

I should have told Ben the truth from the start – except that it's so shameful that he probably would have left as soon as he heard it. And if he had done, then Theo's body would never have left the hotel room, and we would never have returned for the phone and so never discovered the video camera and—

Fuck – what the hell am I doing? Thinking like this is a total waste of time; it's nothing more than a child's game of 'woulda, coulda, shoulda'. History can't be re-written – that isn't what happened: in the real world we got rid of the body, found the camera and I killed Alex. If I'd have called an ambulance when Theo fell, then maybe all of this would be different, but I didn't call 999. Instead I took action myself – because I'm not a victim. I'm not. *Fuck that. Fuck that with bells on.*

–

I thought it would go smoothly tonight, meeting the stud that I thought was Alex, that I'd thought of everything. I had my change of clothes in a bag, with make-up and toiletries and everything I'd need. I took it to work and left everything else at home, my phone, keys, cards – everything that could identify me. All I had was some cash, enough for the night and to get home. There was nothing else. I'd taken off my watch, earrings, necklace and my wedding ring. My hands had felt naked – it was strange, but exciting. I know that sounds bad, but I was thrilled, there was a buzz that ran through me all day as I waited to be Julie Jones again.

I left the office half an hour early and headed to the club. The idea was to get a couple of drinks to get rid of the jitters, and then I'd change in the club toilets and get myself ready for meeting *him*. I planned to send a text to Ben, saying there was some last-minute presentation and I'd be home late, and that he should order something from Desi, our favourite Indian take-away, and that I'd be home by ten. That was the plan. It was a good plan and it should have worked. I wouldn't need to drug him and he'd never know. It would be clean. Ben wouldn't be hurt. I sat at the bar. I ordered a Manhattan, and drank it down in one. There's a two-drink minimum at the club, you pay up front and they stamp your hand – so I got another and downed that too. The maraschino cherry was chewy and sweet and boozy. I thought I'd have one more before I went and changed into my silk panties and figure-hugging dress. Just thinking about it made me hot, excited and thrilled. I downed a third – already a little drunk – and I thought about a fourth.

'You on your own, sweetheart?' A voice said from behind me.

'I'm married, I'm af—' The words died on my lips as I swung around to look into the face of my husband. Ben looked a little sheepish and behind that, in his eyes I saw worry.

'Hi, I… you look nice,' I said, and he did. He was wearing his Paul Smith suit and he'd shaved – not brilliantly – but at least he'd made the effort, for the first time in months and months. I actually can't remember the last time he'd scrubbed up and we went out.

'I thought I'd surprise you.'

'You did. You have, but how did you know I was here?'

'I was waiting outside work for you, I saw you come out and—'

'Followed me.'

I slowly slid my hand off the bar and into my lap. I was acutely aware that I didn't have my wedding ring on.

'I…'

'You're wondering why I'm here,' I said.

'I've been watching you,' he sounded a little embarrassed.

'You thought I might be meeting someone?'

'You drank three Manhattans in—'

'I just needed to decompress, after a really shitty day.'

'I'm sorry, what happened?'

'I lost a big client,' I lied. 'I got looked over for a promotion and I get paid way less than the men doing a worse job than I do.' I laid it on thick, trying to take his mind off how suspicious this looked. And I was worried that he'd already seen that I wasn't wearing my ring.

'I thought I'd meet you and take you out, you know, like I used to. Early Valentine's dinner, partly me being romantic and also that everywhere's booked up on the actual night and I forgot and—'

'That's lovely.' I leaned forward and I kissed him – a peck on the cheek – though I knew it was just to shut him up. I felt guilty enough, without having him play the ideal husband. 'But I just want to go home, I've already reached my booze limit. I'm sorry.'

'Okay, not even one?' He gave me the sad eyes, but I couldn't change my mind.

'No. I'm sorry,' I told him coldly.

We walked in silence to the tube station; it was already cold with little spits of rain in the air. I kept my hands in my pockets, keeping my lack of ring covered. I didn't have my train pass, instead I used cash to buy a ticket – I don't know if he realised that was odd. He didn't say anything.

We were quiet on the train, and on the walk back home. I think maybe he was scared. He knew I was lying – at least I thought he did. My stomach churned all the way home. When we got there I asked him to order a pizza and open a bottle of wine. While he did that I sneaked into the cupboard under the stairs and sent a text to the man I was meant to be meeting, saying I'd be an hour late.

An hour late – *fuck* – I know, I should have left it; I sounded desperate and deranged, but I had to meet him. I had to.

When I got back to the kitchen, I found that Ben had cut his hand opening the wine, a nasty gash, which just showed how nervous he was. We cleaned it up and I put a dab of antiseptic on it. He wanted to put a plaster on it, but I said not to, that he should let the air get to it. Then I poured us both a large glass of wine – and that was when I put it into his drink. Rohypnol.

I hadn't meant to use it again – that was never the plan, it was just a back-up for an emergency, but that was what this felt like. I simply *had* to get out of the house and Ben wanted to talk; and I knew he would talk and talk and talk… so I used the drug. I had to.

He drank the wine quickly, while I just sipped mine, as I was already over my limit. He was nervous – I'd seen his eyes flick to my hand a couple of times and I knew he'd seen that I wasn't wearing my wedding ring – so, I said it wasn't talk we needed but love. I told him I wanted to make love to him, right that minute. He looked a little confused, but so very happy. I hadn't seen such a big smile on his face in a long time.

I took him to the bedroom and we undressed, but the drug was already taking effect. He dropped his clothes, right where he was, already swaying a little. He tried to kiss me, but almost head-butted me in the mouth, then he collapsed. I just managed to push him a little so he fell on the bed.

I left him there. I rolled up his suit and shoved it in the bottom of the wardrobe. I changed into my dress, got some more cash, grabbed my burner phone, and headed out. I still had the Rohypnol. I was going to throw it away… I swear I was… I knew this was the last time. The last time I'd drug my husband, and the last time I'd meet a man for sex. The last time, I swore it.

Then I headed out to the Lampton Hotel.

I step up onto the bridge, into a cold wind that slices at my cheeks. I'm lost, like I'm at a crossroads, but I can't read the signs. I'm still shaking from the violence. It's like I'm a kid again, when I was scared of everything: the dark, the woods, bugs and creepy crawlies; I was petrified of dogs and just about every other wild animal. I had nightmares about the tooth fairy and even Father Christmas, but then Santa had tried to kill me when I was five, so I knew not to trust him.

There was an old guy, everyone knew him where we lived; he was big – huge to a little kid – and had a long white beard and crazy white hair. He cycled everywhere and wore shorts and a big green hat, whatever the weather. My mum thought he lived in a hostel for unfortunate adults with learning difficulties, and that he had no family. She said he was harmless, even though he used to stand in the street and howl sometimes. Mum said we should all feel sorry for him. So, on one cold December day when we saw him, and I had a plate of mince pies that we were taking someplace, I ran up to offer him one. I must have spooked him – probably he didn't hear me until I pushed the plate right in his face – but he went berserk. He was screaming, his spit covered me like he was rabid. He grabbed me, lifted me up and punched me. I was crying and screaming and he hit me again, then shook me like a doll, and threw me down. He broke my collarbone, my cheek and a rib. I wet myself. Mum screamed, someone called the police and he ran… His face was inhuman that day, his eyes burned… just like Alex's tonight. Violence… extreme anger; it freaks me out. Christ, I can't stop shaking and it isn't the cold…

I feel like I did that day Santa tried to kill me. At least I haven't wet myself. Not yet, anyway.

–

I turn right, onto Putney Bridge and start to walk. Head forward, I go… I want to get away from Mia. She's toxic. Tonight has poisoned us – our marriage is over. I can't trust her; I will never trust her again. It doesn't matter that I love her, and that my heart aches for her – I can't see her again. She drugged me, and she isn't even sorry about it. She doesn't care about me; tonight she just used me… *Christ*, that thought is like a knife in my guts, twisting and turning in my belly. She just uses people – even the pervert twins; she basically used them too. Our marriage is done.

'*Jesus Christ…*' I mutter but it isn't a prayer. I don't believe. Maybe once upon a time I did but not now, not for a while. Certainly not since we lost Rosie and— *oh god*, just thinking about my daughter makes me double over, as my stomach cramps. Since she died everything has broken apart. My friends have fallen by the wayside, my work is insular, I'm on my own most of the time. Rosie is gone and I just lost Mia. I was a husband. I was a cartoonist. I was a satirist and writer… and most of all, best of all, I was a father. Now I'm nothing. A big, fat, nothing.

Across from where I stand there's a Premier Inn. I could just go inside and lie down; that would be wonderful, to sleep in crisp white sheets, to wake up to coffee and a croissant. Bliss – but I can't do it. It's too close to the crime scene and – this makes me want to laugh – I have no credit card and no cash, not a penny. Mia has all the cash we had, and I'm not going back to ask her for money. I won't ask her for anything ever again.

All I can do is walk home. It will take hours, but maybe that's good. A long walk in this cold wind will give me the time to think. I look up to the sky; it's a blue-black, inky colour, and I search the heavens for stars to wish on; but there's nothing. Clouds crowd out the heavens.

From behind me there's a sudden sound, like a whirring, and I spin round to see a shadow—

'Hey!' I drop and crouch, holding my hands up in front of my face to protect it from a fist, or a bottle, but the shadow isn't someone come to hurt me; it's just a milk float passing by. Its electric battery whirrs, and the bottles clink together in a kind of John Cage tribute band. The driver looks at me, as I squat like a mutant crab on the side of the road.

'You okay?' he calls out.

'Fine, I'm okay, thanks for asking,' I call back, extra politely, so he knows I'm not some circus freak.

'Okay then,' and he drives off, probably thinking I'm high on something. I watch him go. It's strange; I haven't seen a milk float in ages – probably thirty years or more – not since I was a kid and did the early shift on my newspaper round. I thought glass bottles were a thing of the past too; that everyone got plastic nowadays so we could kill some more turtles, but here we are, there's an actual milkman. I thought everything from my childhood was gone and—

Hell. I haven't got my hood up and I'm walking in the middle of the street like I don't have a care in the world. I'm even doing weird dances that get me noticed by milkmen. *Damn*, I'm so bloody careless. When the body's found, the police will look through the CCTV on the bridge and... I feel sick. This whole thing just keeps spiralling and it won't ever end.

I pull up my hood and hunch over, hiding like a criminal – except it isn't *like* I'm a criminal, I *am* a criminal. I just watched my wife murder a man, and I didn't even try and stop her... *Christ*... I actually helped her. I'm as much to blame as she is.

I cross the bridge and walk up Putney High Street. It's a depressing sight, as in front of most of the boarded-up shops there are sleeping bags and pillows where men and women – even kids – are sleeping rough. There isn't a high street in England now that doesn't have the homeless in every nook and cranny. What a fucking world. And here isn't even as bad as some places in London, Putney is still pretty affluent, but nowhere has escaped the recession and depression. There's a foodbank up here, and a church that has a soup kitchen four nights a week, and I've said a million times that I should volunteer there, but I haven't. I will now. I must. I have penance to do. *Jesus Christ*, I could work in a leper colony for the rest of my life, and I wouldn't pay back this one single night.

I get to the top of the high street, with the hill up to Putney Common in front of me, and I suddenly feel so dog-tired that I need to sit down. The train station is on my left and I go and sit down on the steps outside. Nothing's open yet, but it can't be long before the milk train goes through – that first of the day – and then the paper shop will open and then the bakery, and the day will start. Wow, when was the last time I stayed up all night? It has to be years, before Rosie was born. I really can't do this anymore, no wonder I feel nauseous and everything aches. I swing the bag off my shoulder and feel it thud into my leg and I go cold inside.

The laptop… The bloody laptop; I'm dragging around evidence of a sexual assault that led to the accidental death of a young man. I'm an idiot, it could land us both in prison. I should destroy it. Right now, I should delete the videos and smash the computer. And I will. But first… *oh god*…

I have to see it. I have to see what happened.

I take the computer out of the bag and open it. The video software's still running; I find the big file from the video camera hidden in the wardrobe, and I hit *play*. My mouth is so dry; I wish I had some water. But I have nothing.

I fast forward through ten minutes of blank screen. The camera was clearly turned on for quite a while before Mia and Theo arrived. I keep pushing fast forward until the door opens, and in they walk. Mia's in that dress, the one I saw earlier, so bright and sexy. She looks amazing, and he's so handsome and moves like a dancer; fluid and confidant. I feel guilty watching them at first but then I see there's no touching or kissing between them; it looks formal. A few words are said and then Mia walks to the desk, pulls out the chair and begins to undress, folding each item carefully on the seat. There's no erotic charge here; it's more like she's at a doctor's surgery, getting ready for her gynaecologist. The only clue that this is different is her underwear, it's so skimpy and silky, seductive, and yet she doesn't pose for him; he barely seems to notice it. She takes it off and lays it with the rest of her clothes. This doesn't feel anything like lust or desire; more like a business transaction. I don't understand. And in the cold of the squalid little room, Mia shivers. Naked, she looks thin and pale. Around her eyes the mascara has smudged, and she looks like she's been crying. This isn't sexy. It isn't sexy at all.

Theo says something and I see my wife blush a little. I could turn the sound on but I don't want to. I don't want to hear them; that would be so much worse. He undresses, but doesn't bother to fold his clothes. Instead, they drop to the floor where he stands. His body is impressive and his penis, even semi erect is… well, it's significantly bigger than mine. In all dimensions.

I can see the tattoo on his chest – I already knew that was there – but I hadn't seen his back, where, spreading from his shoulder blades are wings, like he's an angel. *Christ.* Suddenly he grabs Mia and pulls her to him, their bodies entwining and his penis nudging into her belly. He goes to kiss her, but she won't meet his mouth – is she going to push him away, is this where he rapes her? But instead, he kisses her neck and licks down her throat and she grabs his cock.

I close my eyes.

I don't want to watch, but I have to see what happens – it's like being a kid again, and watching the scary stuff through my fingers while I hide behind the sofa. I used to love making my wife come, licking her, touching her, making her shudder and shake with pleasure until…

I look away from the screen. I can't watch. Not now – I don't want to be reminded of what I can't give her. I close my eyes and try to remember when we were all we both needed. I recall going down on her in an old Wendy house in a friend's garden, and on a picnic in the New Forest. We made love on a boat, over the hood of a car, on a scree slope in the Lake District, in the warm rain, on the balcony of a hotel and…

I open my eyes and she lies alone on the bed, sobbing… Theo is nowhere to be seen. He's dead.

Mia

Fuck. Fuck. Fuck.

Why did he say that? Why the hell did Ben put that thought in my head? *Damn him.* Why did he say anything about the website guy, or the accountant, or any other lowlife Alex knows? Why did he say that any one of them could keep the site going, find the unpublished films and use them?

Hell, I'm shaking. Could that really happen? I should have got all this information out of Alex but… oh god. What if I killed him for nothing? What if I actually made all this worse? I want to scream, to cry and punch and kick and… *fuck.* I need to think. Put away all the anger and fear, stop worrying about Ben and— *please god, I must stop thinking about Rosie.*

But I can't, she's crowding out everything else. I just wish she were here. Everything that's gone wrong has been since we lost her – we weren't perfect before she died, but we were still a family and we loved each other. Thinking about her is torture tonight, I have to put her aside for a while – *I'm sorry, darling* – and concentrate on my next steps, because at some point in the next few hours, probably when the tide's low, the police will find Alex's body. How quickly will they identify him? *Fuck –* I pat my hoody pocket; I have his wallet, I have his phone and his car keys. There's nothing left on the body to ID him with. So what else?

Fingerprints. They probably have him on file – but what happens to fingerprints if they're in the water for

200

hours? Even in the bath they go all pruney after ten minutes, so can they use the fingerprints of a drowned man? Do I have days, or only hours, before they know it's him? Do I have time to find the computers and servers they use to store the films on, and smash them up? Do I? Or am I out of time, and out of luck; am I going to end up in prison after all?

Ben

I watch her, on the screen. She's curled into herself. I can see the bruises on her throat starting to come out, not as vivid on her white skin as when I first saw her tonight but... *oh Mia*. The sight of her shaking, as she sobs on the bed, cuts into me and makes my whole body burn. It's too painful to watch. It takes me right back to when Rosie died – when Mia collapsed in the airport. She saw my face, she knew what I was going to tell her and she fell. Crunched into the ground. But at least she had me that day. She wasn't alone.

Like a coward, I stop the film. I screw my eyes closed, trying *not* to replay the scene I just saw in my mind – but it is too powerful. Mia sobs as the purple bruising on her throat darkens and takes shape, becomes more livid. Her face distorts in anger and shame and frustration and loss, as he forces himself on her... in her... *oh god*. All night I have been against her. Not fighting for her, but hindering her. I was there because I loved her, not because I believed in her. I was there from habit and duty. I've tried to run away all night, desperate for this to end, but for my sake, not for hers. I have staggered through the last five hours without really thinking about what she's gone through, and how this kind of trauma affects someone. This attack

– this bastard forcing himself on her – this kind of abuse changes a person. She's potentially got PTSD from tonight – like she's fought in a war, and in a war, all the rules of normal life go out of the window. I am amazed by how strong she is, that she keeps going, keeps fighting. I have to follow her example. I need to be strong too.

I look back at the screen and press play... then I turn the sound up a little and... *oh my god*, her sobs wrack her body; they come from so deep and they make the bed shake. I stop the film again; my hands are shaking. Then I drag the curser back along the timeline, maybe five minutes, and, after a big breath, I press play. But I turn the sound off again, so the film is silent. He thrusts into her; she is underneath him, her eyes closed tight. He says something to her and... there is an explosion. Mia's face turns to pain, and then a furious anger. She starts to hit out at him but he laughs and holds her down. A hand snakes around her throat, digging into the flesh, and I can see the fear in her face as she thrashes like a fish, fighting for air; but his hand tightens and her struggling starts to die away as her eyes roll back in her head. Her movements are fading... He's killing her. He's *killing* her.

Then, with the last push of energy she has, she somehow manages to lift her leg and slide her foot onto his chest, and with the last ounce of life, she kicks. His hands snap apart and he falls back out of frame... He's gone.

On the bed, Mia curls into herself and begins to weep. I stop the film.

It isn't quite what I thought it would be. At first she seems to be participating in the sex, but barely there. She's not looking at him and doesn't seem to be enjoying it; she seems distanced from it... but then something happens.

He says something and she turns wild, yelling at him and punching him. She wants him off her; she wants the sex to end. But I don't know what happened, what changed the situation? I don't understand why she lashed out at him and the way he responded… *Christ*, he's like an animal, overpowering her. He was raping her, I can see that; she was not in any way consenting, she was fighting him off; but what happened? I pull the curser back and put the sound on. I have to watch it again. I don't want to, but I must. *Play*.

He is grunting and moaning, but she's quiet, then he yells, 'I'm going to come – where do you want it?'

'Inside me, please, put a baby in me, give me a baby.'

He stops thrusting at that, and laughs. 'I can't give you a baby. That's my brother does that – I fire blanks, I'm just for fun. I'm gonna pull out and shoot over your sweet—'

'*No!*' Mia shrieks and her hand flashes out to hit him in the face. It's so hard it leaves a red mark.

'What the fuck?' He looks shocked, and then his eyes burn and one hand grabs at her wrist and the other digs into her throat. 'You like it rough at the end, don't you?'

'Get off me,' she spits in his face, as his hand digs into her throat and steals her voice away.

'No way, bitch, we're not stopping this ride. Daddy isn't done.'

'Get off me, get off me, *get off me*!' She screams and thrashes, but she can't stop him from forcing himself back inside her and—

I stop the film. My stomach is churning. It doesn't matter if the film proves Mia killed him in self-defence or not, I don't care anymore because now I know that she lied to me – but more than that, I know *why* she lied. I know why she drugged me. I know why she seems so far away, and why she would risk everything to meet this man in a sleazy hotel.

She wants to be pregnant. She wants a baby. She wants to replace Rosie... but she doesn't want a baby with me.

'Ben,' a voice calls to me.

Mia

I call from the car and he looks up at me. 'Please get in.' I lean across the seat and push the passenger door of Alex's car open. 'There isn't much time.'

He doesn't move. He looks pale and shocked.

'Please,' I yell. I don't know what he'll do or say. I won't be surprised if he doesn't want to come but I hope he will. I really hope so.

'This is the last...' I try to persuade him to come, but my words dry up, as I see what he's been doing. He has the laptop open and... *oh god* – I see it in his eyes – he's watched the film and he knows. He knows what happened... what really happened. He knows everything.

The lights change, and a part of me wants to slam down on the accelerator and peel away. But I can't. I mustn't. Time to face the music, as he gets up and walks towards me.

'This Alex's car?' he asks, as he slides into the passenger seat.

'Yeah, it's the downside of modern car keys. If you murder the owner and steal their keys, you can just walk around pressing them, until their car lights up like a Christmas tree.'

'Huh,' he sighs. I see he has the Adidas bag over his shoulder, but he still cradles the laptop in his arms. I look at the dashboard; it's almost five a.m. Less than six hours since it happened.

'Are we going home?' he asks.

'I wish,' I say as I ease the brake off and drive.

'So where are we going?'

My hands are white, where I'm gripping the steering wheel so hard. I don't answer his question; instead, I ask my own. 'You watched the film, didn't you? From tonight, Theo and me?'

'A baby,' he says, though I barely hear him above the engine. I'm not sure if it's a question or an accusation.

'What were you going to do if you got pregnant?' he asks, and I say nothing. I just look ahead, out of the windscreen. 'Would you have pretended it was mine? Would we have had a one-night reconciliation and a miracle conception?'

I stare ahead. I can feel my jaw tighten, but I say nothing.

'Or... or...' And I hear the angst and pain in his voice even more than before. '...or would you have just left me, and had the baby alone?'

I can't reply. I think my answer would hit him hard, because I think that what I wanted was for everything to change. I wanted to detonate my life. I always knew deep down that, if I fell pregnant, I'd leave Ben. I wanted to leave, but the only way I could do that was to break our marriage, blow it sky high, and maybe that's what all of this is about. Doing something he could never forgive, to put our marriage out of its misery.

'I don't know,' I say, 'it's just so bloody complicated.' I chicken out of telling him the truth.

'Complicated,' he echoes me, but in his mouth the word is empty and soulless. 'You could have gone to a sperm bank.'

'Have some student wank in a cup for me?' I say. And of course I could have done that, if I was doing this all just for a baby it would have been the best thing to do. Except I wanted one last thrill of desire, I wanted to be wanted by a man – I wanted lust again. And then I wanted a new life with my beautiful child, just the two of us. I wanted everything. I'm greedy, and that's what has led me to break Ben's heart and kill two men. My greed has cost me everything tonight.

'I'm sorry, I didn't mean to hurt you,' I tell Ben.

'I understand,' he says, though I don't think he does. I don't think he could. 'But Rosie's gone... and we can't just replace her.'

'Replace— fuck you, Ben.' I almost hit a traffic island as the car slews across the road. The word *replace* makes me burn with anger, I'm not trying to do that, I just wanted... I just... I slam on the brake and we slide into the curb, hitting the pavement hard. 'You don't have the right to tell me what to do.'

He looks hurt. 'I'm not telling you what to do... Jesus, Mia... but this isn't something you can just decide to do on your own. We're both in this marriage.'

I open my mouth to tell him that I'd already decided there would be no happy-fucking-family, that he would never be a father to my baby... but I can't do it. Instead I say, 'It's my body we're talking about, I don't need your permission.'

'Of course it is, I didn't mean that, but getting pregnant... that's something we have to talk about together.'

'Were you going to give me a baby?' I see him flinch at that.

'I'd at least have talked about it.'

'Talked.' I hear the bile and resentment in my words.

'Rosie…' he mumbles next to me. And then, a little louder, 'You said you didn't want another. You were adamant about that.'

I did. I did say that. So why the fuck am I so angry with him?

-

Rosie's birth was difficult – not just the actual delivery but the pregnancy. I had pre-eclampsia, and was in hospital for six weeks, scared. Ben was there every day. He often made me lunch and brought it in a picnic basket, and sometimes for dinner he'd turn up with pizza or an Indian take-away because weeks and weeks of hospital food was more than I could stand, and even today I shudder at the memory of the watery custard and grey mince; everything had bloody mince in it. He always had a laptop with him too, loaded up with stuff to watch – comedy mostly. *Flight of the Conchords*, *Spaced* and *Seinfeld* were my favourites.

Rosie was eight weeks premature. I almost bled to death, and she was put in an incubator while I was in intensive care. Ben had to decide who he sat sentinel over… and he sat with the baby. It was the right choice; it was the choice I would have made too. He watched over her for days and days. He couldn't touch her skin, just see her through the glass of the machine that was keeping her alive. There were holes built in the sides, they slid open, and he was able to wear big gloves, and put his hand through, to feed her with a bottle.

When she was deeply asleep, and he thought he could take the risk, he would run down the six flights of stairs to find me. He'd sit with me for a few hours, and then run back, scared she'd have woken up and found herself alone.

He ran between us, though mostly sat with her that first week, while I floated in and out of consciousness. I still recall the fever dreams of my baby dying.

I was fine after about ten days, ready to go home, but the baby – we hadn't named her yet – was still in the incubator. She was there for a month. Then she had her first seizure. The first of hundreds, thousands even. And the problem was that life still went on. Even when your child needs constant care, the bills still mount up, and all around you friends and family grow older, learn more – they change and leave you behind. Friends get married and have babies – embarrassed that their children are healthy and yours isn't – and they drift away. The world still spins while you reel.

In those first months, our world shrank. It became little more than baby, and Mia and Ben. It wasn't really a choice. There was no list of pros or cons. Rosie – yes, we actually named her a week after we got her home – needed constant care, and twice-weekly trips to the hospital. And it made complete sense that Ben would be the one to stay home and care for her, because he could work from the kitchen table, or a doctor's office, or the park or anywhere. He just needed a sketchpad and a pen. So, after six months' maternity leave, I went back to the office.

And – full disclosure – I liked it. I liked the break from the constant worry; from having to check that she was still breathing every other second. Going to work also meant that I had to get dressed in the morning and take a shower. It made me feel human again, as I'm ashamed to say that my personal hygiene had taken a great knock during maternity leave. It was hard to think about doing stuff for myself when Rosie could need me at any moment. After all those months of being constantly hyperaware of being needed, I wanted to get out and, though I hate to admit it, I had to have time away from her – from *both* of them. Ben didn't have the same needs or the same hang-ups as me, and he was far better at meeting the other mums than I was. He charmed them all in the park, arranged playdates, and remembered juice and snacks and doctor's appointments.

So we switched the traditional roles around a bit, and he was the house-husband. He liked it. He loved Rosie with such a passion, and he had such patience – he could peek-a-boo for hours and hours, whereas I was done in eight minutes. So it was good that I went to work, and made the money, and he stayed home. It was good, except for when she called out in the night, and I went to her, but she still screamed for her dad and wouldn't settle until he came. Or the way that he'd carry her on his shoulders – and he did it for years, far longer than the other kids in the park – but she'd never once go on my shoulders, even though I was easily as strong as him, and I was her mother and… *Fuck*. I had so many resentments back then – but the worst thing of all was when she had a bad seizure and she would scream and scream, and I couldn't comfort her, but he could. He always could, and she would cling to him and weep because she was so scared, and it broke my heart. And hardened it. Bit by bit. I was jealous, I admit it – at least I do now, but maybe back then it was an open secret; we both knew it, but no one said anything. I was a little ashamed and he was a little guilty. But that's life, isn't it. There's always a little guilt and shame tucked inside a marriage.

–

Next to me, in the passenger seat, Ben sits up, alert again, like he's thought of something. 'You met Alex a month ago, but you didn't fall pregnant?'

'I don't really want to talk about this.'

'And last night, did you think you were meeting the same guy?'

I don't respond.

'You did, didn't you? You didn't know they were twins, that's why you didn't know about the vasectomy.'

I feel my whole face redden. 'Okay, I thought I was meeting the same man until we were in the room, then I knew he was different but not... I just wanted... *fuck*... Ben this has nothing to do with you,' I say angrily.

'It has everything to do with me.'

'It's my body. It's my choice. I wanted a baby.' I feel deep in my bones how true those words are. 'I wanted the feel of it growing inside me. I wanted it to kick me at night, make my tits hurt and my back ache. I wanted to feel something that isn't just emptiness all the fucking time. I wanted a baby.'

'Without me?' he asks with such a deep sadness.

'I'm sorry.'

Ben

Sorry. Jesus Christ, how that word burns.

'I know it's your body, of course it is, I just thought there was still an *us* to consider. I thought we were still a couple, a family.'

She doesn't reply; she just looks ahead at the road, like the word *family* is a bad smell hanging in the air between us.

'Have you got the photo?' I ask her.

'What photo?'

'It wasn't in your purse and I thought I saw it earlier. I think you had it in your bra.'

She doesn't say anything, but I know that she has it, and that it's the only thing she took from her old life when she went to meet a man who she hoped would make her pregnant.

It's a photo of the three of us. Mia's holding Rosie, who must be about five in the picture. Her head rests on my shoulder, and we all look so happy – radiant, even. It just captured that moment so perfectly. I'd been moaning that we never had pictures taken of the three of us; that it was always me taking pictures of Rosie and Mia, or Mia taking pictures of me and Rosie. So I asked our neighbour to take our picture, and she did – the perfect family portrait – I have mine on my desk at home, and Mia has hers in her purse. At least, she did until today. Now she pulls it from her bra.

'Here.' She waves it at me. 'Happy?'

I take it from her fingers and look at us, nine years ago. We look so happy. I want that back. I can see why Mia wants a baby, but what about me? Where will I be in the new family picture?

Mia

He curves away from me, looking out of the side window and holding that damn photo to his chest. I drive past a Chinese restaurant I went to with my grandmother for her seventieth birthday – what was that, twenty-five years ago? It was before I even met Ben. The food was so good; I could really eat the crap out of some dim sum right now. Rosie loved dim sum, or at least she loved the ritual of picking up the dumplings with chopsticks, and getting them into the dipping sauce, and then into her mouth – hopefully without too much collateral damage.

Thinking about Rosie is such sweet sorrow. Tears sparkle in my vision, and the light refracts and diffracts all over the place, making the windscreen look like it's shattered. I scrape my sleeve across my face and drag away the tears and the snot. I miss her so much. I am so empty inside, like I've been carved out – hollowed and mummi-fied. I look across at Ben.

'Hey,' I whisper, but there's no answer; perhaps he's asleep. 'Do you remember how the top of her head smelled when we brought her home?' I ask in a whisper. 'Do you remember how it snowed that first day, and we all wrapped up together on the sofa? Do you remember how she felt in your arms, or when she fell asleep on your chest? How long it took to get her to sleep – all that bouncing and those endless verses of "The Animals Went in Two by Two"… do you?'

'Every second,' he whispers back, but he doesn't open his eyes.

There's silence in the car as we drive through the tricky Wandsworth road layout, and out towards Battersea. It used to smell round here, it was Price's candle factory – it was disgusting – but now I don't smell anything. Have they changed the wax recipe? Maybe… I should look it up later, when I have my phone again and can Google the shit out of everything. I drive.

Ben

I look through the side window, as I'm slumped against it. There are still loads of shop fronts boarded up; it's a little

212

better than it was when the virus hit, but mostly just coffee shops and hairdressers. The stuff you can't get online. It's depressing, but still better than thinking about tonight and Mia screaming: *put a baby in me*. A baby. Jesus Christ, tonight life and death is all mixed and swirled together, like you can't have one without the other, all sweet and sour.

She drives us into a tunnel. The lights inside are like sulphur, or burning torches, the kind a mob has when they march up to Castle Frankenstein to kill the monster. I look at my hand and it's yellow. It looks dead, like a zombie hand. I turn to look at Mia and the yellow cast makes her look painfully thin and unhappy, her eyes sunk so deep in her head and— *put a baby in me*. I can't stop hearing her say that.

'Why him, I mean a man like that?' I ask.

Mia makes a snorting noise, like she's disappointed in the level of my questioning.

'Oh come on, Ben, that's the easy part. Handsome, good strong physique, and you get a certificate to prove he's clean and healthy. He gets tested weekly… you don't get that on Tinder.'

'But why—'

'I want a child… but not with you.' Her voice is as cold and hard as ice. I wince and twist away, trying to get as far from her as I can; if it wasn't for the seat belt I'd have jumped out of the car.

She hasn't forgiven me. That's why – why all this – she hasn't forgiven me for Rosie's death.

–

When Rosie was five, the magazine re-titled the strip I wrote, it was changed from 'The Kingdoms' to 'Stay-at-

Home Dad'. I say it was the magazine that forced the new title, but it was really me, as I'd spent almost a year drawing just Rosie and me. Mia had pretty much disappeared from the stories. Fans even tweeted that my real-life wife must have died, and I got sent flowers, and had a lot of offers from women who wanted to be Rosie's step-mum.

The strip had become even more popular then, and I know that Mia was a little annoyed by me killing her off, but she wasn't around, as her job was taking up so much of her life. She got promotion after promotion and was handed bigger and bigger clients. She complained a lot about how much work she had, but that just seemed to be a smokescreen. I think in private she loved the work and the increasing responsibility. I really thought that she felt like I'd got the raw end of the deal; being at home all the time, with a child who could have great days but also some truly scary bad days too. I know she felt guilty that I was home, but I was really happy. I thought I'd got the best of the deal – I didn't want the travel and the parties, the pressure and the spreadsheets. I thought Mia and I made a good team; we both played to our strengths and gave Rosie the best of both of us.

And I was content because I knew Rosie loved me and I thought Mia did too. Maybe it was a different love than Mia and I had before Rosie – it was true that the sexiness and desire for each other had receded – but I believed our friendship and the closeness of our little family was stronger than ever. And our physical closeness wasn't all gone; sometimes we'd cuddle on the sofa in front of a movie, occasionally we'd even have a date afternoon at a museum (if we could hire a sitter) or a walk in the park. I cherished those times – I know we weren't Cathy and

Heathcliff, but it was okay. We both felt content; at least I thought we did.

And then, when Rosie was nine, and Mia had just been made vice president of intellectual property defence in Europe and Asia Pacific, Rosie had her worst seizure. Mia was away, in Prague, and I rushed Rosie to the hospital. She was in intensive care and I just knew there was something really wrong this time. I felt scared, like this was it – like my darling child was walking a wire between life and death.

–

'You never forgave me.' My voice echoes in the car.

We shoot out of the tunnel, the sulphur yellow illumination replaced by the lights from shops and buildings, giving life back to our faces, and making the air sparkle. Ahead, the light turns red, and she slows the car to a stop; then turns to me.

'No,' she says as cold as ice. 'No, I didn't forgive you. I never will.'

I nod. I thought that was the case, but I've never had the courage to ask her outright. 'I understand.' And I actually do.

'You kept her from me,' she says. 'At the end you didn't let me say goodbye... you stole that, and I can't forgive or forget. That's what killed *us*.'

–

Rosie was in intensive care for twelve hours and I didn't call Mia. I just sat, like those days after she was born, when I sat alone by her incubator and waited for her little eyes to open. I could have called Mia – I should have called Mia

– but I didn't. I just waited. I didn't pray, didn't think... I just sat.

Finally the nurses let me in to Rosie's room, but it was only to hold her, talk to her, and to say goodbye. We had one last night together, my daughter and me. I got to hold her, even though I don't think that she knew I was there, but I got to tell her that I loved her. To tell her that I have never been happier than being her daddy. We had those few, precious hours – and then she died. It was about 2 a.m.

I called Mia six hours later. I told her to come home as quickly as possible, but I didn't say why, and I didn't tell her the awful truth of what had already happened. She must have been beside herself with worry, hurrying back from Prague, not knowing what she would find, and I let her sit in that fear. It was cruel and heartless of me. It was utterly selfish.

I met her at the airport, it was the opposite of that scene at the start of *Love Actually*, where everyone leaps into each other's arms, so happy to see their loved ones. Instead, Mia came through arrivals and I was there, behind the barrier, and she took one look at my face and knew. She collapsed, seemed to dissolve into the air as she fell. I ran forward, threw myself down alongside her, and hugged her to me. Together we both sobbed, there on the floor of airport arrivals, as hundreds of people disembarked from planes and had to step around us, because we didn't move for more than an hour. We just held each other and wept for our child.

–

I look ahead at the red light. 'I'm sorry,' I tell her, and even though I mean it with all my heart, I know that it's still empty and worthless.

'I don't care,' she says. 'I don't care about you, about what you feel and what you want. I'm all out of sympathy, Ben. All I know these days, is that I'm not done… I'm not done with motherhood and I'm not done with love and being a woman and I've not given up on sex.' She pauses and watches the traffic light, still waiting for it to turn green.

'I still feel like a mother – I still wake in the night and think Rosie's called out to me; I still put her favourite foods in the shopping trolley before I remember she doesn't need them anymore and… and I see her and feel her everywhere. Everywhere, Ben.'

Mia

The windscreen suddenly fractures as light breaks and buckles. I go to hit the wipers, but realise it's just tears in my eyes, not rain.

'I didn't know it was the end,' he says, just pathetically enough to make me angry.

'Liar.'

'You were away.'

'I would have come back! I would have moved heaven and earth to get back in time.'

'I didn't know it was the end.'

'Our daughter died, you got to hold her in your arms, you got to say goodbye… you had her all to yourself.'

'And you had your career, you had your urgent business trip, you had your dinners with clients and fancy spa hotels.'

'You had her.'

'Yes, I had beans on toast with our daughter after school, and I had the bloody awful recorder concert, and sports day and I got the colds and the chicken pox and the days off school after a seizure.'

'You got her. You got to watch TV with her and hold her hand and—'

'It was your choice.'

'I didn't choose to be forty-two years old and be a husbandless wife and a childless mother… I never wanted that…'

'Neither of us chose that… it wasn't a choice.'

'I miss her.'

'I know.'

'I want to be a mother again.'

'I didn't…' He pauses. 'I just didn't know you wanted another child.'

'I couldn't tell you, couldn't ask you… it's such… I worry she'd hate me, that she'd think I was replacing her.'

'No, she could never hate you, she loved you more than anything.'

I appreciate the lie – because it is a lie: I know Rosie loved me, but she also hated me for all the parties and school concerts I missed. I was AWOL for a lot of my little girl's life but I didn't know it would be cut short. I thought I had all the time in the world.

'I didn't mean to hurt you,' he says.

'I know that – I know there's not a mean bone in your body – but it still hurts. My daughter died when I was at a fancy dinner, schmoozing a table of tech CEO's, while you, dad of the century, were at her bedside.' I pause and see the pain of that memory burn through him. 'And it isn't that I'm not grateful you were there – I'd hate it even

218

more, to think she was all alone, and I know you made her comfortable and made her feel loved.' I take a deep breath. 'But I was alone, at the most important moment of my life, I was alone and I didn't even know it was importan—'

'Fucking move it,' someone screams, as a car screeches out from behind us and pulls level. 'Fucking women drivers,' he yells, as he sees me behind the wheel, and with a squeal of rubber, shoots off through the lights and away.

Ben

'Bastard!' I yell at the car, as it tears away, but Mia just laughs, then puts her foot down and drives off, as the light turns back to red and she shoots through it – speeding up, getting dangerously fast.

'Mia, that was a red light, be careful! The roads are full of CCTV cameras – you're going to be photographed by all of them going at this speed, in a dead man's car the night he's murdered. Slow down.'

There's a beat, while the information sinks in past the hurt and pain, and then she eases her foot off the accelerator, and we go back down to twenty-eight miles an hour. 'Thank you,' I tell her, feeling my heart slow a little. 'And I'm sorry.' I reach over and squeeze her hand, just for a second as she's driving.

'Me too,' she says looking straight ahead. 'I forgive you.'

And I feel tears break through and bleed down my face. I look ahead and watch the road. I wish we had talked this through four years ago, but I'm glad we have now. I feel lighter and I do understand what she's gone through – I mean, we all want love, *that* love, the uncompromising and unquestioning love of someone who adores you. I get it, I don't blame her... Actually, that is finally true. I don't blame her tonight and feel lighter than I have since Rosie died. What a night to get things off your chest.

Rosie, Ella and Theo and Alex. And of course there's Claire and Harry and Lilly... and maybe Alex had kids too... and he talked about their parents and said they were crazy about each other. They've lost both their sons in one night – how will they feel? Oh god, I wish I hadn't thought about them. Loss and grief just spirals out from this, so many lives will be touched by what has happened. How will we live with ourselves after tonight?

–

Nothing's said for a while, as Mia navigates a path through the night. I'm still not sure where we're going, though there is a part of me that's glad that we are at least going somewhere. A shop we pass has a flashing light in it, and I feel that old anger in my belly: *Don't they realise that flashing lights can bring on seizures in children?*

'Where are we going?' I finally ask, desperate to break the oppression of the brooding silence. Holding the steering wheel with one hand, Mia takes Alex's wallet from her pocket and hands it to me.

'There's a business card,' she says and I find it and read it.

'*Alex Carswell. Managing and Creative Director of studslovemums.com*. So are we heading to their office?'

'Yes.'

'What's the plan when we get there?'

'To destroy all the films, smash the computers and servers, and then burn the fucking place down.'

She says it with such relish that I pause, not knowing what to do or say. I think about the two men, Theo and Alex. 'Okay,' I say. 'Let's burn it down.' And I see the faintest flicker of a smile cross her lips.

Chapter Twelve

Ben

The address on Alex's business card is Arches Walk. It's a stretch of the old railway arches that starts under the abandoned part of Clapham Junction station, and stretches down along the tracks towards the river. We park the car and look around cautiously, but there's no CCTV. Some of the arches look like they've been converted into studio space for artists and artisans, but others are dilapidated and dark. Up ahead there's a fire burning in a brazier, and it looks like a few drunks and homeless people are scattered around it. I don't feel safe here — it smells of piss, decay, desperation and loss. It's the other side of the coin from what I normally see in the day; but this is the night realm. I look at the group standing by the fire to keep warm and I think: *there but for the grace of god*... because if a few things were to go wrong in my life, I could easily be there beside them. Really, very easily. Maybe tomorrow.

It's dark, underneath the arches. The moon seems to have gone AWOL, and the only light is a sodium yellow streetlight above us, sending shafts through the slats of wood and corrugated iron that creepily stretch above our heads. The light doesn't stretch far enough into the darkness, so the arches themselves remain pitch black.

'I wish we had a— *ugh!*' Mia hisses, and slaps her forehead, annoyed with herself. 'I've got his phone.' She pulls Alex's phone out of her hoody pocket. 'I can't open the home page without his passcode, but you don't need that for the torch.'

'His phone? Why have you got his phone? Is it still live?'

'Of course it is, and when the police use it to plot his evening, they'll have him coming here as the last thing he did. That might make them get the time of death wrong or throw them off in some way. Anything that muddies the waters helps us.'

'Jesus Christ, Mia, you've watched too many Scandi noirs.'

She shrugs and then swings the arc of the torch beam into the darkness. 'That's better.' She runs the beam over the far wall. 'But I still can't see any bloody numbers anywhere.'

'We could ask someone,' I say.

'What, one of the drunks?' She scowls at me, and swings the light up and down and across and—

'Fuck.' She kicks something in the dark and it skitters into the side of the building, making an echoing clang. I can see the guys huddled around the fire look over at us. Shit, if they turn out to be zombies I will die. Literally die.

'This is stupid,' she says and I have to agree. We've been walking up and down for the last ten minutes, and haven't found the office.

'Let's go back towards the car, see if it's closer to the older section of the station,' I suggest, and she sighs and kicks at the ground again.

'Maybe—' I start.

'Don't you dare try and be upbeat,' she cuts me dead. 'Cute, funny and hopeful are not welcome.'

'Okay, so no trying to make the situation lighter, or suggesting there might be some hope, I got it.'

She fades into the shadows. All I can see is the pale light from Alex's phone, bobbing up and down like Tinkerbell. This feels hopeless – even if we do find their office, how do we think we're going to get in? And even if we can get inside, what are we going to do? Are we seriously going to burn the place down and hope that's it – hope the films are destroyed? It all feels pretty desperate, and time is running out. The night is fading fast and Alex's body will be spotted as soon as day breaks. I suddenly have a thought. 'Sandi,' I say.

'What about her?' Mia asks.

'You said you found Alex and Theo through her?'

'Yeah.'

'She might know where their offices are.'

Mia looks dubious. 'I doubt it, but even if she did, we can't ask her. That implicates us – leaves a trail.'

'Damn,' I bite my lip; it hurts. 'Does Luke know?'

'What?'

'That his girlfriend pays men for sex?'

'I don't know, I didn't ask.'

'I like Luke. I have no idea what he sees in Sandi but whatever it is, he's a good bloke and he doesn't deserve this shit.'

'He loves her,' Mia says.

'Love?' I hear the cynicism in my voice. Love sounds like a dirty word tonight, like a prison sentence, or a sexually transmitted disease. 'He shouldn't be with her,' I say, all righteous. 'Not if she's going to act all—'

'What?'

'Slutty.'

'For fuck's sake, Ben. *Slutty* – I thought a lot better of you than that.'

'Me too, but I find I'm pretty upset when I think about my wife and her friends paying men for sex.'

'Oh come on, I bet you wouldn't be so sanctimonious about a guy paying for some teen to suck him off. It's safe and professional. It isn't swiping right and finding the closest guy that can get it up.'

I walk away from her, boiling inside. I'm angry, but also ashamed at what I said; this is far from my finest hour. Then another thought hits me, and I turn back to Mia. 'She wasn't trying to have a kid, was she?'

'God, no, can you imagine Sandi as a mother? She'd *eat* the poor little thing! No, I just don't really think she's the monogamous type. She loves Luke, in her own way, and it isn't like she's having an affair.'

'No, it's not an affair – just high energy sex with male prostitutes.' I don't think anyone could miss my sarcasm, but Mia just shakes her head sadly.

'Maybe she needs that in her life; maybe without it her life with Luke can't happen. I don't think she's unhappy with him, just bored maybe.'

'And that's better than an affair? Some wild, anonymous fucking sometimes?'

'Well, isn't it? It isn't an emotional betrayal, just a physical one.'

'Physical?' I can hardly believe what she's saying. 'Isn't any betrayal as bad as another? It can still ruin everything.'

Mia pauses in the dark; she steps towards me, and a bar of light slices across her face.

'Do you think that's true?' she asks. 'That all betrayals are equal?' She looks at me for a few seconds, before she slides back into the darkness. I don't say anything. Is Mia meeting Alex and Theo just as bad as me fooling around with Ella; is it the same betrayal? I don't know.

'Hey, it's here,' she says from the shadows, sounding very pleased with herself. 'I found it.'

As I follow her voice, I realise I don't even pause; I follow her blindly into the dark.

Mia

I almost miss the set-back alcove, but the torch beam from Alex's phone slides over a name-plate, which shines dully for a moment. I look closer and find the sign stuck to a metal shuttered door at the back of the arch: *Home of studslovemums.com*. Finally, we're at journey's end.

'Over here, come on,' I call to Ben, and hear the crunch of his footsteps as he follows my voice. I can see that there's a metal shutter, half pulled down across a locked gate, with a doorbell to one side. There's a padlock on the gate. I pull the keys I took from Alex out of my pocket and try them. The third one fits, and with a snap, the lock falls open.

'This is breaking and entering,' Ben hisses from behind me.

'First of all, I've got the key; second, there are two men dead tonight, so we're way past worrying about breaking and entering.'

'But—'

'You can stay out here, it's okay, I can handle this,' I tell him as I pull the door open. It squeals, metal on metal, like a sound effect from a cheesy Hammer horror film. I hesitate for a moment, not because of the fingernails-on-blackboard sound, but I'm afraid there's going to be a guard dog or an alarm. I hover, on the threshold, waiting for a vicious bark or an electronic scream, but there's nothing. I nervously push forward and step inside. There's a musty smell, part damp and part old sweat. I go to close the door behind me, but Ben grabs it.

'I'm coming,' he mumbles like a teen with FOMO, and pulls the gate closed behind him with a prison door clang – another classic sound effect. It makes me want to giggle, but of course, that's the adrenaline and the fear washing through me; none of this is in any way amusing.

I slide my hand along the wall, trying to find the light switch, but can't, so I turn Alex's phone torch back on, and run it across the wall. Ben goes the other way, his arms out like a zombie, and after a few seconds he clatters into something hard – '*Be careful!*' I hiss, and then there's a click, and a ball of light from a desk lamp illuminates a run-down office. The air flickers with dust from the filthy carpet tiles, each step we take makes an enormous ball of dust rise into the air; I don't think this place has ever seen a hoover, or a duster.

'Here,' Ben says and turns a switch on the wall, making ceiling lights flicker into action, though only half of them actually work. It's weird, like we've time-travelled back to 1972, into some crappy office-based sitcom set. The room's beige and dull. Wood panels line the walls but they're splintered in places, and water damage speckles them. The ceiling is made up of Styrofoam tiles that are broken and stained. Everything's covered in a nicotine sheen. It must have been new and clean once, but now it's neglected, filthy and sad.

'There's a kitchen through here,' Ben calls out, and I go over to see the tiny little room. It's beige too, and splattered with grease. There's a small sink that's crowded with mugs and plates, all looking like they should have been washed six months ago. There's a microwave on a shelf, and the little window is stained with what looks like pasta sauce, but it's so thick that it's impossible to see inside. There's a cooker that looks like it's been slimed with fat and grease. The counter top is so covered with dust it's impossible to tell what it's made from, and on it sits an electric kettle which, weirdly, looks so clean that I'd believe someone just bought it today. Next to it there's a giant wholesale-size jar of coffee, and a pile of UHT milk sachets like you get on airplanes. In front of the kettle there's a single mug that reads: *World's Best Dad*. I wonder if it's Theo's mug – did little Lilly or Harry buy it for him? I should smash it. I'd like to smash something.

Instead, I leave the sad little kitchen, and head to the flimsy partition that stretches across a part of the main room, closing off access to a smaller office that sits behind. Something tells me that's where we'll find what we're looking for.

As soon as I step inside I have to fan my face – it's so hot in here. I turn on the overhead light and it spits and crackles as the fluorescent tube warms up. Inside, there's a cheap desk and behind that, pinned to the wall, is a nude calendar – but from years ago when such things were *saucy*, like a bygone age where a woman in a mink coat flashing a nipple and some leg was seen as strong stuff. Considering the graphic porn the twins make, it seems almost quaint, up there on the wall – a kind of old-fashioned innocence. Next to it is a large picture of Alex and Theo with their arms around each other's shoulders. They look like the mirror image of each other – like some Victorian trick photography from a freak show. And behind the desk is the source of all the heat.

'This is what we're looking for,' Ben says as he follows me into the sauna of a room, and sees the wall of computer servers banked around the desk. 'This'll be where they upload everything.'

'Can you delete it all?' I ask.

'I'll try.'

'Just *try*?'

'There'll be a password and maybe even encryption. I know my way around computers but I'm no hacker.'

'Alex and Theo are too stupid to make it complicated,' I say. 'Look around the desk, it'll be written down somewhere.'

'And if it isn't?'

'Then all we can do is smash them all up, and burn the place to the ground.'

He shakes his head ruefully. 'And if there are other servers, in other places?'

'Then… I don't know, alright? I don't know.' I feel so tired. 'I just… just do what you can Ben… please.'

I walk back into the main room and feel so light-headed I think I might faint. It's so hot in—

Thunk.

'Fuck.' I freeze. I listen hard. I'm sure I heard something, a *thunk* that sends me into a funk. It sounds like footsteps but not quite; more like multiple doors are being closed, one after another. I stop breathing…

At the back of the main office, in the shadows, where two of the fluorescent tubes are broken, a door opens. Behind it, I can see a bare bulb and what looks like cement steps, heading down into a basement, or maybe it leads to another warehouse built into the arches. Framed in the doorway is a silhouette, and then a man moves into the light.

He's wiping his hands on a piece of colourful cloth. He wears an old-fashioned vest shirt and chinos held up by a belt. He's about fifty and heavy, looks like he could have been a boxer once upon a time; he's got that bulk in his arms and chest, though now it's turned to fat and he has heavy man-boobs. But even with the extra weight I know who he is; I can see them in his face – he's the father of Theo and Alex. His hair is receding a little now, but I bet it used to be full and lush like theirs, and they share the same jawline and eyes. Without doubt, he's the father of the two men I killed tonight.

He's sweating like he just ran a marathon, and all out of breath. He stops and takes an inhaler out of his pocket and squirts it into his mouth, but then he looks ahead and sees me for the first time.

'Who are you?' He wheezes, and has to take another pull on his inhaler. I look him dead in the eyes, unable to say a word.

'Who are you?' he asks again. 'I don't know you. Why are you here? I mean, it's not even morning and…' He looks confused. 'Did we have a meeting, have I forgotten something?'

I slip into my best 'high-paid solicitor who knows everything' persona. 'No, no. We don't know each other. I'm a friend – well, more like a business colleague of your sons. They asked me, well us – my husband and me – to look at something for them.' I say with a breezy smile.

'Look at something? But it's so early, what's that important?' he asks as concern creases his face.

'You know what they say about the early bird and that damn worm,' I reply with an encouraging nod. 'There's a computer problem – with the servers – and they wanted them back up ASAP. You know that time's money. You're their father, aren't you?'

'Tony,' he says and he balls up the cloth in his hands and throws it onto the desk. The delicacy of the cloth, and its vibrant patterns, had hidden the fact that his hands are like sledgehammers. 'So, who are you?'

'Mia. My name's Mia and my husband is Ben.'

'Ben?' he asks and looks around, suddenly fearful he might get jumped by a man from the shadows.

'No, Tony, it's okay, we aren't here to do any harm or hurt anyone. Ben, can you come out here?' I call back into the office and Ben slowly steps out. Tony looks at him hard.

'What were you doing back there?' Tony asks Ben, who looks guilty. I wish Ben were a better actor.

'Ben's looking at the servers… I'm a lawyer and they asked me for some advice.'

'Legal advice?'

'Yes.'

Tony frowns. 'I'm gonna call Alex.' He pulls his mobile from his pocket and starts to dial.

'No,' I say sternly and he stops, at least for a second, but what am I going to say to stop him calling Alex? I need to get to the heart of this quickly. 'Do you know what they do Tony?' I ask, my voice now cold. 'What your sons do in the hotel room in Earl's Court. Do you know?'

That jolts him. His eye twitches involuntarily, I can see goosebumps prickle across his arms, and his lower lip wobbles a little, like a jelly. He knows what his sons do.

'They're good boys,' he says.

'Good?' I ask him, feeling the hackles on the back of my neck rise.

'Yes, good and kind – to their late mum and me.' He nods earnestly as he talks about his sons. I can see his genuine love for them. It annoys me.

'That's a very slim definition of good and kind,' I say.

'It's not been easy,' he whines a little.

'Are you making excuses for them?' I ask.

'No, no, I ain't, but it feels like there's something you want to accuse my boys of but you don't have the guts to say it outright.' He straightens up and looks me directly in the eye. I hold his gaze, unblinking.

'Your sons have sex with older women.'

'That ain't against the law.' He snaps, his cheeks flushing a little with anger.

I pause; he looks more like Alex now, with his face set and stern. 'The women pay them for sex.' I say, my voice level and clear. I don't want to let anger blunt my argument.

He looks down at the floor. 'That ain't right, they don't do that.'

'And they film the women.'

'No.' His head snaps up. His nostrils flare like a bull about to charge.

'And the women are abused—'

'You get out, this is nothing but—'

'Theo raped my wife.' Ben slams his hand on the desk, forcing both of us to turn to him.

'No,' Tony shakes his head hard, screwing his face up. 'He wouldn't have done that, not my Theo.' He glares at me, his eyes getting red and puffy. He wants me to take back the accusation. I look at Ben; I'm angry that he's gone straight for the jugular, but there's no putting the genie back in the bottle now, and I'm damned to hell if I try and appease this man who raised two rapists.

'I'm sorry to tell you this, but your son forced me—'

'No, *no*! You take that back. He didn't do nothing bad. Maybe you got caught doing something you shouldn't have been. Maybe you lied to your husband to get out of a hole. I don't know, but I do know my son never raped you. He never raped no one, never hurt no one. Not my Theo. Not him.'

'He filmed me – filmed him and me having sex – without my consent, without my knowledge.'

'That ain't rape.'

'It's a violation.'

'It ain't rape. It ain't nice – ain't good manners – but it ain't rape.' He looks pleased with himself, relieved that he's rebutted the attack on his son.

'I think the courts will decide on that,' I say and he looks daggers at me, but I can see he's scared underneath. 'The filming is one thing against your sons; a lot of women were abused and cheated by them. But the rape is real. Tonight, Theo met me at a hotel and we started to have sex, but I asked him to stop... He refused and I tried to push him away and...' I see the man's head droop a little. '...he wouldn't stop.'

'He... he's a good kid. He was so good with his mother when she was ill, so good.'

'But you know what he can be like.'

Tony's eyes flash as he looks up at me. 'Women have always thrown themselves at him – I bet you did – because he's so handsome. He can have anyone he wants, celebrities and all, so why would he go with an old—' Tony stops and looks ashamed. 'I... I'm sorry,' he stutters. 'That was rude. I didn't mean that.'

'It's okay. I'm sure he could get a lot of women. Beautiful young women,' I say, and look down at my formless, drab clothing. I have cried so many times tonight that I bet I look like shit. Tony knows how good-looking his sons are, and I agree. What would either of those men want with an old woman like me?

'So, where is he, my Theo?' Tony asks, looking down at his feet. 'His wife called a couple of times, she'd expected him home. I told her not to worry and just go to bed… I thought he was with someone but…' The older man looks up. He's scared for his son. 'Where is he? He's alright, isn't he?'

'He…' I start but I'm not sure what to say, then Ben barges in.

'A friend of ours is with him – babysitting him, if you like,' Ben says.

'You ain't hurt him?' Tony looks scared, he's starting to sweat.

'No, but he isn't very forthcoming with information. We'll let him go, Tony, if we get what we want. Otherwise we'll turn him over to the police.'

'What do you mean? What do you want? Money? I've got a little, but it's not much.'

'We don't want money,' I tell him, but he just looks confused. 'I want the film destroyed. The one of me.'

'I don't understand.'

'Your sons film women and put them on the internet, it's their business, and I bet they make good money from it. But it ruins people's lives. You know that, don't you?'

Tony looks down, ashamed. 'It's not got anything to do with me; the boys run it together. I don't get all this new technology.'

'But you know what they do. Your boys make and sell pornography.'

Tony turns red, even his ears, and beads of sweat run down his forehead. 'It don't do no harm.'

'It does a lot of harm. I could lose my job, I might have lost my husband tonight – it could kill my dad.'

I see tears join the sweat to roll down his cheeks. 'I'm a lawyer Tony – I wasn't lying about that.'

'It ain't illegal,' he says gruffly, not making eye contact.

'Of course it is: these women don't give consent. Your sons would get ten years minimum, and a high security prison too – this isn't tax avoidance or fraud; they'd do hard time.'

'I love my sons, no matter what they've done.'

'I don't—'

'His wife, Claire, she's a good kid, she don't know what he does.'

'But you do, Tony, don't you? You know about the films.'

'They all wanted it, some of 'em even paid to be with them and on the site. They wanted it,' he says, looking from Ben to me, and back again.

'Is that what your boys told you?' I ask, and Tony shifts uncomfortably. He won't meet my gaze.

'They weren't ever disrespectful – neither of 'em. I taught them better than that.' Tony insists, and I almost laugh.

'I think forcing yourself on a woman is pretty fucking disrespectful.' I see him wince at my use of the word *fucking*. I feel sorry for him; he probably did try and teach them to be better than this, but he failed. A pity for everybody.

'Are you two parents?' Tony asks.

'No,' I say as Ben says 'Yes'. Tony looks confused.

'We lost her,' Ben tells him, father to father. 'She was nine, almost ten. It was four years ago.'

Tony looks genuinely pained by that. 'I'm sorry, that's hard. I know how I'd feel if I lost one of my boys.'

Next to me I feel Ben's entire body clench, and I know he's thinking about how Tony will soon learn that both his sons are dead. I know Ben wants to tell him; that he thinks that will help, but we can't do that until we've destroyed everything here. I don't care that this poor man has lost all he loves. I can't – there's too much at stake. I know how that sounds, how selfish I am. But I won't stop until everything is safe for us. No, that's a lie – until everything is safe for *me*.

'Tony, I have a mum and dad and friends and a job,' I tell him as I try to engage his compassion. 'All of that could be destroyed, by your sons putting a film of me up onto the internet.'

'I don't know anything about any of that.'

'Don't you?' Ben asks incredulously. 'Because the films that are on the internet, they're stored on machines inside that office.' And he points through the door into the hot, cramped room, just a few feet away.

'No... no, this is their place, I hardly come here.'

'So why are you here now?'

'I...' There's a beat – just for a second – and then he replies. 'The call from Claire, about Theo. I told her not to worry, but I was a bit concerned; he hardly ever goes AWOL like this. I decided I'd come over and see if he'd pulled an all-nighter. I just live on the other side of the tracks. I got a key that opens the garage, that's what's through there.' He points back to the door he came through.

'The computer's got a password,' Ben says. 'I need it to delete the film of my wife.'

'Just her one?' Tony asks.

'And one other,' Ben tells him, thinking about Sandi.

'Was she raped too?'

'No,' Ben admits.

'Then I don't see why her film is a problem.' Tony stands as tall as he can.

'You're right,' I say. 'Our friend probably even paid for the attentions of your sons. I think she had a great time – I think she loved them fucking her.' I see him wince at *fucking* again. 'I think she would fuck them again.' Another wince. 'But she had no idea they were filming her; she had no idea it would go online and millions of desperate and nasty men would masturbate over her, in back bedrooms and offices and seedy hotel rooms. She had no idea the people she loved could see her at her most intimate. She had no choice.'

'That's wrong, it's bad, I know that – but not prison bad.'

'You're fooling yourself, Tony. Your sons didn't get consent from any of those women – and that's rape. In my world that is rape.'

'No.'

'Yes. So it's not just my film; I want to erase every single fucking film on these computers, and if I don't get them all down, then your sons will both go to prison.'

'Are you threatening me?' Tony curls his hands into fists and his jaw hardens into steel.

'Your sons will go to prison. That's no threat, that's a fact,' I say with as much venom as I have. He looks into my eyes, and for a second he's just like Alex – a wolf – and then the fire starts to die and his mouth twitches, like he's desperate to stop his face crumbling.

'They aren't bad kids...' he says. 'They were so caring when they were younger, and when their mum was ill they looked after her. I was useless. I couldn't cook or clean... but they learned... they nursed her. They're good, kind... but no one ever said no to them, including me. They always got what they wanted, and girls have always thrown themselves at 'em – it turned their heads. It's a curse to be that handsome.'

'I'm sorry, Tony,' I tell him, even though I think his sons were devils.

'What's the password, Tony?' Ben asks with a mateyness that's quite impressive. Maybe his acting is better than I thought. 'Tell me, and all this can end, and Theo can come home.'

Tony's lost for a few moments in his own head, in memories of the boys when they were younger – sweet young cherubs – before they got tall and handsome, the hormones kicked in and easy sex turned their heads. 'I don't know their passwords,' he says low and slow.

'Shit,' I hiss, showing my annoyance and frustration, but Ben is calm and asks.

'What about their phone, or Netflix – have they got something they often use for things like that? Lucky numbers or a name they love?'

'I...' Tony reddens and looks away. He's not a good poker player; even I can see he knows something.

'What is it, Tony?' Ben asks. 'Is there something they often use?'

'I don't... I don't know exactly... I mean, I really don't know nothing about computers, but on something like the Sky box, they use their mum's name.'

'And what's that?' I ask, but I'm too quick and desperate. I sound like the Child Catcher and Tony draws away, instinctively feeling he shouldn't tell me.

'I don't… I should call Alex. He can come here and do it, clear the computer or whatever. He loves his brother and he'll be really sorry about all this. He might not even know about the…' He can't say *rape*. 'He'll do the right thing, they both will, if we get a chance to talk it through. If you let me talk to them I can sort this. They aren't bad boys. They aren't.'

Next to me, I hear the air catch in Ben's throat and I turn to see a tear start to well. He feels sorry for the old man – put into such an awful position, where he has to choose between his sons and what's right. I can see that Ben's wavering. He likes Tony too much, feels sorry for him. And I do too – but not enough to lose my life over. Has Ben forgotten that he can't talk to his sons? Not without a fucking ouija board.

'No,' I say, cold and hard as I can. 'No more stalling on this. Tell us the password. *Now*.'

Tony looks upset, and turns to Ben for help. 'But the boys will know what to do, I'll just…' and before I can do anything, there's a phone in his hand and he's hit a one-touch speed dial.

There is a moment of calm when nothing happens, and everyone's eyes are glued to the phone in Tony's hand. I don't breathe… and then a ringtone blares out and my heart shrivels in my chest.

Tony seems surprised for a moment. He turns towards the door, a look of expectation on his face. He thinks his son is walking through the door right this second. He thinks it's an amazing coincidence. But it doesn't open.

Instead, confusion creases his face, until he realises that the phone is ringing from inside the room.

He looks at Ben first, who gives his fellow dad a half-shrug. And then he looks to me, and I see a coldness creep through him as he realises the phone is ringing from the pocket of my hoody.

'Turn it off,' I tell him.

'But that's...' He looks at the phone in his hand, and then back to me as I see both confusion and fear on his face. I take the phone from my pocket and turn it off.

'That's my Alex's phone,' Tony says slowly. 'I don't understand... Why do you have it?' He takes a step towards me. I step back – he may have gone to seed but his arms still look like they could do me a lot of damage.

'What have you done to my Alex?' Tony's moment of confusion turns to a cold, steely anger.

'Your son is fine, Tony. What's the password? What was your wife's name?' I say, trying to keep the man calm and get the information we need to get out of here.

'Where's Alex?' he yells.

'Your wife's name?' Ben repeats. 'What is it, Tony?' and he steps between the deranged father and me.

'Where is my son?' He drops his head slightly like a bull about to charge, and rounds his shoulders so the now tightly wound fists rise in the air.

'We politely asked both Theo and Alex to take the films down and they said no, so they're both being held—'

With incredible speed, Tony's right arm shoots out, as he jumps forward, but he doesn't punch Ben; instead, his hand grips around his throat. 'I said, *where are my sons?*' and he squeezes hard.

'Leave him alone,' I scream as Tony forces Ben down onto his knees. I can see the fingers dig into his neck and already Ben's fighting for breath.

'I will crush your husband's windpipe. I will squeeze until his eyes pop out of their sockets, now tell me where my boys are?'

I'm stuck, paralysed. I watch Ben's face turn ashen and then purple. Tony pushes down more and his left hand joins the right to choke the life out of Ben, who starts to thrash like a fish pulled from the ocean and dropped onto a wooden deck.

He looks like Rosie in the midst of a seizure – my poor, poor baby – and I could let Tony kill him. I could, as I stand here watching them both. I could let him squeeze the life out of Ben. I wouldn't grieve, not really. I don't think there's any grief left in me – losing Rosie used it all up. I loved Ben, but now I have no idea what love is. Maybe that was what I wanted from a baby – but that won't happen. Not now. It's not fair to bring a child into the world when you're a murderer. Two-time murderer – let's keep the facts straight – and if I let Tony choke Ben to death, that's like three deaths on my conscience.

Three dead because of me... and as I think that, Ben's eyes bulge in his head. I just watch... I don't move to stop Tony choking the life out of him; instead I feel a kind of excitement, a kind of sense of justice.

'Meee...' Ben gasps with his last breath and the eyes roll back in his head. His arms stop shaking and he flops like a scarecrow. Dead.

Chapter Thirteen

05.30 a.m.

Ben

'Meee... ahhhhhhhhhhhhhh...'
  Synapses flare –
  image of Rosie in the park
  my best friend Steven eating a sandwich at playtime
  Mia in bath
  shudder of legs
  light
  dark

Mia

I'm a widow... a widow...

But what will that mean? Because at this moment I'm just numb. I don't feel anything, but is that it? Is the cold in my heart all I have to look forward to from this moment on? Or will I thaw, and will the remorse and grief come flooding back and engulf me, because I loved him for so many years, and with all my heart. When I go back and look at photographs of *us* will I miss him? Will I re-read 'The Kingdoms' and laugh and cry and say what an amazing man he was, what a great husband, what a kind person? Or will I always remember that he let my daughter die, that he kept me from being there? Will I always remember the faults, the *what-he-didn't-do's* and the *he-shouldn't-have-done-that* stuff... will Ella be a toxic cloud over my head forever?

Will I even think of him at all?

Tony releases his hold on Ben's throat, the violence and anger starting to dissolve in him. Ben's body collapses, lying still. His shirt's all rucked up from thrashing about, and I can see his tummy and belly button. He doesn't look peaceful. On the desk there's a paperweight – it's actually a ten-pin bowling trophy – it says 'Surrey Champion 1987'. The base is a heavy marble plinth, with a metal bowler on the top. I grip it, and swing with all my might. It catches Tony on the back of the head, just above where the neck joins. As the marble base hits his head, there is a pretty sickening crunch, and the stone section shears off the trophy and flies into the wall, leaving a dent and a bloody mark there. Tony topples forward, blood pulsing from his head, and for a second I am back with Theo, in that room, watching the blood pump out, spilling like a lake across the floor. Tony doesn't move.

I kneel down, to inspect my work. The wound isn't as bad as Theo's. There's blood, but he won't bleed to death... I think. I mean I'm pretty sure of that, but he should be out of it for some time yet.

I look down at the two unconscious men. Tony's blood is smeared across Ben; it makes him look like he's run through a slaughterhouse. Blood vessels have burst in Ben's eyes and it looks like he's crying tears of blood as his final act of remorse. Seeing him like that makes my heart break.

'Oh my god, Ben, I didn't mean... I just...' I drop down onto my knees, just by his chest, but I freeze. When

Rosie had a seizure, I couldn't hold her while she shook and moaned – it was always Ben who held her. What do I do? I put my hands on his chest. Isn't it chest compressions to 'Staying Alive', but what are the fucking words? I can't remember. I can't even recall the fucking tune. I hate disco. *Fuck*.

I push and push and push and then breathe into his mouth. Push and push and push and breathe. *Come on*. I'd give him my life, I would. I really would. *Stay alive*, I beg and pray to whatever is out there. *Please stay alive*. My tears roll into Ben's mouth as I compress again: Chest – chest – chest – breathe. Chest – chest… come on Ben – I can't be alo—

'Arrrrrrrrrrrrrrrrrrrrrrrrr—'

He suddenly sucks air into his lungs as he fights to start breathing again. Alive. *Fucking fuck* – I brought him back! I brought him back to life… At least I've saved one tonight. Two to one; that isn't so bad, is it?

Ben

My lungs burn, like I've sucked down fire, and my throat's shredded.

'Ben… Ben…' I hear Mia, but I can't see her. My eyes won't focus, like the room's full of fog and all I can see is a fuzzy outline of something that could be human.

'Ben… I saved you.' I feel her hands grip my shoulders.

'You…' My voice rasps, '…let… him… choke… me.'

'I…' is all she can manage to defend herself.

I try to get up, but I can barely move; my hands are shaking too much. My head throbs; the veins stand out in my neck like vines. I thought I was dead, I thought my head was going to pop like a champagne cork – and she could have stopped him before she did. 'You wanted me dead,' I manage to croak.

'No... I...' she chokes, as the tears strangle her voice. Suddenly it feels like it's raining, as her tears drop from her cheeks and splatter on my face – but instead of being moved by it, I just feel fury.

'Liar,' I hiss as loud as I can. 'You watched him do it. That was your sick way of getting revenge.'

'No.'

'You wouldn't lift a finger to help me, after I came out tonight to—'

'*No!*' she yells and kicks at me – hard into my leg. It hurts. '*No!*' and she kicks me again.

'You wanted me dead, all neat and tidy,' I say despite her blows.

'No, liar – you fucking liar.' She drops down next to me and raises her fist and hits me hard in the chest. 'You fucking liar!' She hits me again, and again. Her fists rain down on me and I curl into a ball and let the blows come, as they spread to my legs and side and back. She pummels my body with all her strength – all her rage.

'No,' she moans. 'No... no... no... noooooo...'

Finally, she's finished, and she folds over me like an origami crane, and cries into my hoody until it's sodden; then she curls into a ball and lies next to me, back to back, like angry spoons in a cutlery drawer.

'I'm... I'm sorry,' she manages through the snotty tear-less sobs. 'I don't... I don't... I did bring you back – I saved you. In the end I saved you... I did. Ben, please forgive me. I'm not a monster, I'm not.'

And she heaves with tears for the loss of herself and her heart. I can hear how desperately she needs me to forgive her – but I can't. Not yet. Maybe never. Instead, all I do is lie here, looking at the ceiling. There are stains all over the tiles and I think I can see a dachshund in one, and a cross between Winston Churchill and The Hulk, dressed in a tutu, in another.

Huh, my brain will do anything rather than deal with all this emotional hurt. I want to run away, hide in dreams and stories like I always do… but I can't. We need to talk and – *Jesus Christ* – I have to confess to the giant lie that has dragged at my heart for the longest time. I must tell Mia the truth.

'I could have…' I say, feeling Mia curled beside me – like we're in bed, but lost to each other. 'I could have called you. I could have got you to come home and be with Rosie before she died. I think there was time… there was a moment, before I went in to sit with Rosie for that last time, when I could have called you, but I was… I was hoping against hope… and I was scared and… I delayed calling. I'm sorry.'

–

I remember standing in the hospital with the phone in my hand, thinking I should call Mia and get her back from Prague… actually thinking she would hate me if I didn't – that *I* would hate me if I didn't – but still, I didn't. Instead, I put the phone back in my pocket, and went into the room to sit with Rosie. I didn't know for sure it would be the end, but I did know that if it was, I didn't want to share her with anyone. I wanted Rosie all to myself. I wanted to hold her, and I knew if Mia were there that she'd dominate, that she would take over and be the one holding Rosie and shouting at the doctors and causing a fuss. She would have railed and roared against the end, and I wanted to say goodbye to my amazingly brave daughter quietly and with dignity. But how do I say that to Mia? That I feared fighting with her for our daughter's last moments?

—

'I was selfish, Mia. I didn't think about you, just me. I am so sorry,' I tell her and then feel her body shake against me with huge, wracking sobs.

'I'm so sorry, Ben… I just… I let you die. I let Tony squeeze the life out of you. I should have hit him before but… I think…' She laughs, but not a happy laugh. 'I think I'm broken inside, Ben.'

'I think we both are,' is all I can say. 'I think it's grief.' We lie, side by side, and where we touch it's like a fire. It warms us somehow, the closeness of our bodies alongside each other. Maybe we'll never move again. Maybe we'll—

'Aargh…' Tony groans.

'Shit.' Mia rolls over and gets to her feet. 'We need to tie him up.'

She runs to the desk and searches inside it. A few seconds later, she rushes back with a handful of cable ties. She pulls Tony's hands behind his back and uses the ties like handcuffs. Then she takes the fabric he'd thrown onto the desk when she first saw him. It's an African print cotton. It looks like it was really pretty once, but now it's smeared with what looks like oil, and something that's either ketchup or blood. She rips a strip off it, forces it between his teeth and ties it behind his head, gagging him pretty effectively.

Then she comes over to me, for a second I actually think I'm gonna get the cable ties and gag treatment too

– and I think I see that thought flit across her face – but instead, she offers me a hand and helps me up.

'Does it hurt?' she asks, as her fingers move to my neck, but I pull away from her touch.

'I'm okay.' I manage in a raspy whisper.

She nods. 'Yeah, okay, so we still need to take those films down.'

'Password,' I croak.

'He told us.'

I frown. 'No, he didn't.'

'He said it's his wife's name.' She smiles like the cat that got the cream.

'But we don't know her name.'

'We do, look in the corner.' She points into the gloom, where about a million dust bunnies roll around.

I'm not sure what I'm looking at until I get closer, and see that it's a shrivelled old helium balloon. Most of the gas has seeped away, but there is just a little left and it sort of floats a millimetre above the gross carpet tiles, held in place by a zig-zag of spider's webs.

'I don't get it,' I say and swipe at the webs, making a swirl in the air current, that tips the balloon up slightly and the metallic lettering on the skin shines enough to read it.

Happy Thirtieth Wedding Anniversary, Tony and Angela. The balloon bobs slightly and the letters vanish again. But I have her name now – let's see if it opens the magic door. I head to the small office, and sit back at the computer and try to open it again. The screensaver is a picture of the family; Tony and Angela in the centre, and Theo to one side with a woman and two kids who must be Claire and Lilly and Harry. Alex is on the other side and he has a huge grin for the camera. His arm is around the shoulders of a very slight black woman, and her face is turned away from the camera like she doesn't want to be included in the photograph. Alex's hand is on her boob and squeezing it. *What a shit*, I think and then remember he's dead, and we killed him.

I type *Angela* into the password box and hope it's an open sesame. It is. It unlocks the home page and I'm inside. I open the folder for 'hot milfs' and there are at least a hundred subfolders, a hundred women secretly filmed, some of them multiple times. I open the folders and scroll through the names, amazed by how many there are… and then I find the emails.

Most are from women begging and pleading to be removed from the site, a few threatening legal action, and then there are two news clippings that have been kept. Two women who committed suicide, leaving behind stunned husbands and children, who had no idea that their wife and mother was so unhappy. And even though the newspaper reports say nothing about the films or the website, I know why those women killed themselves, and it makes me feel sick. Theo and Alex were responsible – they killed those women as surely as if they'd put the nooses around their necks, or thrown them onto railway tracks. Those bastards deserved what they got. Tonight, Mia has been an avenging spirit, a hero-nemesis, fighting for these lost women. For a second I think that we could be on the right side in all of this, on the side of the angels. Then Tony groans from the other room, and I remember they're his boys, and I remember Theo's family, and maybe Alex actually loves the woman whose boob he squeezes in the photo. Whatever's happened tonight, Mia and I had no right to play judge, jury and executioner. We aren't on the side of the angels.

I look through the letters, from women who have found the films of themselves online. One of them says a work colleague found it and exposed her to the firm and her family. She's lost everything, and I feel like I want to write to her and tell her I'm taking these films down, but I know it will do no good, it's too late; she's already been vilified for her simple desire to be loved, and to be pleasured. And taking these films down won't get them off the internet, as they'll have been shared to hubs, sites that collect porn and make it free for everyone.

'How are you doing?' Mia calls to me from the main office.

'I'm in the computer.'

'Have you found the films?'

'Yes,' I tell her, but I don't say how many there are, or how depressing it all is. And she doesn't need to know about those who have tried to stand up to these bastards and been beaten down, or even taken their own lives.

'I'm going to delete the masters, and then take them down off the servers,' I shout through the doorway. 'It will take a while; there's a lot of them.'

'And Sandi?' she asks.

I don't answer immediately, but I have found her folder. In it are four films. I thought about emailing a link to Luke, but I didn't. Maybe a few hours ago I would have, but after all this I won't. What's the point in being *that* guy? I can't sit in judgement. So, I delete Sandi's films with a single swipe. *Gone.*

Then I turn to the folder named *Julie*. The film from a month ago is inside. She's lucky that it hasn't been posted already, but I can see the long queue of films they have ready to post and some stretch back six weeks. They have been busy. I sweep the curser onto the film to delete it, but I pause. A part of me wants to see Julie, this other woman, my own wife's doppelgänger. But that would be another unjust intrusion into her life, and I have no right to do that. So I delete it. *Gone*.

And then I go through the others – ping, ping, ping – all gone. I clear all the films off the computer, and then the servers. I clean out everything this computer has access to except… 'Mia,' I call. A few seconds later she appears, covered in cobwebs and dust.

'What?'

'There's something here, on the computer, under everything else. Below the hot milfs site, under all the films.'

'What?'

'I don't know, it's encrypted – state-secrets-level encrypted… like, dark web-hidden.'

'Can you hack it?'

'Who the hell do you think I am? I haven't suddenly gone all Jason Bourne.'

'So what is it?'

'I don't know. It could be the financial stuff, I suppose, the client lists and credit card details and all that stuff.'

'But it could also be hidden copies of all the films?' she asks glumly.

'I don't know, I have no idea. I don't see why they'd have two layers of protection on the films, but I can't be sure. Whatever they are, I can't access them.'

'Okay… so what now?'

'It's clobbering time,' I tell her.

I pull the computer tower out and, with one well-aimed kick, break it open and pull out the hard drive.

'Yours, milady,' I tell her and with a shriek, she stamps it into tiny pieces.

'This is great,' she tells me. 'It's actually quite cathartic.'

Then we start on the servers, opening them up and pulling out all the linked hard drives. When they're all out – and it's more than a hundred – we start to smash and crash like a couple of Hulks in a china shop.

Mia

Smashing up the computer servers is just what I need. After ten minutes of crazed abandon, I'm a sweaty, steaming mess, and everything has been reduced to tiny broken shards of plastic, wire, and metal jigsaw pieces. It feels good, I feel alive again, I feel—

'Aargh!' comes a yell from the other room. We both rush in and— oh Christ. I freeze as Tony is… is… I can't…

'Mia, I need your help,' Ben yells as he gets down to the older man who is convulsing and—

'I can't, I can't,' I hear myself mumble as I start to shake. I'm back in time, to the first massive seizure Rosie had, and I couldn't help her – my own baby. I was frozen. I couldn't bear seeing her thrash and shake and her eyes roll in her head. It had to be Ben who held her hands and sang to her and – *oh fuck* – that was why he was the one to stay at home: because I froze, when I was needed. I couldn't—

'Mia, help me. *Mia!*' Ben screams, breaking me out of my memory.

'I… I…'

'Get scissors; we have to cut through the cable ties. Mia, find something to cut through them,' Ben yells, but I'm rooted to the spot. I can see the foam flecking Tony's lips, and the way the ties cut into his wrists, and the fear in his face – he doesn't want to die. Ben rips the gag out of his mouth and he yells in pain, thrashing and twisting like he's on fire.

'*Mia!*' Ben screams and I turn, like I'm wading through quicksand, and make it to the desk. I think I saw scissors before, but when I open the drawers I don't see anything, it's as if I don't remember what scissors look like or what they do or anything.

'Ben, Ben I can't... I don't have... Ben?' I stammer and then I feel him next to me, his hands on my shoulders. He moves me, so he can dig into the drawers himself. In a second, he pulls out scissors. Then he's gone from beside me, as he rushes back to help Tony. I hear the moans from the older man, and his feet skittering on the carpet tiles as he convulses. Ben tries to calm him, singing and talking to him, just like he did with Rosie when she had a seizure.

'Shh, it's okay Tony, calm down and relax, shhh...'

I close my eyes. He bounces her on his knee and sings: '*The animals went in two by two, hurrah, hurrah.*' And together they make the animal noises and choose who goes in – will it be the goats and gnus or the ants in their pants? Or—

'Tony,' Ben's voice is strangled, angry and full of pain. I keep my eyes tightly shut, but I can't hear the moans anymore.

'Tony...' Ben hits something and then breathes hard... I know it's his chest and he's giving him CPR but I still can't look. 'Mia, you have to call someone, call an ambulance. Christ, Tony – come on. Come on.' He pummels his chest again. I listen but there is nothing from the older man... no gurgle or half breath.

'Mia,' Ben says, with pain in his voice, and I open my eyes to see he's kneeling beside a dead man. Tony's eyes are open, but there's nothing in there. In that moment he looks more like his sons than ever before – in death they are so similar.

'I couldn't save him, Mia, I couldn't… I couldn't.' He sounds lost and heartbroken.

'You tried, you tried so hard,' I tell him.

'I broke his ribs – I think I broke his ribs.' Ben turns his face to look at me, so full of remorse. 'He didn't deserve this… not Tony.' And he starts to sob. 'He was just trying to be a good dad, that's all he could do. It wasn't his fault the kids went off the rails… he was just… he just—'

'He tried to kill you, Ben. He strangled you to within a breath of your life.'

'He was just defending his family. He thought we'd done something bad to them – and we had. We killed them, Mia – his two sons – and he loved them.'

'His sons were abusers.'

'But *he* wasn't… He didn't deserve to die. He was just a dad,' Ben says, and I see the pain of one dad acknowledging the loss of the other. I see his pain, but we don't have the luxury to feel sympathy.

'Ben, Ben, look at me.' I gently cup his chin and tip his head to look at my face, as I feel his tears pool in my palm. 'This was a tragedy – this has been a night of tragedy. We didn't mean to hurt him; it was probably his heart. We didn't kill him. He died of natural causes.'

'Natural causes? Christ, Mia, we tied him up, and you knocked him unconscious with a ten-pin bowling trophy.'

'We're doing this for all these women.'

'But two wrongs don't make a right – and we have blood on our hands,' he says.

'I agree, two wrongs don't cancel each other out, but remember what this was all for—'

'For god's sake, Mia, don't say we are doing this for others; this is all for us, for you. We are doing this to save you… for your reputation and… My god, what have you made me do?'

'I haven't made you do anything. We didn't know he was here; we should have been in and out. This was all a mistake.'

'A mistake? My mistake was coming when you called.'

'So, what are you saying, that this is all on me? Everything?'

'I'm just saying that the only reason that I'm here is out of loyalty to you.'

'Liar.'

'Okay then, so it's loyalty and love for Rosie, who would not want her mother in prison.'

I glare at him, my blood boiling. 'Fuck you, Ben, don't you dare use our daughter to win a point in a shitty argument.'

He stares at me with eyes that burn like the sun… but then they cool and melt into black holes – like the history of the universe in a moment. 'I'm sorry. I didn't… I'm just…' He can't finish the words. Instead, he looks down into Tony's face. Drool and spittle dot the dead man's cheeks and chin. Ben uses his sleeve to wipe his face clean before he closes the dead man's eyes.

'You've got his DNA all over you now,' I tell him and he just nods distractedly. 'We have to get out of here.' I want to bloody shake Ben, as he looks like he's going to collapse. 'When does the sun come up?'

He shrugs. 'I don't know, maybe six thirty?'

'So we don't have long, it's almost six now.'

He looks at me, so lost and unhappy.

'Snap the fuck out of it, Ben.'

'I can't.'

'Ben, you have to. I'm sorry you're upset, I really am, but we have to get out of here. We don't have the time to clean like we did at the hotel, and we've touched everything in this place, and I mean *everything* – including all those servers and computers that we then smashed into tiny fingerprint-sized pieces. It would take hours to clean, and even then I doubt we could erase everything. And the second they ID Alex's body they will head here. The clock is ticking.'

'So what do we do?' he asks.

I don't hesitate. 'We torch the place.'

'What?'

'We burn it – that will get rid of everything.'

'And Tony?'

'He burns too.' I say coldly.

'My god, Mia, we can't do that,' Ben moans, mortified. I reach across to take his hand, but he pulls away from me and walks away. He stands with his back to me and I can see his shoulders shake a little.

'I'm sorry Ben, but it's the only way.' I try to keep my tone neutral. I can see how hard this is for him, but I can't let his inherent decency bring us down. I put my hand lightly on his back. 'He's dead, and the dead don't care anymore.'

'But there are others…' Ben is desperate to hold onto the image of this family man.

'His wife and children are dead, so they don't need a funeral,' I say.

Ben turns to me, his eyes pleading. 'But we know he's got at least two grandchildren.'

'And they've got their father and uncle to bury already, don't you remember? We killed them earlier tonight.'

'Jesus… Mia, how are you so cold and callous?' he asks, pulling away from me.

'I'm not. I'm passionate and compassionate – but I save it for those who deserve it. For those I love. And tonight that's you and me.'

I see him waver for a moment, hearing me say I love him, but he still can't agree to burning the body.

'But he wasn't a bad man Mia. Tony loved his family.'

'And he almost killed you, don't you remember him choking the life out of you?'

Ben screws his face up. He bloody well does remember being half-choked to death – but he can still forgive him. 'He thought we'd hurt his boys,' he says.

I shake my head, frustrated that he doesn't see the bigger picture. 'His sons deserved what happened to them.'

'But not him,' Ben says.

'He raised two rapists, how the hell is he innocent of that?' I snap.

'He was a father—'

'Yes… a father…' I sigh, feeling so tired all of a sudden. 'Look, Ben, I didn't leave the house tonight thinking I'd see three dead men—'

'And be responsible—' he cuts in but I stop him dead by grabbing his arm. I'm angry now.

'Yes, we played a part in his death, and, it was a shit thing to happen. But it has also saved him a fuck of a lot of grief.'

'What, he should be grateful he died before he found out that both his sons had been murdered tonight?' He pushes my hand away and stalks off.

'Not grateful but… oh fuck, you know what I mean.' I kick at the desk. Both of us seethe with frustration at the other – that we can't see what the other sees. We stand here, both in our own heads for a few seconds, before Ben breaks the mood.

'So what do we do?' he asks.

'I already said what I think we should do. Set a fire, with some kind of fuse or time delay, so we can get away and establish an alibi.'

He looks at me incredulously for a second. 'Fuse? Time delay? My boys' book of knowledge didn't have a section on burning down buildings. Jesus Christ, what alternative reality is this? Eight hours ago we were law-abiding citizens.'

'And shit happened,' I yell at him. 'And three men are dead, and now we need to burn a fucking building down and establish an alibi for when it happens. That's the reality – that's our life now. Fucking cope with it.' I'm shaking as I scream at him. I've totally lost it.

He doesn't reply immediately; he watches as I try to get control of myself again. Then, with a low voice he asks, 'How do you do it? How have you just adapted to this?'

'I just have. I want a life after tonight. I don't want to die here too.'

'And what does that *life* include? Is there a place for a husband?'

'I… now isn't the time for this.'

'But it has to be, I need you to answer my question: What about me?'

I hold my breath. I do know the answer to this, but I had hoped he wouldn't ask, because the truth is that there is no *us* anymore. Not for me, and I'm pretty sure that's been true since Rosie died. For four years we've just been living inside the echo that was left of us from happier times, and now it's finally faded and there's nothing left.

'Can we talk about this later?' I say. 'After we find out if the police are going to arrest us? Because that will take the choice out of our hands.'

He sags slightly, maybe my non-answer has told him what he needs to know. 'Okay,' he says. 'So how do we burn this place down and not be here?'

I take a deep breath. 'I think the first thing to do is search the place for anything that'll burn – oil, petrol, booze – anything.'

'Okay.' Ben nods and we start to search.

–

Five minutes later we have a bottle of sunflower oil, a half bottle of whisky and a bottle of rum. We also have a box of matches and a box of candles, a pile of old newspapers, and the rest of the African cloth. That's all we have. I am totally out of ideas.

'I think we can do this,' Ben says with a weird look on his face, which is mostly guilt, but there's some excitement too. I mean, who doesn't want to burn a building down at least once in their lives?

'So, what's the plan?' I ask him.

'I've got two, so if one fails, the other should work,' he says very seriously.

'Okay.'

'On the stove we put a pan of oil and water. We put the gas on high so the water will evaporate – I have no idea how quickly, but when it's gone, the oil should catch light.'

'The second option?' I ask.

'A candle standing in a bowl of oil. When it burns down enough it should set the bowl alight.'

'You think that'll work?'

'I guess so, but you do know that I've never done this before.'

'Okay, I suppose if we pour the oil and the booze all over everything and we scatter the newspaper and… you know, it should all burn.' I look up at the ceiling and see a smoke detector. 'We have to get that down.'

Without a second's thought, Ben jumps on the counter and pulls at it.

'Come on you little— crap—'

It comes off the ceiling, along with a lump of plaster that rains down on my head. When he opens the plastic casing there's no battery inside.

'Well that's stupid,' he says, frowning. 'What's the point of that? The place deserves to burn down.' Ben changes our smoke detector batteries every eighteen months, and he buys new alarms every five years.

'Okay, let's burn this mother down,' I say, and we get everything ready. While Ben's in the kitchen, I pour the bottle of whisky over Tony and then the rum over the computer hard drives. After five minutes of preparation it's all done. The office stinks of booze and oil.

'You light the cooker, I'll do the candle in the bowl,' I tell him.

'Mia, wait—' Ben says and I take one look at his huge sad–dog eyes and I know that I don't want to hear what he has to say.

'Ben, there's no option. We burn it and we get to be free.'

'And us? What's the plan?'

'We go home, we shower and change clothes, then we head out to get coffee – I think I want waffles – and we make sure we're seen, and we use our cards to pay for stuff and our phones ping off all the cell towers they can. We look like a couple that spent the night at home. We eat, then we go home and my plan is to sleep for a solid twenty-four hours. Then, if the police haven't come to see us, we talk.'

'About?'

'Everything. About Rosie and why I've been so sad and so upset with you.'

'About having a baby?' he asks.

'I guess. And we talk about Ella too.'

'And about our marriage?'

'Yeah, we'll talk about *us*,' I tell him, even though I already know what I will say and how that will hurt him.

He drops his head. When he raises it again he looks like he's calm again. 'Okay, that would be good,' he says with an almost-smile.

'But first we have to do this.' I point at the candle in the oil. He nods and watches me, as I strike the match, it flares and—

Zeeeeeep – zeeeeeeep – zeeeeeeeeep

For a second I feel lost and then I realise what the sound is, and dip my fingers into my hoody pocket and pull out the burner phone. I'm scared.

'Only one person has this number,' I tell Ben, as my hand starts to shake and my heart pounds. I put the phone to my ear.

'Mia… Mia?' a voice calls for me, sobbing, almost uncontrollably.

'Sandi… Sandi… Calm down,' I tell her. 'It's me, it's me, I'm here. What's up?'

'He's got a knife, he stabbed Luke and he says he'll kill me. He broke into our house; Mia, he made me call you.' I hear the fear overwhelm her.

'What does he want?'

'Mia, he says he wants you here – you and Ben and Alex. He says *now*, or he kills us.'

Chapter Fourteen

06.00 a.m.

Ben

'What's going on? Mia, who is it?' I ask, but she doesn't answer; instead, she whispers one last thing into the phone.

'I'm coming.'

She closes the phone, and looks like she wants to kill someone.

'Who the hell—'

'Sandi, it was Sandi,' she says in an intense voice.

'But what's happening, why the hell was she calling?'

'I…' She stops and I can see the monumental effort it takes to pull herself together, almost like she's been unpicked at the seams. 'Someone's at their place.'

'What? Who?' I ask.

'I don't know, but they want Alex there.'

'But how do they know about us meeting him? Who the hell could it be? The money guy? The web guy?' I'm panicking.

'Whoever it is, they know the business. They must do. They must have access to the client list – that's the only way they could have got to Sandi.'

I close my eyes. Why the hell can't we just get some time to breathe between disasters?

'There's already three dead tonight because of me. I can't let her get hurt too,' she says, and her jaw tightens so hard it might snap. 'Luke's been stabbed.'

'How badly?' I ask, feeling weightless. 'What did Sandi say? Should we call an ambulance?'

'No.' She's positive.

'But what if he dies, too? What if he's number four?'

'He won't.'

'You don't know that,' I tell her.

'No, no I don't.' She shakes her head slowly. 'I have to go to Sandi. I have to put this right.' She looks at me, and for the first time in hours, maybe in years, her face is clear of all emotion. I'm so used to seeing it swarm with anger or shame or guilt or resentment or something... but she looks twenty years old again, like she did when I first saw her.

'Thanks for everything,' she says.

'What are you saying?'

'I need to go and face the music, alone. You go home and—'

'I thought you wanted waffles.'

'I did – I do. God, I want waffles, but...'

'Come on, we need to get over to Sandi's,' I tell her and take her hand. She doesn't pull it away; instead, she nods and walks to the door, a little dazed. I can't let her go alone. We're in this together, right to the end. That's what Rosie would have wanted. We head to the door, but then I remember.

'Hang on,' I turn and take a last look at the studs love mums office. I take a match out of the box and strike it – it flares bright and hot, and I go to touch it to the candle.

Then I take another, and go into the kitchen and turn on the gas. We can at least burn this bloody place to the ground.

I go back to Mia, and lead her out into the last vestiges of the night. It isn't really dark anymore; on the horizon it's starting to lighten. The day's coming. Soon everything will come to light.

'You've still got his keys?' I ask, as we walk back to where we left Alex's car. It was only about forty minutes ago but it seems like days or weeks have passed. Mia just nods, slouching beside me, looking down at her feet. I guess she's thinking about Sandi, and if we'll ever get out of this nightmare.

At the car, Mia opens the driver's door and gets in. I hesitate, as I realise something. I walk around to the back of the car, where I aim a vicious kick at the number plate. There's a heart-warming splintering of plastic and the plate breaks down the middle. I pull it off the car and throw it on the backseat.

'What are you doing?' Mia yells at me like I'm crazy.

'There are cameras for the congestion zone – they take dozens of photos of every car number plate each night. They can track everywhere you go, so we should be careful. We don't want to lead the police from here to Sandi's.'

'Yeah, you're right,' she says. 'That's smart.'

I go around to the front and kick at that plate too. It's harder, and takes a few whacks, but it breaks before my shoe does, and I pull it off and throw it onto the backseat alongside its sibling.

'You know, you really missed your vocation: you should have been a criminal,' she says and actually smiles.

'And if we get caught, you can even defend us and get us freed,' I say, trying to keep the joke going but suddenly she frowns.

'Except I don't do *useful* law,' she says. And I do remember saying exactly that to her a few months ago. I slide into the passenger seat.

'Hoody up, eyes down,' she reminds me, and I pull the hood up and over as far as it can go, like I'm some monk from *Assassin's Creed*. She steps on the accelerator and we jerk away from the kerb and we're off. We don't speak, we're both lost in our troubled heads, imagining the worst, and yet still hoping Luke and Sandi will be okay. The sky looks like a dribble of milk has been poured into jet black coffee. The sound has changed too; I can hear a thrum of traffic, as folks head out to jobs. Soon kids will be getting breakfast and heading out to school. Life goes on.

'I spy with my little eye,' I whisper into the gloom and Mia makes a sad half-laugh. It was what we used to play on car journeys with Rosie, and there were so many trips to hospitals and consultants. We'd play 'I Spy', and Rosie's variation, which was *I hear with my little ear*, though that could get very silly, very quickly. But her favourite game was *skittles* – AKA 'yellow' car, as you got a point for every yellow car or van or truck you saw, though the pinnacle of that game was to see a yellow Mini – and then you'd scream *mini cheddar* and get five points. And right on cue, I see a yellow Mini on a side street… but I don't yell. Today isn't the day for childish games.

Instead, as Mia drives us towards Sandi's, I look out of the window, lost in thought. So bloody lost, as I think about the situation with Ella, and lying to Mia, and how we dealt with the loss of Rosie and—

'We're here.' Mia's voice pulls me out of my head. I was lost in an alternate universe of what-ifs and maybes, so the journey had happened in a blink of an eye. I look around and don't recognise where I am, even though I've been to Luke and Sandi's place many times, but tonight it all looks different; it might as well be an alien landscape. I'd swear that I'd never been here before – but that's crazy. Isn't it?

The car engine stops, but Mia doesn't take the keys out of the ignition. 'I'm going inside,' she tells me.

'We both are.'

'No, you're staying here.' She grabs my hand as I reach down to undo my seatbelt. 'I'm going inside, and if I don't come out again, then you have to go to the police and tell them everything.'

'But that's—'

'If I don't come out, then I'm dead, and so is Luke, and so is Sandi.'

'Mia—'

'You have to stay alive, in case I don't. Then you have to tell the truth, about what happened with Theo and why...' Her face collapses for a second, and then she draws it all back together. 'Tell the police that I wanted to get pregnant, but I got cold feet, and I asked him to stop and he wouldn't.'

'And after that?'

'That it all snowballed.' She drops her head. 'I'm sorry, Ben, I didn't mean to drag you into this, I just knew you'd stand by me and... who else would I turn to?'

I nod, not trusting myself to say anything more.

'Five minutes, then go to the police,' she says as she hops out of the car.

'Five minutes isn't much time.'

'Plenty of time to die,' she says melodramatically, then makes a little snorty laugh, as she realises just what a diva she's being. She shrugs – and then she turns her back on me, and walks to the house.

She gets to the front door and taps on it. There's a pause, and then it opens, only a little, just enough for her to squeeze through, and then shuts behind her. I'm alone.

It takes me a couple of minutes to realise that I don't have anything that actually tells the time, as Alex's phone is in the pile of broken computer servers waiting to burn. I can't recall if there was a digital clock on the dashboard, so I slide across into the driver's seat and turn the key in the ignition, so the dials light up. It's 6.20 a.m. The sky is getting lighter all the time, and the birds are getting louder. I see bedroom and kitchen lights coming on all along the street as morning alarm clocks go off to start the new day. I watch them, and imagine the normal lives going on in those homes. Families who slept last night, couples that shared a bed and woke up next to the one they loved. Kids who had bad dreams, wet the bed, stayed up late reading under the covers or watching YouTube on their phones. Just normal life stuff.

It's 6.23 now. She told me to go after five minutes. To go and get help because she's dead. Dead. But it isn't five minutes, it can't be. Another few minutes can't do any harm. I watch the clock and wish it weren't digital. I wish there was a second hand, but there isn't; and so I just watch the numbers made up out of those bars, wait for them to change and be—

6.24.

My heart wallops in my chest. I should go to the police. I should do what she asked me to do… but I can't. Instead

I watch the clock and wait for it to change to 6.25. But do I wait for 6.26, and 6.27 and 6.28? Do I wait until I can't wait anymore and I'm hungry and thirsty and need the toilet?

She's dead. Mia's dead. They're all dead.

I didn't care about Theo, not really. Oh, I cared about the imaginary family I made for him in my head – Claire and Lilly and Harry – but that was just my middle-class guilt. I cared for the man I'd created in my head, but once I'd seen the film, and heard how he treated women – how he treated Mia – throttled her and raped her; after that, I can't say I care about his life. I didn't care about his brother either. Neither of the boys warranted my pity – but Tony, I do mourn him. He seemed an okay guy, just trying to do his best for kids who had that awful curse of being far too good-looking for their own good. But you can't hold a parent responsible for good genetics, in the same way that you can't blame them for bad. Life sucks.

The digital bars of light move again: 6.25 a.m.

I don't believe in God. You know. I just don't. Rosie had a weird friend at school, this little ginger-headed kid, who insisted that the 'glory' would 'save us all' and he said it with such a look of happiness on his face. I don't know what happened to him. When Rosie died I tried to get all her friends to the funeral, but he'd just vanished. It was a pity; I'd actually hoped that big smile of his was going to make me feel better.

6.26 a.m.

I promised Mia that I'd go, that I'd get her story told… but I'm not moving. I can't. My fingers are curled around the key and I'm not turning it. I'm thinking about how Luke put his hand on my shoulder, as I wept for my lost little girl, after Rosie's funeral, and how Sandi held Mia as she sobbed. That's who friends are and what they do.

6.27 a.m.

I look up at the house, as the first ray of light touches a window; the sun is rising at last. It burns the night away. I imagine I see Mia in the window and she waves to me, *it's okay…* but she isn't there. It's just a trick of the light.

I should leave. I promised I would – and I have tried to keep my promises tonight. But I can't keep this one. I have to go in and find my wife, because there is something I have to tell her. All of our secrets have *not* been laid out tonight. I still have one that burns my heart. I lied to her earlier – or at least, I didn't clear up an assumption she'd made. I can't leave her now, because I might never see her again – and she has to know the truth. She has to.

6.28 a.m.

I look to the house. I hadn't seen it happen, but now the front door has swung open, leaving a black hole in the front, a gaping maw. I can't see inside; there's no light or movement, there's just a big black nothing. I stare into it.

6.29 a.m.

I uncurl my fingers from around the key and flex them, to get the feeling back. Then I open the car door and step out. From somewhere close by, I hear a cat hiss, but I don't think it has anything to do with me. I walk slowly forward, like I'm approaching the gallows, and maybe I am. I get to the front door, and it's really creepy, because inside is jet black, like looking into a cave that slides into the ground, and winds down to the base of the earth.

'Hello,' I call out, listening for something – anything – but there's nothing.

'Mia?' I yell and then, 'Sandi… Luke?' but nothing comes back, not even an echo. It's like the house soaked it all up and devoured it. I don't know what to do; I don't know anything – except I can't leave Mia here. Not while there's a chance she's alive in there.

I step inside. Into the dark.

Chapter Fifteen

06.30 a.m.

Ben

'Mia,' I call into the blackness ahead, but there's no response. Of course there isn't, because they're dead and I'm committing suicide by following them. But I have no choice. I hold my hands out in front of me and slowly shuffle forward. I don't want to go too fast, in case I fall over something.

'Luke!' I yell. 'If you can tell me you're alive that would be good.' I strain my hearing into the dark, but there's no answer. My hands slide across the wall and find a doorway to the right. It's the kitchen, and I go inside. I hit the light switch, but nothing happens; I guess the power's been turned off. I move slowly to the side, and feel along it, until I find the stove. I remember it's a gas hob. I know that because we roasted an aubergine to make some baba ghanoush one night. I feel the knob and twist it. The gas starts to hiss, I hit the ignition and whoosh – we have light. Of course it's pretty dim, and makes the room look like Tiny Tim should be in the corner, but I can see the table and chairs and – blood. Even in this low light I can make out the blood spots on the floor. They are not like the lake of blood around Theo, these look like they're from a wound, as if the victim moved away from their attacker, leaving a trail, like liquid breadcrumbs.

The spots of blood arc across the floor and into the hallway. I go to follow them, but stop. I see something on the back of a kitchen chair that isn't right. There's a jacket looped over the back; it looks black in this dim firelight, but it's actually a dark burgundy, and the lapel is edged in metallic silver, I've seen the jacket before. At least, I think so. I reach out my hand slowly, which is stupid, as it isn't like I'm reaching out to stroke a vicious dog or something, it's just a jacket. On the lapel is a plastic square, a name badge. I angle it towards the light, so I can read it. *Ali*.

'Ali?' I call at the top of my lungs. 'Ali, it's Ben, from the hotel. We met earlier, you helped me. You and Nadia. Ali, it's okay, these are my friends and my wife. They don't have anything to do with Alex or his brother. We aren't part of this, we just got suckered in tonight.' I listen, but there's nothing. 'Ali.' I yell. '*Ali!*'

'Ben,' there's a low call; the voice wavers with broken emotion. I think it's Sandi and it's coming from upstairs. I move, throwing caution to the wind, as I rush away from the light of the flame and back into the pitch-black hallway, except now there seems to be a slant of light above my head.

'Sandi! Sandi?' but nothing comes back. 'Sandi, is Ali with you?'

'He…' and that's all she says, as I get to the top step. Above us is a loft conversion that Luke uses as an office, and on this floor there's the master bedroom, a spare room, and what was at one time going to be a nursery, but is now Sandi's exercise and junk room.

'Arghh.'

I hear a moan; it's coming from the spare room and I rush at the door and hit it as hard as I can. The door cracks in the middle and the lock splinters and pops out – falling to the floor. I storm in, off-balance, hitting the opposite wall with my shoulder – *damn*, it feels like I dislocated it, but that doesn't matter.

I take in the sight of this room in an instant. Luke is on the bed – it looks like he was thrown there. The duvet is red with blood, and there's a tourniquet around his leg, but it isn't tight enough. It looks like he's been stabbed in the thigh and he's lost a lot of blood. Sandi's on the floor; she's holding his hand and her chest is all bloody, but I think it's his blood. She looks out of it. Her eyes are wild and she's shaking.

'Sandi, Sandi… *Sandi.*'

Her eyes swim wildly, she has no idea who I am.

'Sandi!' I slap her face, hard and stinging, so her eyes come back to me, and her mouth starts to quiver.

'It's my fault—' she sobs.

'That can wait. Luke's losing too much blood, you have to make a new tourniquet and make it tighter.'

'I can't.'

'You bloody can and you bloody will.' I am so angry all of a sudden, I pull her up off the ground and put her hands on his leg, into the slick blood. 'Pull yourself together and do some good,' I yell at her, and grab at a part of the sheet that isn't soaking in his blood and tear a strip off it. In the corner of the room, I can see Mia. She's unconscious. There's a trickle of blood coming from a gash in her forehead, and I'm guessing she was hit with something. Maybe—

—but then I see Ali, and I'm shocked, because I have never seen such pain in the face of a human being. He's crouched down with his back to the wall, and his head is in his hands as he rocks on the balls of his feet and wails softly. He holds the knife pointed up to the heavens like a lightning rod. I wonder if that is what he wants – for God to strike him down and end everything.

'Ali… Ali…' I say as I bend down next to him. 'Ali, do you remember me, from the hotel? It's Ben – you helped me.'

Ali rolls his head towards me. His eyes are almost entirely white, only the smallest pinpricks of colour in the centre. I think for a moment that it must be drugs, but when I hear his voice I recognise what it really is – fear.

'She said he's dead,' he whispers. 'She said Alex is dead.' He looks so completely bereft. His fingers loosen and the knife clatters to the floor. I slowly move my hand down and slide it away from him, under the bed.

'Sandi, call an ambulance—'

Ali's head springs up, and he looks at me with huge eyes like a frightened child. 'Please,' he mouths and, though I can barely hear the word he speaks, I can clearly see the pain that rolls through him.

'Call an ambulance, Sandi, but not the police. We need to get Luke to a hospital. Tell them he'll need blood en route – if you know what blood group he is make sure they know.'

She hesitates, not wanting to leave Luke for a second. I see the love written across her face, and feel such shame that I thought about telling him she didn't love him.

'You have to call them Sandi – right now.'

She kisses Luke lightly on the forehead, and then she runs.

'Everything is lost, everything is gone,' Ali wails. 'If Mister Alex is dead then she is dead… and if she is dead… then I am dead.' He rocks back and forth on the balls of his feet. His mind seems to have snapped.

'Who?' I ask. 'Who's dead?'

'She was everything! She is why we risked it all to come here, without her there is nothing, nothing…' Ali speaks, but it isn't to me, or to anyone in the room; he seems to say it to the air.

'Ali, Ali, who's dead? What's happened?'

'I am sorry I hurt your friends, I am so afraid… she is everything.'

'Who is *she*?'

'Khadra… she is Khadra, it means *lucky* in our language, but we have no luck for a long, long time. I couldn't keep her safe, I tried, I tried so hard, but now she will die.' He looks at me and I see fire burn in his eyes. 'I wish it was me.'

'Why will she die, what do you mean?'

'He told me.'

'Who?'

'Mister Alex, he said, if anything happen to him, then she will die and we will never find her. She will starve to death, slow like a dog and—' Ali breaks down, and his sobbing steals away everything else. I put my arm around his shoulders as he weeps; I don't know what else to do. I hear Sandi come into the room, and she sits next to Luke, and holds his hand again. There is so much pain in this room, so much grief.

'Uh,' a groan comes from across the room and my heart flips over. *Thank god, thank all the gods, Mia isn't dead.*

'*Fuck…*' Everything is black. I try to open my eyes but forks of lightning jag through my brain, so that's a terrible idea.

'Mia… Mia…' A voice that sounds like Ben is talking to me, but the words are like little knives that cut my brain into slices. *Stop talking*, I scream – or maybe it's just a loud thought. I don't know.

I try, again, to open my eyes, and they kind of tear open like a Velcro shoe, but I can't focus; everything zooms in and out.

'Mia… Mia… How many fingers am I holding up?' Ben asks and I squint.

'A million and one,' I tell him.

'How many really?'

'You were supposed to get the police.'

'I couldn't.'

'You promised.'

'I couldn't do it, I had to help Luke and—'

'Three,' I tell him. 'You're holding up three fingers, and my head hurts so fucking much.'

'Good. I mean, sorry, but good you're awake, I think Ali—'

'He threw me against a fucking wall, Ben.' I put my hand up to the huge football-sized bruise, now ballooning out of my temple. '*Fuck.*'

'I am sorry,' someone says from the fuzzy part of my vision. I move my head to try and see who it is, but that just makes it hurt even more.

'Let me…' I feel a hand on my forehead, and I pull away – I don't want to be touched, not be anyone.

'You've got a nasty cut on your head Mia, I just want to—'

'Leave it,' I rasp at Ben. My head doesn't matter. 'Luke was badly hurt, is he…' I can't say the word *dead*.

'I called an ambulance…' Sandi says in a faltering voice from somewhere far off.

'Sandi, be strong,' I tell her, and then I put my hand on Ben's shoulder, so I can lever myself up to my feet.

'I have to tell you something,' he whispers to me as I get up. 'Personal, about—'

'Later,' I tell him. 'This isn't the time.'

'Okay.'

I feel nauseous for a second, but it passes.

'You,' I angle myself to talk to Ali. 'Why the fuck did you break into their house, threaten my friends, make them call me? What the fuck was it all for?'

'I told you… I need Mister Alex.'

'You also said you meant me no harm, but you still threw me into the fucking wall.'

'Yes… I am sorry… but you said he was gone. I ask where Mister Alex gone and— Dead… you said he was dead.'

'So you bounced me off the wall.'

'The news was… was the worst news I could hear, that he is dead.'

'But Ben said you helped him at the hotel… he thought you hated Alex.'

'Of course I hate him, he is the devil; but he has my daughter.'

'What?' That wakes me up, and I push my headache away. 'What do you mean, he has your daughter?'

'All of us, all who work at hotel and others, many more who clean other hotels, work in factories, make clothes, and younger women who have to do much worse…' He looks sickened by what the younger women have to do,

278

and I think it must be forced prostitution. 'We are illegal. We run from death in our home countries… I am from Somalia and my family had to leave. We prayed and hoped for peace – for somewhere to live where we would not be afraid. We risked everything, gave everything we had to come here. But here is not good, worse than the war, here we find a kind of living death.'

I lean into Ali, close enough to see the whites of his eyes. They're bloodshot and hopeless. 'You said Alex had your daughter.'

'We pay everything we had to get here, everything – I sell everything. They take it, but then say it is not enough. They want more, they want so much more, and they come in the night, just one day after we get here, and they take the children and the young women.'

'Oh my god,' I gasp.

'They give us jobs – tell us we must earn our children back – but they demand huge money, so much money I think we never pay it back. I think we never see our children again. I think I have lost my daughter. But we cannot give up hope, and we beg them, plead with them to give us back our children. All they give us is a telephone call once a week. I speak to my Khadra for only ten minutes, and it is supposed to be today, after my shift. It is all I live for, and it does not come. I try to talk to Alex, to beg to see my Khadra. It is her thirteenth birthday tomorrow. I want to offer to work more, give my blood, my kidney, anything to see her.'

'Oh Jesus…'

'But there is no Alex to beg. He does not answer his phone, he is gone.'

'And your daughter, where is she?'

'We do not know. All we are told is that our children are kept underground – that is what they tell us – all they tell us, and when we speak to our children we ask them, but they do not know where they are. They have no window to see out. They are kept in dark, and my Khadra has bruises, sometimes cuts, and her eyes are full of fear. They are not the eyes of a child anymore, but when I ask about how she is treated, why she has bruises, she says it is nothing... nothing... We have such fear for them. I do not sleep, my dreams are so bad I take pills to keep awake. And now I think I will never see her again. Alex said, if we do anything to him, they will die. He told us, they will starve if he does not go to feed them. I am so afraid for her, for all of them.'

Ali's voice breaks, as gut-wrenching sobs roll through him – I can see he's in a state of collapse. What have we done to these girls? Are they going to die because of us? Will tonight's death toll just rise and rise and rise? I can't bear it.

'Please tell me you lied,' he pleads with me. 'That Mister Alex is not dead, that you know where he is. I know he went to meet with you. After you left, he came to hotel. He said he was going to kill you... but you are not dead. You are here, you are alive, he is missing... but not dead... please not really dead. I beg, not dead. Because if he is, that means Khadra is dead too; and if she is dead, then I will follow.'

'No, no you mustn't,' I tell him. There's a limit to how many lives I can be responsible for ending tonight. 'We can find her. We can save them,' I say, and I think it sounds positive, but for the life of me, I don't know how to save her. I look desperately at Ben, hoping he might have an idea. But he looks helpless too. Oh my god, I just wanted to hold a baby in my arms to stop the loneliness. Was that too much to ask for? I shake my head, trying to blow the cobwebs out of my brain, though it just makes it explode with pain. *Fuck*, but it actually does clear away the goop, at least a little.

'Ali, you were looking for Alex, so how did you come here, to Sandi's house?' I ask.

'She's your friend,' and he nods towards Sandi, who sobs ever harder. 'I saw you both together, weeks ago but I have good memory, and I watch them. I watch Mister Alex and his brother like a hawk. I keep a notebook of all their meetings with women; I think I might find clue to where they keep my daughter. But nothing has come of that so far – until tonight – and you come to hotel for second time. I remember you from before, and she brought you there that night.'

'Yes she did, Sandi introduced me to Alex.'

'Yes, and that night, I asked you to sign register, but you leave it blank – but she had signed it before and she leave her address.'

Sandi snorts and grips Luke harder, feeling like this is all her fault – and it bloody well is. What a fucking idiot, leaving contact details at a sleazy hotel where you go to have sex with a stranger.

'So you and Sandi both went to the hotel a month ago?' Ben says angrily.

'She had a drink with me, before I met Alex that first time, she took me there… it was actually good of her.'

'Christ,' Ben shakes his head. 'Good of her to introduce you to her favourite male prostitute.'

'Leave it Ben,' I snap. 'Can't you just forget you hate me for ten minutes?' *Christ*, he makes me so angry… I have to block him out, because Ben's anger is too big a distraction. Instead, I turn back to the hotel receptionist. 'Ali, can I call you Ali?'

'My name is Aaden, but the hotel already had the name tag for Ali, so I wear it, but I am not Ali.'

'Aaden then, please think carefully, is there anyone else who knows where your daughter may be kept?'

'No, I only see Mr Alex. And his brother, Mr Theo – but he does not know where my daughter is.'

'How do you know that?'

'I ask him, I beg him – he has children, I see his children, I give them lollipops when they come and sit in my reception. He says he knows nothing about the children his brother take.'

'And there's no one else?'

Aaden drops his head. Then from somewhere far off, we hear the siren of an ambulance.

'Thank god,' Sandi mutters and squeezes Luke's hand. I look over at him and I think it's come too late. The ambulance squeals to a halt outside the house.

'We have to go – now,' I bark, as I grab Aaden by the hand, and pull him up to standing. He's limp like a scarecrow, all the fight knocked out of him. Then I whisper to Ben, who looks like he's sulking on the other side of the room. 'We have to go.' And I pull Aaden away, as the paramedics reach the front door.

'Up here, please hurry,' Sandi yells out to them.

'Come on,' I tell Ben, who looks back at Luke lying on the bed. I can see that he doesn't want to leave him. 'The paramedics are here, we can't do any more.'

The three of us hide in the other room, as the first paramedic runs in and sees Luke. He yells to his colleague, and then rushes to the dying man. The second paramedic runs up the stairs with a case, and as soon as he's past us, I tug at Aaden, who follows wherever I lead.

'Come on, Ben.' I rush us down the stairs. We can't be here; it ruins everything. Our alibi is nothing if we're seen here. I just hope Sandi keeps her mouth shut about us. I push Aaden out of the front door and into the new day – and fuck, it *is* day. Those damn birds won't shut up, and I can hear people on the move as traffic thrums from somewhere not far off. Back in Putney, I'd guess that someone is walking by the river now – bloody dog walker probably – and will look over and see Alex floating there, and they'll call the police. The clock has run down, there's no time. No fucking time—

'Get in the car,' I bark at Aaden, but he just stands there blinking in the early morning light. I look to Ben to help, but he looks out of it too – they're both fucking zombies. 'Come on,' I yell at Ben, trying to break him out of the funk and I push him. He clatters into Aaden, knocking him over and pitching his phone out of his hand. It falls, hitting the ground and the screen breaks.

I look down, and through the broken glass I see a photograph. The girl looks about ten or eleven. Smiling broadly, she shines in the bright sunshine of the photograph. She is lovely.

'Is that your daughter?' I ask him, as I bend down to pick up his phone. 'She's beautiful and…' I feel cold creep through me. 'That dress…'

'Yes, it is Khadra, and that dress is her favourite; her mother made it for her before… before she was killed in the war. My daughter always wears it.'

'Oh god.' My insides are made of ice. 'I think I know where she is.'

'What?' Ben says.

'My Khadra?'

'We have to go – *now*.' And I sprint to Alex's car. 'Come on,' I yell at the other two as I jump into the car and start the engine.

'Where are we going?'

'Hell, we're going to hell.'

Chapter Sixteen

06.45 a.m.

Mia

I speed. I go way too fast, and I know I must be triggering a whole shitload of traffic cameras, but none of that matters. All I can see, in the road ahead, is that smile. Khadra in the sun, so happy. I see Rosie in her – they would be about the same age, they could be best friends... oh my god... we may be too late.

I made a dress for Rosie when she was six, even though I'm crap at sewing, and it wasn't nearly as well made as the one Khadra's mother made, but Rosie wore it all the time, and when she outgrew it we opened up the seams and used the fabric to make her a bag, so she always had it with her. I had forgotten that. I'd forgotten all the lovely things she and I did together. How she loved to read next to me while I worked, how we made flash cards together for tests, and how we'd sew together. We baked bread, and used to play games every night while Ben cooked dinner... how have I forgotten all this? Why have I erased the good times, and only remember the lost times? All the long boring meetings that meant I missed her sing in the choir, or when I couldn't get to parents' evening, or the time Ben told a teacher I was dead – it was a joke, but it wasn't funny. It wasn't funny because it was true; I was a little dead inside. I wasn't there with them, and I missed so much, but I loved her. I loved her with all my heart and—

'Yargh,' I snort the tears back. I have to drive.

'Are you okay?' Ben asks. Aaden's phone is in his hands, and he stares at the picture. Ben looks over at it too.

'Is it the same?' I ask him.

'I don't know, it looks like it – but I couldn't swear to it,' Ben says, and I want to fucking strangle him for that, but instead I run a red light and squeal around a corner. Aaden is petrified in the back seat; he has no idea what we're doing. I can't tell him, in case I'm wrong or… or… we've killed his daughter.

'Come on, come on, come on,' I whisper to myself and make all kinds of deals with God – I'm such a fucking hypocrite. *Let her be alive and I'll be good, I promise. I will go to prison, I will make amends, I will pay for what I have done – just let her live. Just let Khadra live.*

'There,' Ben yells, as we squeal around the last curve and we see the railway arches. Dawn light hits them, the glass explodes in a rainbow of colour. In the light of day they look so normal, not like the hellholes I imagined last night.

'Smoke… I see smoke…' Ben screams and my heart stops beating.

I only half brake, as the car skids, and I am out of the door in an instant, not caring that it cracks against the wall. There is a prayer in my open mouth – and I know I don't believe but *fuck*, I am making all kinds of concessions here – and I say it over and over as I dive for the door: *Let her live. LET HER LIVE.*

286

It's hot to the touch. I've seen the films – I know I will open this and there will be a fireball. I don't care. I curl into a ball and push it open and fall inside.

WHOOSH—

Flames and smoke billow out, but I roll through it – my skin browns, like on a roast chicken – I know it will hurt later, but none of that matters now. I am up, and my eyes flood with water and my throat crackles with the curling smoke.

'Mia,' Ben screams from somewhere, but I can't see him. I drop to my knees and crawl. I have to aim for the back of the room; that was where Tony came from, and I remember that when the door opened, he was silhouetted by a bare bulb, and there were stairs behind him. And – I close my eyes again – I see him as he stood there, in that first moment, and in his hands was a bright cloth, torn and filthy. He wiped his fingers on it and threw it onto the desk… in my mind's eye it freezes in mid-air. It is the same cloth as in the photograph. It is the dress her mother made for her – the dress that Khadra wears in the photograph. The dress I used as a gag for Tony, when we trussed him up.

I crawl forward. My hands are burning. I don't know where it is, but there's a hidden door here somewhere. I know there is; he came through it, here in this wall. I put my smouldering hands out and feel all around.

'Mia,' another scream from Ben and I hear choked coughs. I find an edge. I feel up the wall and find a depressed section that must work as a handle.

'Please don't be locked. Please.'

The door opens. Bad air shoots from inside, mustiness and the acrid smell of urine. It's dark and I feel around for a light but there isn't one. So I step into the dark again. Like Orpheus I descend into Hades.

Chapter Seventeen

07.00 a.m.

Mia

The air is fetid and cold. It smells bad, but not of death – not of blood, anyway. I didn't know, not before tonight, that blood smelled so bad, not before Theo emptied out in front of me. But that isn't what I can smell down here – this is fear and human waste.

'Hello,' I call out into the nothing. 'Hello, is somebody here?'

There is a sound – not a spoken word, it's something more akin to a hissed groan, but it is human. It's the sound of someone only half alive.

'My name's Mia, I've come to help…' I call out, but I can't see anything. 'I came to get you out.' I walk down concrete steps, tapping on each one to make sure I don't pitch forward into the black. To one side there's a wall but the other side is open.

'Khadra… are you here?' I call, and in response there's another moan. I think smoke is following me down but in the darkness I can't tell for sure. I might be bringing death down with me.

'Khadra?' I call, as my foot hits the bottom of the cellar. I feel around – there must be a light. *Snap.* I pull a cord and a feeble bulb lights up the stairs and a little area around them. The cellar seems to stretch a long way back and I cautiously head into the gloom.

A soft moan comes from directly ahead of me. I reach out my hand and touch something metal. It feels like a bar, so I trace it sideways, along to a series of shelves and, in the gloom, I can just make out a torch on one of them. I snap it on and a lance of warm light shoots through the bars and onto a cot in the centre of what seems like a cell. I swing the torch beam, trying to find a handle but all I see is a padlock.

I get in as close as possible and shine the light onto the cot; there's someone lying on it. I can smell the human waste strongly now, and I see there's a pot by the bed.

'Hello,' I say to the figure on the bed. 'Are you—'

The figure moves and the beam catches her.

'Oh my god.'

She's naked and thin – so painfully thin – and her hair is lank and unwashed. On her skin, even though it's dark, I can see bruises and on her arms and legs there are cuts and what look like burns.

'Khadra,' I say softly and she turns her face to mine and – it isn't her. This girl is older. 'Who are you?' I ask, but she says nothing.

'Here, please here,' a voice comes from out of the dark, further ahead. 'I am Khadra,' she says from the shadows. 'Help us.'

I skirt around the central cell and see shapes. *Oh my god* – there are so many of them, perhaps a dozen human figures move in the dark. I raise the torch and see girls and young women, all naked or in rags, each of them undernourished. I want to cry, but what kind of example would that be to set to these brave women? So I hold it in.

'Please, help us,' one of them cries.

'Of course, do you know where the keys are?'

'The devil has them,' one says.

'The fat pig, he never lets them leave him.'

'Who?' I say but I know who she's talking about; I think I knew the moment I realised Tony had Khadra's dress. I knew what I would find here, I just didn't want to believe it. 'Do you know where the lights are?' I ask and they tell me where to look and after a few seconds I find the switch and—

-

So many people can tell you where they were when they heard that Neil Armstrong walked on the moon. Before that it was the death of JFK, and before that it was VE day and so on, back into the smoke of history. Key moments sear themselves on your memory; they define you and your place in the world. They stay with you until your last moment on this earth, and even if you get some terrible disease that wipes away the very core of your being, these are the last memories that leave you. For me, I will be left with this moment: seeing these girls here and now. This is my moon landing, this is the last thing I will see before I die. It is branded on my brain.

-

'I... I... I need to get the keys, I will be back,' I say to these women, as I turn away from them and run to the stairs and... *oh fuck*. Now the lights are on I can see the cameras set up, and the beds with chains and costumes and sex toys. On the walls are photographs of men, groups of men and I see Tony right in the centre, with a girl and… I want to be sick. This is sick.

I run up the stairs. 'Ben!' I scream. '*Ben!*' The smoke is thick and curls through the air, but the heat's gone. The fire is out and I see Ben, the vision of him distorted by the smoke, but he's wafting the door back and forth to disperse it. Aaden is there too, helping. Both are covered in soot and it looks like Ben's hoody caught fire.

'Ben,' I say and he turns and I grab him and hold him. For a second I collapse into him, I'd love to just have the biggest cry on his shoulder and have him take care of me… but I can't. There is too much to do. I pull away.

'Aaden, she's there, Khadra's downstairs.'

'Oh praise be to Allah, my friends,' he says and I have never seen such pure joy on a face before.

'But she has not been taken care of. She may be hurt, but she's alive.'

He nods and then rushes down the stairs to see her. I turn to Ben. 'Get me the keys from Tony.' I look over and see that the fire got to the old bastard's clothes but not his flesh. A pity, I think. 'He abused them, Ben. Those girls. He took them from their families and he… he raped them and filmed them. He had men in to— oh Ben, he's even more of a monster than his sons.'

'I'll get the keys,' Ben says, emotionless.

'Good, I need to call Refugee Watch and Amnesty International. We need asylum specialists – we need protection for these girls, compensation and the right to stay in this country. We can't let the home office spirit them away – they aren't getting pushed around anymore. I swear it Ben.'

He looks at me, and slowly a smile breaks over his face like a wave and washes the pain away. He smiles at me like he used to, a million years ago, when we were everything to each other. 'They're pretty lucky they were found by such a great lawyer then,' he says and I think he means it.

'Huh,' is all I can say in reply, and then I rush back down to the girls.

Ben

I walk over to Tony's body. He smells of charred hair. I look into his face, and I feel like I don't know the world anymore. I felt sorry for him. I felt deep compassion for a fellow father. My god, what a terrible judge of human character I am.

As I turn him onto his side, the smell of burning clogs my throat again and I want to gag, but I manage to reach into his pockets and find the keys. Then I head downstairs and… *hell*.

I am stunned by what I see, and the depth of the depravity hits me. Along one wall are photographs, of Tony and other old fat men and one of the twins – I think it's Alex, but I can't be sure. They are… no, it's not something I can even describe.

Ahead, in small cells, with little more than stained camping mattresses and blankets, are a dozen or so kids. That's what they are, kids – ranging from about twelve to seventeen maybe.

'Ben, quickly with the damn keys,' Mia shouts.

'Here they are.' I hand the keys over and she immediately starts opening the cells. The first released is Khadra; she was holding her father's hand through the bars, and he was whispering to her or maybe it was singing – it sounded musical, but none of the words were clear. Maybe it was a song he sang to her when she was a baby, I don't know. But the emotion that sweeps them both up, as she falls into his arms, is beautiful. Aaden is beside himself; he hugs his daughter and at the same time sobs for the pain she has been through. I look at Mia and her eyes are blazing like I haven't seen in twenty years. They were like that when she first talked about the law and how she could help people.

'Ben, open the other cells,' and Mia hands me the keys and then she hugs Khadra and she looks like a mother again as she coos into the girl's ear and gently examines her body. She soothes both father and daughter, telling them it will be all right, that they will be safe, that she will protect them.

Aaden is petrified of the police but Mia says he has nothing to fear. She has made calls and, even as she talks to them, at the main entrance, lawyers are already arriving and someone from Amnesty and someone else from Citizens Advice – they are here for Mia and her children.

'We cannot afford—' Aaden starts but Mia waves everything away.

'All free,' she says. 'Everyone will work for nothing; these children have been harmed in our country, by our citizens, we're the ones who'll pay.' And she grips Aaden's arm and he leans forward and with the faintest of bows, he kisses her cheek.

'God sent you,' he says.

And she doesn't contradict him, just smiles and leaves him to talk to the other girls, as her team begins to enter the building. And as I watch her marshalling her forces, instructing lawyers to do this and do that, I wonder if Aaden was right. Maybe she was sent here tonight, maybe this is the test – not of our marriage – but of her humanity. Or maybe that's just foolish, and it's nothing but luck that she's saved these young women and removed their tormentors from the face of the earth.

I look on, amazed, as my wife takes charge of all of this, and then she turns to me and gives me my orders – go get some food and drinks for everyone. Of course, I'm glad to have something to do. I run. I get all the way to the corner, before I realise I have no money and no cards. For a second I feel lost, and then I turn around and run right back. I go inside – there are so many people here now – and the girls are starting to be helped up the stairs. I go to Tony's body, and fish around one more time. I get his debit card and I go and buy as much on contactless as I can. I figure the bastard owes us all. I buy all the bottled water and fruit I can, as well as nuts and cereal bars. Then I drag it all back and start to hand it out. The girls are overwhelmed; one of them flinches as I offer her a nut bar.

'I'm sorry,' I mumble to her, but I see the fear in her eyes and I don't want to make any of them feel uncomfortable. So I hand the bag of goodies to a young woman who's just arrived – she looks like a legal intern – and she gives out the rest.

I move back to the wall. Standing there, I watch Mia, as she orders people around, making calls to newspapers and high profile MPs. At some point a policeman arrives and a group of ambulances. The police are kept away from the girls, while the medics are allowed in, to care for them. They won't be allowed to go to hospital until each one of the girls has been fully documented, and some of them need translators, so paralegals are running this way and that making calls and sending emails. It's crazy and, in the eye of the storm, Mia conducts it like an orchestra. And then she sees me, and for a moment that confidence flickers and she glitches like static in a film. Someone's talking to her, but she breaks that off and comes over to me. This is it: I have to tell her my last secret.

'Mia, I—'

'Shut up,' she hisses and her eyes flash. She bends forward and whispers in my ear.

'Alex's car, under the driver's seat. You must go now.'

'Okay, I—' But she's turned away and has already been subsumed by all those who need her. I can see her confidence is back, as she points this way and that, sending people to get things and call so-and-so and do what needs to be done. She was lost last night, but now she's found herself. There is a crisis and she will deal with it. My secret will have to wait for a while. Now I have to go and look under the seat in Alex's car.

I walk past Tony's body, which still lies there. There is spittle on his face and in his hair. I think a couple of the girls spat on him. I can't blame them. I stop, and I spit on him too.

–

Outside, I actually have to squint and hold my hand up to protect my eyes from the glare of the day. It's a watery February sun, not exactly warming deep in the bones, but it's bright and makes my skin feel alive again. I tip my head up to the sun and just stand there, feeling it slowly ease the bruises out. I am drop-dead tired. I could just lie down in the corner and—

'No, come on,' I tell myself and I drag my failing carcass over to the car. The doors aren't locked and the keys are still in the ignition – we're lucky it's still here. There's a police cordon about thirty yards away, stopping anyone coming in, and checking those who leave. They can't know about Tony yet or they wouldn't allow Mia to keep them away. I kneel down and slide my hand under the seat and find a roll of something. It's a Ziploc bag. I unfurl it and—

'*Christ.*'

In the bag is the hammer, the one used to break Theo's teeth. There's blood on the head and… and… my guess is that my fingerprints are on the handle. I remember she gave it to me and… shit… shit… shit… shit.

On the back seat is my Adidas bag. I grab that and push the bag with the hammer into it. Trying to be as casual as I can, I run back inside. My heart's beating so fast and hard, I can't hear anything but the drumming.

I head into the kitchen. The walls have bubbled and melted, burst in places, and the ugly décor made even uglier. I remember there's bleach under the sink. I take the bottle and pour the whole damn lot into the Ziploc bag and drown the hammer in it. There's a fizz, as the bleach attacks the blood, and maybe the plastic of the bag too. I watch it, as tendrils of red drift off the metal head. She was keeping this as insurance, so that if we were caught then she could have pinned it all on me. Or maybe she would have kept it as leverage, to keep me quiet or she'd hand it to the police. Either way, it would have been a pretty awful thing to do – not something you do to the man you love. And maybe it gives me the answer to a question that's been in my head all night. I think it's clearer than pulling the petals off a daisy. Actually, after all the angst of the night, all the will-she, won't-she, does she love me… I'm finally okay with this. I know where I stand.

After a couple of minutes in the bleach, I tip the hammer into the sink and then run a bowl of water with washing-up liquid in it. I wash the head really well and then dry it. Making sure not to touch any part of it, by holding it with a disgusting old tea-towel, I take it into the office, and put it with a couple of screwdrivers in the desk drawer.

At least she gave it up, I think. I could be angry – she drugged me, dragged me out of bed, made me complicit in murder and then let a man kill me. Actually, put like that, I should be furious, but that's been our problem since Rosie died. We were both so angry with each other, that we've never been able to see past that. Maybe tonight we finally have and—

'Oh hell.' I realise that Mia isn't the only one of us hoarding incriminating evidence. I have something that could send Mia to prison too. I have the SD card from the camera in the wardrobe, and the overhead cameras. I also have the laptop, and even though I deleted the files, that might not be enough. I'm an idiot – the police are so close and they've got a perimeter set up. *Shit.*

I sit in the corner, keeping out of the way of all the lawyers and paralegals who are starting to process each of the young women here.

I open up the laptop; it's only got six per cent battery left. I take the SD card from the overhead cameras, and slip it into the slot on the side – I pull the files up and select them all to delete... but at the last second I click *play*.

And there she is. Mia's on the bed, having sex with Theo, in that disgusting room. I can see her face more clearly from the angle above, and it shows me that her eyes are closed, but I don't see any pleasure on her face.

I see worry, I see anger and a touch of shame – she's not enjoying this – and then he says he's going to come. I stop the playback.

I already know what happens – he's had a vasectomy so he can't give her a baby. *Only fun*, he'll say, and she'll fight to get him off her. I don't need to see that again. But something makes me fast forward, past his attack and after she kicks him off of her. Then I hit play again.

Mia is curled into a ball on the bed. She doesn't look at the man on the floor, but I can imagine the blood is starting to flow from the wound in his skull. I can see it start to spread in my mind; it begins as a halo, and then that begins to balloon outwards as the blood seeps from him.

I watch Mia sob on the bed. She looks so thin, there's nothing remotely sexual about her as she cries – there is just misery and pain. It must have hurt her so much, when he said he couldn't make her pregnant. She risked it all tonight – even after I found her at the bar, she brought me home, drugged me and still went back out. She was desperate… and he ripped all hope out of her hands. That's why she sobs on the bed… I've seen enough heartbreak tonight, I don't need to see any more. I stretch out my finger to delete the file and—

There is a soft moan. I barely hear it, but Mia does. On her bed of anguish, she raises her head to look at what, or who, makes the sound. I can't see, as it's off-camera but I see his foot twitch, just in the corner of the frame. I hadn't even realised it was there, but it moves. Theo isn't dead.

'You bitch…' He moans from the floor. 'You are gonna fucking wish you hadn't done that.' His voice is slow, full of pain, but he's alive. 'By the time me and my brother are through with you, you will beg for death.'

I watch, not breathing, as Mia gets off the bed, her face crimson with anger, her hands curled into claws. I turn up the sound as loud as it goes. She stands at the very edge of the screen; I can't see her face as she speaks to him.

'Don't you dare threaten me, you bastard, you can't even get up.'

'I will.' He groans a little, as he tries to move. 'And when I do get up, I will make you pay for that.'

'I already paid, you fucking monster. You have no idea the price I paid to come here tonight.' And she kneels down beside him. 'I came here and you cheated me. You are a total waste of life,' she says, her voice calm and clear.

'You are gonna die, bitch.'

'No,' she says. And I watch her move. I see an arm reach to something and she grunts and there is a sound, like slamming your hand on a table.

He moans in pain. Then she does it again. There is a sickening crunch and Theo's foot twitches. He makes a groaning sound, like a sigh. His foot moves again and… nothing. She staggers back into the frame and her hand… *Oh Jesus*, her fingers are coated in his blood and I see strands of hair there too. I can't breathe.

She killed him, in cold blood.

I couldn't see it, but I know what she did. She snaked her hand into his hair, pulled his head off the floor and then slammed it into the ground. She did it twice to make sure she broke his skull. This wasn't an accident… it was murder. That was why she never even considered calling the police.

'Oh my god…' I don't know what to think. He did rape her, and he threatened her, he might well have killed her; but it was still in cold blood, and the forensics would have shown it wasn't a single blow to the head from a fall.

She lied to me, she's lied to me all night. So what do I do now I know the truth?

'Ms. Kingdom, Mia Kingdom,' a voice calls from outside. 'This is James Manders of the Metropolitan police. My men and I are coming in now, no more delays.'

Jesus Christ. I pull out the SD card and I put it on my tongue like a communion wafer. I actually offer up kind of a prayer, and then I swallow it.

I hear Mia yell back at the policeman, like a fishwife, forcing him back, but I know it won't last long. I see the other lawyers and advocates come up behind her; the police don't know what's going to hit them. Then someone yells that the Channel 4 news team has arrived and the shit really hits the fan.

I put my head down and work. I wipe down the laptop and then grab a screwdriver and open the casing. I pull out the motherboard and hit it with the hammer I just cleaned. Then I turn the memory into dust and lastly throw all the bits of crap into the burned pile of smashed server hard drives. It takes just a few minutes. All the evidence is gone. Mia is free.

But this is not over.

I see Mia turn away from a policeman and come back to talk with other lawyers. I have to tell her.

'Mia,' I call.

'Not now, Ben.'

'Yes now.'

'Later, I am—'

'No.' The tone of my voice makes a dozen lawyers look round at me, and some of the girls whimper, worrying that some new arsehole of a man has come to make trouble. I lower my voice and say in little more than a whisper, 'I'm sorry Mia, but you owe me one minute. After twenty years you at least owe me that.'

Her eyes flare in annoyance, but she waves people away and stands there staring at me. 'Okay, one minute.'

I sit on the floor and untie my shoe.

'For fuck's sake, Ben, I've already seen the ring, please don't do this again.'

'It isn't the ring, I brought something else.' I pull off my other shoe this time and then snake my fingers down into the base of it.

'Oh come on, Ben, what is it this time? A slice of our wedding cake or—'

'Shut up, Mia,' I say as I stand up, holding a small square of plastic. 'It's nothing of ours.' I hold a small photograph in my hand. I'm not sure now that I can show it to her. I freeze.

She sighs. 'Thirty seconds left, Ben. Whatever it is we can talk later; these girls need—'

'I don't think so.' I say and I lean in close so that nobody else can hear us. 'I got rid of the hammer. Thank you for not using it on me.'

She shrugs. 'I'm sorry I kept it. If it helps, I had decided a while ago I'd get rid of it.'

'None of that matters anymore; what you need to know is that I erased all the films from tonight and destroyed the laptop. The films should be gone, so I think you're safe, but you need to talk to Sandi and Luke and make sure they have their stories straight.'

'I heard from Sandi already.'

'Luke?'

'It was touch and go, but they think he'll make it. They've given him a full transfusion.'

'Thank god.'

'I know. So that's your minute up,' she tells me and then nods her head at the photograph in my hands. The back is to her so she can't see the image on it. 'What's in your hand that's so important?'

'I love you,' I tell her.

'I know you do,' she says. 'And I loved you.'

'Past tense?'

'Past tense.'

I pause, to give myself a second to think. 'I thought you'd say that, I just hoped… you know.'

'I'm sorry,' she says and I know she means it.

'I'm sorry too.' I stop and take a deep breath. It's time to tell her my final secret. 'Mia, I know you're about to go and save these women, but before you do that I have to show you this photo. It's the other thing I brought with me tonight, as well as my wedding ring. It's the other thing I couldn't just leave at home.'

'Is it the same one I had – the picture of the three of us that Becca took?'

'No,' I tell her, amazed that I'm finally going to let go of this secret that's weighed me down for so long. 'I'm sorry Mia, but it isn't that photo.' And I turn the small photograph around in my fingers. I see her eyes narrow for a moment. She looks bemused; she can't understand why I'm showing her a photograph of a baby boy she doesn't know. And then suddenly the truth hits her.

'His name's Sam. I haven't even met him.' I tell her.

'Oh, Ben.' Her face creases, folding in on itself, a myriad of emotions run through her, as she realises what she's looking at. Who she's looking at.

'You were right, about Ella and me, we didn't use anything that last time – but you assumed she had an abortion, and I didn't stop you thinking that because I was so afraid of hurting you.'

'Oh, Ben,' she says again, as a tear breaks free and runs down her cheek. Another lawyer tries to step in but she brushes them away.

'I told Ella it had to end, and it did, but she was pregnant and left the agency. She didn't tell me; instead, she went home to her mum in Devon. I didn't hear from her for months, I forgot all about her and what we did – and then out of the blue she called. She told me I had a son.'

'Oh, Ben.'

'I didn't know what to do, so I told her I didn't want anything to do with him. I meant it; I didn't want to lose you, but she sent me this photo a few months ago.' I stop; my throat is ragged with the smoke and the pain of my words. 'I've kept it on me all the time since. When you're asleep I look at it, and I dream about the boy, Mia. I dream about him growing up without a dad – but what am I supposed to do when I love you? And I haven't stopped loving you, Mia. I loved Rosie so much, and I went mad when she died. I wanted to stay with you, to keep her alive – I was so desperate but...'

'Shh.' She folds me in her arms like I'm a child needing comfort; she pulls me into her so tight I can feel her heartbeat. 'You have to go,' she tells me with such gentleness.

'I know – I will. I'll stop by the house and get some things; I'll let you know where I am.'

'I mean you have to go to your son. You have to see him and make a connection. You should be a dad again.'

I sob-moan as I hear her say *dad again*, it forces up and out of my throat, I can't stop it. 'I'm sorry,' I say.

304

'Don't you dare be sorry, you bloody idiot. You are a wonderful father and you can't desert him. If you do I will never talk to you again.'

'I never meant to hurt you.'

'I know that. Of course I know that. But I did hurt, we both hurt so much. I don't blame you anymore, I'm so sorry that I ever did.' She squeezes me so tight, just for a second, and then releases me. 'Go to Sam. Send me a photo of him in your arms.' And then she turns away, and returns to the crowds of lawyers she's brought together to help these girls. She doesn't need me now, which is good. And I don't think she needs a baby anymore, she's got a dozen step-children all of a sudden, and in particular, she has Khadra to care for and fight for.

I think this night is done at last. I can hear the police start to form a crowd at the doorway, ready to force their way inside – and I know it's time for me to go.

I wave to Aaden, who looks dazed and doesn't see me. I see Nadia, who must have arrived while I was out getting the food, and she hugs a girl tightly to her chest. Good for her. Good for them all. I give myself one final moment, to remember all of this, and then I leave.

I remember what Tony said, about the garage behind the office. I run down the stairs and past all those other women who are smiling now, as they slowly come to realise that they're safe. I run into the back and find the door. It's pretty well hidden, but I know it must be there. I force it open and then use my sleeve to wipe away any fingerprints.

I get into the garage, but it isn't what I thought it would be. It's more like a tunnel and it leads some way underground. This must be how they moved people, how they trafficked their slaves.

I race down the tunnel, and at the end there's a door – thankfully, it isn't locked. I push through, again making sure to leave no prints, and I'm in some kind of cellar. I go upstairs, hoping the door won't be locked, and find I'm in a house. I'm in Tony's house, and it looks so ordinary. There are pictures of Tony and Angela everywhere; you would think them such a happy normal couple, unless you knew, unless you'd seen the girls in the cages. The thought makes me nauseous. I don't want to think about them ever again. I don't want to stay in this house a second longer.

I open the front door, using my sleeve of course, and close it behind me. On the doorstep, I pull the hood up over my head, and hunch slightly. I am outside the police cordon, but still I need to be quiet and unseen. I will be nobody again. It's something my wife taught me. Then I step out, into a brand new day.

Mia

I walk away from Ben and I don't look back. Yesterday, his confession would have made me want to kill him, but now I just wish him well. God that feels good, to finally forgive him. I have been so angry for so long. The rage has been a fire in my belly for four years, and where did it lead? To the deaths of three men. I am a murderer, and the stain of that will never leave me, but I have the chance to make amends, to save these young women and maybe, *maybe*, to be a mother again. I don't want to jinx it, but Khadra needs me, and the other girls need me. I can be a kind of mother to them all. I don't want to hold onto the anger and the hate anymore. I can let it go. I can forgive Ben, and more importantly, I can forgive myself.

There's suddenly a commotion as the police are finally forcing their way in, but we've documented all the children, and their parents, so it should go smoothly. We aren't letting any of these people get hurt again. That's a promise.

I told Aaden I have a spare bedroom, and that he and Khadra can stay with me. He said I'd already done enough, but I insisted, pretending I was doing it for them, when it's really just selfishness. I look over at Khadra. She needs a shower, and she needs a good meal and a home. I have that. I have it all, but no one to share it with anymore. And if I'm honest, more honest than I've been in a long time, what I want – what I really, *really* want – is just to smell her hair after she's washed it. That sounds weird, doesn't it? And it is, I guess, but that's what I want: to smell a young woman's shampooed head, and heat up a pizza and watch some TV together. That sounds like bliss right now.

'Time to go outside,' someone calls, one of the interns I think. Khadra leans on her father's shoulder. She looks exhausted. I move alongside and take her hand. She lets me. I wonder if she likes beans on toast. I'll find out. Together we step out into the air of a brand new day.

A letter from P.D. Viner

Eighteen months ago I was about to give up writing.

After the success of the Dani Lancing/Sad Man stories I had wanted to make a change in direction and not have such a prominent police procedural element in my books. So I wrote *The Funeral Director* – which I thought was my best book yet. Set in Furie New York and featuring a sixty-nine-year-old, lonely Funeral Director investigating the death of his best friend (and New York Senator)'s grandaughter (in real life my father-in-law is a New York funeral director and I have spent many happy months living in his Fun Home and tagging along with the local police). I thought this book would be a crime classic… but nobody wanted it. Boo-Hoo.

So I thought I'd take a break from crime and work with my daughter on a couple of kid's books (sociopathic dinosaur and depressed last king of the dragons). Again it was just disappointment after disappointment. I was at a pretty low ebb after the twentieth rejection – perfectly poised for the oncoming storm of Covid and loss of all income. But I love writing, it is who I am, and so I went back to the basics, and I wrote a claustrophobic story about a couple whose life is crumbling about them, and it all comes to a head one night – maybe their last night together (my marriage is fine, thanks for asking).

I submitted *The Call* far and wide, and as you can see it finally did find a home – and what a magnificent home it has with Hera – but there were a good few months of holding my breath, and braving the onslaught of a lot of *sorry, but no's*. (You have to be ready for knocks in this business) though I was really disappointed by the fact that so many publishers and agents just never responded, not even a form letter or 'ta very much for submitting' email. There was nothing. So, for all first-time writers (and returning writers like me) out there - all I can say is: you must have the hide of a rhinoceros and the self-belief of a sociopathic dinosaur to survive this business. Hats off to anyone crazy enough to write a book, and for all of you out there ruining your backs hunched over a laptop... good luck, I hope your dreams come true.

As this letter appears at the end of the book, I assume you've now read *The Call* (and you aren't the kind of pervert that jumps to the back of the book to read the acknowledgments and author letter nonsense first) so I really hope you liked the book. No, actually I hope you *loved* it and want all your friends, family, co-workers, teachers from school and anybody you have ever fancied and wondered what they look like naked – to read this book. And I hope you will do all you can to make that happen. For example; write five-star reviews on your favourite book site (or bathroom wall), give copies as gifts to those you love and tattoo your favourite line of dialogue on your body, somewhere saucy.

If you have read my previous books (published by Ebury and Crown) then I hope you liked this at least as much as those. And if you haven't read me before... what are you waiting for? *The Last Winter of Dani Lancing* is fabulous, *Summer of Ghosts* is a great read too – go buy multiple copies.

If you want to ask me any questions, bitch or moan about my shortcomings, ask me to talk to your book club or read at your wedding; then you can contact me by visiting my website: www.pdviner.com or www.studslovemums.com

You can see what I'm doing next by checking me out on Facebook (https://www.facebook.com/phil.viner.1) and on Twitter @philviner. You never know, I might do a competition, or confess to a murder – so maybe you should follow me. FOMO is a terrible thing.

Thanks lovely reader, after all, it's all for you.

Acknowledgments

I am so lucky.

I have a fantastically supportive wife (with a real grown-up job) and a teenage daughter who is (mostly) delightful and picks me up when I feel low.

I also have a group of writers who are there to encourage, support and help me rage against the machine. My biggest thanks goes to them: Jane Lythell, Kate Harrison, Laura Wilkinson, Sarah Rayner and Susan Wilkins. They wouldn't let me stop writing – and for that I'm eternally grateful. They read my book when it was just a baby and helped me nurture it. When I had a first draft I also got amazing support (and sharp criticism) from two other great writers: Araminta Hall and Stephanie Lam. Thank you so much.

The last part of my journey came when I joined Hera, and as someone who has been published before (by multiple traditional publishers) it was a real joy to have a team who were professional, energetic, enthusiastic and genuinely helpful and insightful. Thank you Keshini Naidoo, Danielle O'Brien, Jennie Ayres, Vicki Vrint and Steve Mulcahey. I have been so fortunate to collaborate with the team on *The Call* and I can't wait for the next book to come out.

Lastly let me thank Mia and Ben for letting me tell their story. They were incredible.